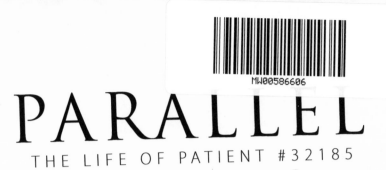

PARALLEL

THE LIFE OF PATIENT #32185

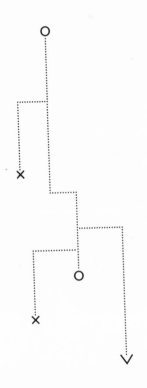

A B R A   E B N E R

Text Copyright © 2009 Abra Ebner

Crimson Oak Publishing

Pullman, WA 99163
Visit our website at www.CrimsonOakPublishing.com

The characters, events, and locations portrayed in this book are fictitious. Any
similarity to real persons, living or dead, or real locations is coincidental and
not intended by the author.

Ebner, Abra 1984 -
Parallel, the Life of Patient #32185 : A Book / by Abra Ebner

www.ParallelTheBook.com

printed in U.S.A

1 2 3 4 5 6 7 8 9 10

"It is not humanity at fault,
It is he who cannot accept the world that is to blame."

- A.E.

July 12, 2009

My name is Jordan Mckay, and if you've found this, then you have seen the consequences of what led me to my death. There may be things about me that you will find strange, but if you could understand the life I've lived, then you will know more about the nature of my makeup. I am different from everyone; special, unique. I am what I have come to understand is called a Shifter.

Within the boundaries of our life from birth to death, we can travel from one age to the next, leaving a foggy line between our present, past, and future. Here we are able to see how events can change the world, or at the very least, change just one life. If we can manifest a thought hard enough, then we can go there. This is the key to our talent.

I am not completely certain how many of us there are, or why we were created, or even where we came from. I can only guess that it's a glitch in human kind and a chance at playing God. In this world, we learn to fend for ourselves and fight for our basic need for selfish gain. For me, my gain was the love of a woman. A selfless act in my eyes only, but now as I grow to learn what it's done to her, I can see that it was all a mistake that I can no longer take back.

Either way, I have seen that there is a pattern for disaster in this world, and a fear so dark it could swallow the night. I have learned now that you cannot hope to erase all the wrong, only replace it with another. After all, you cannot change your luck; you can only try to change the events that caused the misfortune in the first place.

Manipulation of time is a powerful tool but something I fear is deadly if not completely understood. I hope to reach out to those like me, to save them as I have failed to do for myself, and to tell them that no matter what you do, you cannot hope to make things better. My personal belongings will tell the story...

Jordan McKay

**Statement from Dr. Ashcroft,
Vincent Memorial Hospital, Boston
August 3, 2009
11:56 p.m.**

Agent Donnery:
    When did you meet him?

Dr. Ashcroft:
    I met him at twenty-five.

Agent Donnery:
    But it say's here that you knew each
other since you were six? How is that?

Dr. Ashcroft:
    I met him a couple times throughout
time, but if you understood what Jordan can
do, then you would understand what I mean
when I say that we met for the first time
when I was twenty-five, and he was twenty-
seven. At least according to his driver's
license.

Agent Donnery:
    What do you mean, according to his
license?

Dr. Ashcroft:

Think of Jordan's life as a timeline, only his timeline has been chopped up and rearranged in an order that does not fit science. He could leap around from one place to the next, each place revealing something that has changed, each a parallel life of the one you were just in. When I met him at twenty-five he may have been in the body of his twenty-seven year old self, but his mind had just been six. It's a terrifying thing to have happen to you when you think of it.

Agent Donnery:

I see. So what happened? How and why do you believe, or I suppose know, all this is true? (laughter) It just seems far-fetched is all. I'd like to hear your side of it.

Dr. Ashcroft:

It's hard to believe, I know, but considering the fact that you're from a branch of the C.I.A. that is set up in order to research just such happenings, I believe that there is more out there than I can even try to understand, and that you actually do, or can, believe me.

Agent Donnery:

I can see your angle. It is true that the somewhat fictional nature of

what happened here is not too uncommon.
Our world has been polluted with so many
chemicals and synthetic agents that you
would not believe the things I've seen,
the things you never thought possible,
but of course, you'll never know of them
either.

Dr. Ashcroft:
    (laughter) Except this.

Agent Donnery:
    True, but I also expect your explicit
secrecy on the subject.

Dr. Ashcroft:
    I'm a doctor, Agent. I'm good with
confidentiality.

Agent Donnery:
    Then we understand, so please, tell me
about Jordan McKay.

Dr. Ashcroft:
    (pause) It's difficult for me to
accept, even still, but my life was stolen
from me. If I had known all along about
what was happening, I suppose I would have
tried to stop it, though it would have
been hard. I have been lied to, led down a
path that I no longer see as my own but I
am now forced to live. When I was a little
girl I used to think I was lucky, that all

the great things in my life were God's choice for me, but now I see that God had nothing to do with it.

Agent Donnery:
    So you believe that you were at the mercy of Jordan instead?

Dr. Ashcroft:
    Yes, he made the decisions, took over God's roll, so to speak, but I only saw it as my reality. I did not know I was like a modern day puppet. (pause) There is nothing left of my real destiny but the stories of a man describing a life I thought was no more than a faint memory, imprinted on my mind like a dream.
    When I think back, I can remember it all but it hurts too much to imagine. As I sit here I still can't believe that I fell for it, that I took the easier path that ended with a life that was false.
    In the end, I suppose all I can do is live with the cards I have been dealt. I'm in love with my fate, the fate that took me on this parallel path into a place I was never meant to be. I only hope that grace can still find me here, and that I will be forgiven. After all, if God was no part of it, then I guess love is the devil's creation.

Agent Donnery:
    I see, so you loved him too?

Dr. Ashcroft:
    Yes, I suppose that no matter what,
I would have always found myself drawn to
him. It was fate after all.

Agent Donnery:
    Will you tell us how it happened?

Dr. Ashcroft:
    I can try.

Agent Donnery:
    (pause) Here, these are the journals
you requested, that we found in the
office, splayed across the floor.

Dr. Ashcroft:
    (pause) Thanks, I (pause) I'm sorry
it's just that that the last time I held
these, everything changed and my whole
world came crashing down.

Agent Donnery:
    I understand. (pause) We've gone
through it and tried to make sense of it
all, but unfortunately it jumps around
and it seems things may be missing, or
are out of order. Many of the dates are
very old.

Dr Ashcroft:

(laughter) Agent Donnery, I'm
certain it isn't out of order, that's
what you need to understand. See here,
each page is numbered in order from
beginning to end. You cannot go by date
because his world never worked that way.
(pause) Here, let me begin telling you
what I know, what he knows...

I was ripped from the park bench where I sat eating the melting popsicle and dreaming about my life, now thrown through a dark tunnel, landing with a sudden crack on the seat of a bus. I grabbed my head in agony, the blood pounding through my swollen veins, making me lightheaded.

A woman in a pink nurse's uniform ran toward me. "Sir, are you okay?"

Her concerned green eyes blinked rapidly, and her figure blurred as I tried to focus on her face.

"Sir?"

She referred to me as sir, but I was only six, or so I had thought. The pain in my head subsided and I sat up, looking at my hands. At first I was confused by the size of them and the aged appearance of my skin, but upon closer inspection, I found they were still my hands, as the scar I had gotten when I was four lingered on my palm but was faded as though healed over time.

"Sir?" she asked again, her voice reverberating loudly in my aching head. I quickly put my hands into the pockets of my jeans to hide them, also shocked by the size of my legs as they protruded from the seat.

What was going on? I looked at her as I finally nodded, swallowing to ease spit down my dry throat as I looked around the bus, unable to handle her stare for too long.

Was I dreaming? I had to be dreaming. I pinched my leg through the pocket of my pants but it didn't work. I then thought about the fact that if I were dreaming, I wouldn't be wondering if I was because in dreams you typically aren't as conscious as I felt now. As far as I could tell, I was wide awake.

As my eyes darted around the bus, I noticed that the nurse and I were the only ones on board. I could see the driver eyeing me from the front seat through his large rearview mirror, judging me in a way that reminded me of the mean teachers at pre-school. Looking away, nerves overcame me and I grabbed my head as it throbbed like a swelling bruise. The driver cleared his throat and shifted in his seat, and I knew I was making him uncomfortable.

"He's alright!" the lady yelled to him, also noticing his discomfort.

The driver looked relieved as she said this, and he nodded, focusing his gaze on the road ahead.

I rubbed my eyes with my giant hands, feeling as though my brain had somehow expanded in the split second since I had leapt from the park bench to here and I feared it might leak through my ears. It seemed that all I had once known had tripled in size as though someone had plugged a microchip into the back of my head, filling it with years of information and knowledge.

"Sir? What is your name?"

I looked back into the woman's green eyes, finding them piercing and beautiful as a feeling I had never felt before rushed over me like a hot wave of water. I shrugged, finding myself at a loss for words, my memory too scrambled to speak. I had no recollection of how I got here, no clue as to where I had been.

"May I?"

The woman motioned to search my pockets and I nodded, feeling like a scared little boy. She felt in the lapel of my coat for something, finding whatever it was and pulling it back toward her. I was wearing a green coat that I recognized as my father's, except I now filled it out like I never had before, my body like that of a grown man. My brow began to sweat below the black baseball hat on my head, so I pulled it off, resting it in my lap as I pressed my sweaty curls back, my hair an unacceptable length and a far cry from the maintained crew cut my father had forced me to wear.

A wallet now lay in her grasp and she flicked it open, fishing inside with her dainty fingers, her fuchsia nail polish chipped around the edges. I watched her as she scanned through the compartments, my gaze turning to her face where I noticed a scar. It spread from the right side of her nose back to her ear, leaving a large discolored patch of skin that had tried to mend itself over time, as though a burn from her childhood. Her hair was a deep auburn that was pulled back in a messy ponytail and fastened with a pink rubber band. A few thick strands fell on the right side of her eyes, shielding what it could of the scar, though the attempt was useless.

"Is this you?" She pushed the wallet toward me and I tried to focus on the tiny image as I looked down at the card behind the clear plastic cover. There was a dusty driver's license squeezed into the slot and I touched it with my dirty finger, finding the dates and photo all wrong as I furrowed my brow, my stomach now nauseated. I swallowed hard, reading the name and recognizing it as my own; Jordan McKay, blue eyes, brown hair.

I opened my mouth and narrowed my eyes.

"Er...yes."

I swallowed, frightened by the deep tone of my own voice as I brought my giant hand to my throat, shocked by the Adam's apple that now protruded from the front like a broken bone.

"But..." I brought my hand back to the image and tapped my finger against the plastic, looking at her.

Her green eyes scanned my face.

"It looks like you," she assured.

I nodded, taking her word for it.

She sat down beside me and looked about the bus with frantic eyes. She seemed to be trying to formulate some sort of plan for me, her lips parted as a gentle breath escaped into the air. She looked down at the wallet one last time, her mouth forming words as her eyes traced the blurred letters of the driver's license and address. She perked up then, causing me to shy away out of sudden fear.

"Driver, next stop please!" She looked out the dusty

windows that reflected the neon lights inside, searching for some sign of where we were on the route. I couldn't stop watching her and I wondered what was wrong with me, and why I still felt the same strange wave of warmth crash over me, again and again. Another sudden sharp pain racked my body but this time in my stomach, and I winced, grabbing my side.

"Oh!" The woman touched my arm and my mind forgot about the burning in my side and instead focused on her warm hand. "Are you alright?"

I nodded and gave her a shaky smile, forcing down the pain. She focused back on the bus, looking out the windows. I watched her blink as I continued to shut out the pain and swallow the sick taste in my mouth.

My grandmother had often taken me on bus rides, so I was used to the ride and motion, though my large body was hard to keep still. I looked back down at my hands and legs, wondering what had happened to the time between ages six and now. I must be dreaming but it felt real, as though that time had been stolen from me, like what I imagined would happen if I had been in a coma. I wiped a bead of sweat from my brow, my hand scratching across the stubble that grew on my face. I felt my chin, amazed by the feeling of it as it scrubbed my fingers, reveling in the fact I was man enough to grow a full beard.

The bus screeched to a halt and she hooked her arm under mine, lifting me from the seat as I stood on weak legs, the altitude a far cry from that of a three-foot tall preschooler.

It was then that I caught a glimpse of my body in the fogged reflection of the bus window, my eyes shocked by the large figure staring back at me. I froze for a moment, taking in the reflection of myself in the green coat, my hair just below my ears, and my face rough and tanned. This could not be real, this could not be happening to me. I was lost.

She led me down the stairs as my body shook. We stepped into the cool night, my hot skin welcoming the cool air as it soothed the warm feeling that still plagued me. She looked from side to side, looking at house numbers as she craned her neck to see over each stoop.

She exhaled sharply, and I could tell she was annoyed but I didn't want her to leave either. She brushed the hair from her face, mumbling something under her breath as she pulled me to the left. I stumbled over my big feet as we went past one stoop after the next, stopping at each to assess the house numbers.

Finally, her pace quickened and I struggled to keep up as a few fat drops of rain fell from the sky.

"Oh thank God," she whispered, stopping before the last stoop on the street and looking up at the numbers.

The few drops of rain turned to a sudden downpour, and she pulled me by the arm up the steps to the door. This time she didn't bother to ask as she rummaged through my coat pockets and found a key. She fumbled with it in her hand, the shiny silver catching what little light there was on the street. I heard the metallic clink of it as it met the lock, turning with a soft thud and releasing the jamb.

She pressed the door inward and pulled me with a firm grip as she searched for a switch. Light erupted across the apartment as she succeeded, and my eyes fell on a scene that felt comforting somehow, as though my brain and body recognized it but my soul did not.

"Ok," she breathed, releasing a relieved breath. "You're home." She looked around the room and removed her sodden coat and scarf. "Do you mind if I borrow your phone?" Her hair was dripping from the few stray strands on her cheek.

I looked at her and then around the room, wondering where a phone even was, unable to recognize anything but the feeling in my gut that this place was mine. I nodded and shrugged, finding there was little else to do.

She let go of my arm and I steadied myself on my feet as she walked in a brisk pace toward what looked like the kitchen, trusting her instincts as to where a phone could hide. I blinked and looked around the room, taking it in and finding that as I looked closer there were a few things I did recognize like pictures and a few trinkets; all now tattered with age.

Looking up I saw that there was a mirror across the room above a fireplace, and I made my way toward it, moving my hand from one object to the next, hoping each was sturdy enough to support me. Though my large hands had scared me, I found they were much easier to use and could grasp things in their entirety. I supported my weight with my arms, the muscles flexing as they never had before, like He-man's did in my comic books back home, wherever home was.

As I got to the hearth, I placed my hand on the sill, like

a newborn baby learning to walk. I could hear the woman in the other room on the phone, whispering in hushed tones that were both frantic and a little scared. I turned my attention to the reflection before me, recognizing nothing but the child I had known underneath, my eyes telling the truth as they still held the twinkle I had known.

My face had grown considerably and the once soft youthful skin was replaced by stubble and pronounced features. I nodded to myself, finding that overall I was pleased with the way I had turned out, relieved that I was in fact quite handsome despite what my father had said. I watched as I blinked, almost fearing the man in the mirror, still unable to completely accept that he and I were the same entity.

I turned my head and inspected the side view. My nose had the same small hook it always had and my ears were just as big, though the size of my face had now caught up to them. My deep grey-blue eyes were full of the youth I had seen everyday though now pressed into the mask of a man I struggled to know. I did not look much older than twenty-seven, but it was hard to tell as I had never been twenty-seven before.

I saw the woman exit from the kitchen through the reflection of the mirror, coming toward me with reddened eyes and a saddened brow. She kept her gaze away from mine as though ashamed by what had just transpired over the phone, afraid that if she looked at me, she may fall apart.

She tried to gather herself as she cleared her throat. "I told my husband I was working late and missed the bus so I'd just work through the night."

My gut ached with guilt as my eyes followed her lips as she spoke, a soft crimson that reminded me of my mother's when she was upset. I could see in her tired eyes that her husband had been a horrid man. I knew this because I had seen the same look from my mother. Her husband was probably drunk and mean as my father had been and it made my heart throb with pain. I doubt he noticed how beautiful she was, the kiss of a freckle on her cheek, the sharp green of her eyes.

I turned to face her, finding the overwhelming need to give her a hug, to comfort her when it seemed no one would. I put my arms out toward her, and to my surprise she fell into them and began to sob without hesitation, as though I were her best friend. I felt awkward holding her, my body looming over her small frame and my arms wrapping around her almost twice.

After a moment she pulled back and wiped the tears from her face, her scar reddened by the blood that had rushed to her cheeks. "I'm sorry, I must seem crazy; inviting myself in and hugging a complete stranger." She blinked and looked me in the eyes.

"Oh..." I paused, still surprised by my own voice. "It's alright." I cleared my throat. "To tell you the truth I don't what happened to me, either, I feel as out of sorts as you."

She blinked some more and narrowed her eyes. "You must have some sort of amnesia or perhaps you had a seizure?"

Her attention turned away from the phone call and back to me. She grabbed my cheeks and looked into my eyes, inspecting them before grabbing my hand and leading me to the couch in front of the fireplace. She sat me down, taking the cushion beside me, her movements graceful.

"Forgive me, but something about you seems different." She put her hand out and grabbed my cheek to turn my head to face her.

I shied away from her touch, but she was stubborn.

"You have the eyes of a child, but the body of a man." Her eyes were full of a depth I doubted few could understand the way I did now. It felt so sudden, so strange to feel this way about someone I hardly knew. I found it hard to justify the connection, but there was one. It was as though I had grown up with her as her best friend, been there for every stage of her life.

"I..." I paused, finding the words I was about to say absurd.

She looked at me with an eager stare.

"I don't expect you to believe me, but I was six just a short while ago, and now I'm here and I'm..."

"Twenty-seven?" she finished my sentence.

I nodded. "Sure, I suppose."

"It was on the license," she nodded and pursed her lips, taking a moment to think before looking back to me, content with her answer.

I glanced around the room and took a deep breath. I could tell she didn't believe me, more likely she just believed

I was crazy, but it didn't matter. I needed to say it because to me it was real. "I think I may not be in the right time, if that makes sense. Do you think that's possible?"

She laughed. "I'm not sure but I wish that were true." I saw her roll her eyes and turn the scarred side of her face away from me. "I wish I could change things and go back in time." she allowed herself to imagine it.

I laughed in return. "What would you change? You seem wonderful." I was surprised that she was willing to entertain the idea and it distracted me from the fear in my stomach.

She smiled and I could see tears welling in her eyes. This stranger before me felt like much more than that, as though she were an old friend, someone whom had risked many things to save me tonight, to make me feel as though I was not lost.

She let out one chuckle. "I would change everything."

My heart stung as she said it, feeling the hurt and pain in her words. It did not seem fair that such a beautiful creature could become so forgotten by God, left to fend for herself in a world where no one would lend a hand.

"I would take back all I've done." She ran her hand along the hem of her nurse's scrubs. "I would change this." She touched her face and ran her hand across the scar. "It changed everything for me, took my beauty, my confidence." She pressed back tears. "I used to want to be a doctor, but when you look like a monster, everything is hard."

I watched her with focused eyes, my heart breaking at her every word.

"And my husband…" She shook her head.

"You deserve better." I knew what to say because I had longed to tell my mother the same thing for years but I never got the chance before she died. I always thought that when she got cancer it was God's answers to her prayers. My mother wanted to die; I saw it in her face everyday and now I saw it in the woman's as well, the look of an empty soul that had been left alone in this world.

She nodded and sobbed into her hands. "I'm twenty-five with so much future left to live but I fear I don't want to, I fear my own mind. I have tried so hard that now I have given up. What other choice do I have but to accept my awful fate?"

I placed my hand on her back. "If I could I would save you," I mumbled, and in my mind, I made it a point to save her. No matter what life I was now living, this was my single focus from here on out.

She laughed with tear stained eyes. "I would love you for that."

She looked at me then, and for the first time since reading Cinderella, I felt what love at first sight was like.

"This seems strange, but I think we were meant to meet." My breathing was shallow but I knew enough about fate and life to know that everything happened for a reason.

She smiled, revealing perfect teeth, "You don't even know my name."

I smiled back. "Well then, what's your name?"

A sly look crossed her face and I knew it meant trouble. "Well," she paused, still thinking. "If we were meant to meet, and you're not from this time, let's make a game of it. Let's say that the next time I meet you, whatever time that is, then I will tell you my name."

I laughed. "Makes sense. But how will you remember?"

She winked at me, "Fate will remind me. No matter what happens, meeting you now has left a mark on me that will never fade, just like my scar. No matter what time, I won't forget you. I promise."

She put her hand in the air like a pledge before lowering it back into her lap. "For the record, a part of me really does believe you. I like to think there are still amazing and unexplainable things in this world."

"Well then, you may be the only one that does believe me. I couldn't imagine anyone else would." The conversation hit a lull as we both thought over what was just explained.

She shifted on the cushion of the couch. "Is it alright if I stay here?" She looked me in the eyes, finding a reason. "I mean besides, if you have had a seizure, you'll want me here to watch you to make sure you don't have another."

I shrugged. "Sure, I don't mind." Truthfully I wanted her to stay, not just because I liked this woman but because I was also frightened to be alone.

She shook her head with a smile. "And to think, earlier today I figured God was a fraud. I guess this is his way of proving me wrong."

I raised my eyebrows and thought about my own predicament. "Yeah, me too."

She laughed again, and it made me feel good, as though

her laughter had touched my very soul. There was another couch opposite the one on which we were sitting, and I eyed it. I was sure I had a bedroom somewhere, but I desperately wanted to be close to her, to hear her sleep. After another moment of silence I made a move to get up, but she stopped me.

"You stay here." She rose from the couch and grabbed a blanket that had been thrown over the back and laid it over me, tucking the edges. She then walked over to the other couch and let herself fall into it, exhaling as her back met the cushion, dust flying everywhere.

We laid there for a moment before I heard her breathing change, and when I looked, I saw she was asleep. There were dark circles under her eyes and I could swear she looked dead, but I could understand. This woman beside me had given me all her heart, her last ounce of understanding; just as I was sure she had to everyone she'd met.

I pressed my head against the pillow, feeling lost. Why was I here? Why was I living this dream? I pinched my arm, but nothing happened. What if this was real? What if I had somehow traveled into my future, as I had longed to do for so long? I always wanted to know that there was life beyond what I knew at home, beyond the hell that was my childhood. Perhaps I had manifested it hard enough that now here I was, living it.

I shut my eyes, concentrating now on the past and the life I had known. The room began to feel cold and things around me to shook like an earthquake. I opened my eyes and looked at the woman, but she did not wake. It was then that the same feeling overcame me and my blood began to boil in my veins. I opened my mouth to scream, but before I could utter a word, I was back on the park bench with nothing but a popsicle stick in my hand and an orange stain on my khakis where it had melted.

I dropped the popsicle stick to the ground, my legs dangling from the bench. I put my hands to my forehead that was now ripping open with pain, much as it had on the bus. My stomach lurched then, my body doubling over as I rolled off the bench and to the ground. A cold sweat coated my body, and I begged for my life to end, to stop the pain. I lay frozen for a moment, concentrating on my breathing, until the aching began to subside and I was able to take a deep breath and open my eyes.

To my relief, no one had noticed that I was here and it was hard to know what had happened in the time since I left. I looked at my pants and I could feel my cheeks flush as the orange syrup became sticky between my fingers. I propped myself up off the ground with one shaky arm, dirt clinging to the stain on my pants as I rested for a moment.

It was then that the pain was replaced by fear, fear of what my father would do when he saw me. I wiped the sweat from my brow and got to my feet where I ran to the nearest drinking fountain. I clasped my hands together and gathered a handful of water, splashing it on my pants and praying the stain would leave. After scrubbing as well as I could, I let my pants dry in the sun, looking at my pale young skin and remembering the way it had looked just moments ago.

I thought about the woman, searching my brain and finding her existence felt real, not like a dream that would quickly fade. My fingers still tingled with the memory of the way her hand had felt, her soft skin. It was real.

My head was still pounding but I found that all the knowledge I had gained on the bus had stayed with me. I looked toward a nearby sign, finding that reading it became easy, each word a recognizable symbol rather than the complicated mess it had been at kindergarten. I crunched my brows together, realizing the power of the talent that was now within my grasp. I was confused as to why or how this had happened to me, scared that it wouldn't go away, but then again, did I want it to?

I kept breathing, not knowing what else to do. Everything felt like it was happening so fast that my mind raced with the possibilities, finding that perhaps at a time like this, finding reason was a waste of energy. If I were dreaming, as I hoped I was, then why could I see and feel everything with such vivid detail? I looked at the scar on my hand, seeing that it was now fresher than it had been on the bus, youthful and new like before.

An idea came to mind then and a childish smile spread across my face, my large ears flexing toward my hair. I needed to test this, to see what it was I could do, to see if it was something I could control. My body still ached from before, but I didn't care, the feeling of adrenaline was too strong to ignore. I lay back in the grass and closed my eyes, allowing the world around me to dissipate as I began to think.

I concentrated on the day I got the scar and the neighbor dog that had bit me. They had put the dog down because of it, claiming he had never done anything like it before, but my father didn't care. He had threatened to kill it himself if they didn't, and they believed him. I had felt horrible about his death everyday since because it hadn't been the dog's fault. If I hadn't poked it in the eye, it would have never cared and it would have never died. I had loved that dog because I could relate to it, trapped inside a fence all of its life, never able to reach the world beyond.

A deep pain welled in my heart, and I felt a tear form in my eye as the feeling of guilt overcame me. I opened my mouth and took a deep breath, pressing down the feeling and concentrating on it. It was then that the ground began to shake like an earthquake and I felt my heart begin to beat faster, as though beating in reverse. The blood in my veins began to rush toward my head and the ground left me, as though God had grabbed my sides and thrown me like a baseball, thrown me back to that day.

I winced as loose gravel dug into the palms of my hands, landing on the hot pavement of my driveway. Forcing my eyes open as they watered with pain, I looked at my palms, now burning from the gravel wedged deep inside. I bit my lip, forcing back tears as I saw and felt more like a child, younger and less able to handle the pain. The urge to have my mommy overwhelmed me.

I focused on the blood dripping toward my elbows, my arms now tiny. The world around me was spinning as it had in the park, but it took less time to calm as my body grew used to the changes. The blood in my veins felt hot and furious, alive in a way that reminded me I was still human. I looked around and saw my tricycle had been pushed onto its side just to my left, the wheels still spinning, telling me I had been riding it.

I wanted to smile but found I couldn't, the excitement of the whole situation too overwhelming. It felt like déjà vu, only in reverse, my memories and intelligence from the future remaining with me. It was as though I was hovering above myself, watching my life as a four year old run in my head like a movie I'd seen a hundred times. I was fascinated by what was happening, fascinated that I had defied science in a way that had changed my whole life.

A sharp bark came from my left, and I craned my head to look as I wiped the blood from my arms on my overalls. Rover continued to bark at me through the fence, his tongue wagging between each howl in the same way I remembered. I pushed myself off the ground and brushed off my pants, assessing the new scars one last time, and realizing they would be with me for the rest of my life.

I walked toward the fence, noting that my legs weren't as long as I had been used to, and making sure to take the right number of steps. Rover's tail began to wag, excited that I was coming to say hello. Placing one hand on the fence to steady myself, I pushed my other through the gate and patted him on the head.

"Its okay bud. I won't hurt you." My voice sounded like an infant, though my words were now well articulated, absent of the lisp I once had.

Rover licked my hand and began to whine, almost as if happy that I hadn't poked him in the eye like before. I laughed, allowing his cool tongue to ease the stinging that still remained on the palms of my hands, his nose sniffing the blood and his eyes watching me as though sorry. I smiled, finding that I had done all I needed, I had forced change and the future would surely reflect that. It was then that I heard the voice of an angel behind me, and I jumped, feeling as though I'd heard a ghost.

"Jordan honey, are you all right?"

It was the same line she had said in the past, except

this time it was because of the bike accident and not the dog. A cold chill rolled over me as I turned and swallowed, my mother rushing toward me, plucking me from the ground like a sack of potatoes. I wrapped my arms around her neck and began to cry, finding that I missed her more than I ever thought I would.

"Mom…" I cried, "Mommy."

"Shhhh…."

She rubbed the back of my head, flattening my soft hair behind my giant ears. I reveled in the feeling, breathing deep and taking in her familiar scent. She rocked me from side to side and I shut my eyes as hard as I could, drinking in the moment but finding it too hard to handle much longer.

"Mommy." I paused as I snuggled closer to her ear. "You deserve better," I whispered.

She pulled me away from her, shock coating her face as her grasp cut into my arms with desperation. "What did you say?" Her brows were pressed together, her brown eyes storming under her thick lashes.

"You deserve better. Mommy. I want to leave." I was terrified to say it but this was my chance.

She pressed her lips together as she fought to blink back tears. "Okay." She began to nod as she looked toward the sky, then back at me. She opened her mouth to speak again, her lip shaking. "Okay honey, we'll leave."

I leaned against her chest one last time, squeezing her as hard as I could. It was then that I realized I had done more than save Rover. I had saved her. I shut my eyes and clenched my teeth, trying to get back to age six and wondering what I would find.

I felt my blood begin to cook, my stomach now sour and my head sweating. The ground began to shake as I felt the familiar pull on my sides, taking me back to where I came from, back to six.

I crashed onto the grass from what felt like twenty feet, the malleable ground around me molding into the shape of my body. The breath was knocked from my lungs and I gasped for air, my skin tight as though stretching from a youthful age four to now. As I lay there lifeless on a bed of grass, I was at least relieved that it wasn't gravel and pavement this time, counting my blessings. I kept my eyes squeezed shut, not willing to open them to the fact that she was now gone.

I let a painful breath escape my lips, my whole body covered in a cold sweat as I shuddered. I could feel the afternoon sun fill the air with warmth, and I waited for my heart to slow. At this point, breathing was my only goal, nothing else mattered.

"What are you doing?" A shadow fell over me as a young voice rang in my ears.

I jumped, lifting my head from the cool grass and shielding my eyes from the sun. A young girl of about four loomed over me, her blue shirt catching the wind and rippling around her waist.

"Hi," she spoke again, smiling.

"Er...hi," I replied. I lifted myself from the ground with a wince, brushing the grass from my pants and seeing that they had now dried from the popsicle incident of before, a moment that now felt had happened hours ago.

"What are you doing?" she asked again, eyeing the dented grass where I had laid. Her auburn hair blew in the wind, and she brushed it from her face, revealing her bright green eyes. I swallowed hard, finding those eyes easy to remember, my mind racing in disbelief.

"If we're meant to meet…" I whispered under my breath, repeating the words the woman from the bus had told me. She was right; if we were meant to know each other, then surely we would meet again. I just didn't figure it would happen so soon. "I uh…" I stuttered, my eyes becoming wide as I realized who she was. "Hi."

She giggled and clasped her hands behind her back, twisting in her spot as her skirt fanned out around her. "You're funny." She crinkled her nose and tilted her head, "You remind me of someone." She was missing a front tooth, and I found it cute.

I laughed. "Really?"

I looked at the palms of my hands as I squeezed them into fists, finding they felt strange and seeing that I now had two large scars on the palms of each. I flipped my palm over, the scar from the dog now gone without a single trace, as though it had never happened, though the memory of both incidents still remained. My eyes lit up then.

"So what's your name?" I was so eager to know that I spit the words all over her. Thankfully, she didn't seem to care, reacting with a giggle as she wiped it from her face.

"I'm Kenzie," She announced, lifting her nose in the air.

Her face was perfect, like an angel, and I couldn't help but smile. This girl did not yet know the sorrowful future that was ahead of her, and her eyes were still full of life.

"I'm Jordan," I replied, stretching my hand toward her for a shake.

She wrinkled her nose and shook her head. "How do I know you don't have cooties?"

I let a half smile cross my face, thinking that cooties hardly mattered considering that fact I had already spit words all over her. "As far as I know I've never had friends, so I'm pretty sure I never caught any."

I looked across the park toward my lane, noticing the moving truck at the house down the street from where I lived. I had never seen Kenzie before today, and I figured the moving truck involved her somehow. Was that a coincidence? I shook my head and refocused.

She laughed then, and grabbed my hand, shaking it as though it were a bell.

"Kenzie…" A woman I assumed was her mother stepped out from behind a tree. "There you are darling." She walked up behind her and hoisted her off the ground, giving me a smile. "Who is your new friend, Kenzie?"

Kenzie took a deep breath. "This is Jordan. He says he doesn't have cooties."

Her mother laughed and smiled, pinching Kenzie's nose in a loving manner. "Well, Jordan, I'm sure she'd love to stay and play, but it's already after four and we need to finish unpacking."

Kenzie let out a discontented sigh. "Mama, I hate unpacking."

Her mother laughed again. "I promised you a candy bar if you were good, remember?"

Kenzie's vibrant green eyes lit up and she let out a gasp of excitement.

Her mother looked back at me. "But maybe we will see you again Jordan. We're new to the neighborhood." She turned and pointed toward the house, "That one there." She knelt down and shook my hand then, giving me a warm smile that reminded me of my mother on her well days.

I nodded, still shocked that Kenzie was the girl from the future. They turned then and walked away and I watched them until they left the park. Feeling exhausted, I knelt back to the ground and sat, thinking about all that had happened.

Fate was trying to tell me something, but I didn't know what. Kenzie was important to me somehow, but she had not known me at twenty-seven, as though this meeting, now, had never happened. I furrowed my brow. Had she met me now because of meeting me on the bus? Had I changed the past by changing the future, just as I had changed the future by going into my past? Or had her future always led her here and something else had prevented me from meeting her? I could already see she was someone I wanted in my life, so why hadn't our paths crossed again? Why hadn't we become better friends?

I pondered this for a moment before remembering the time and realizing that I myself needed to get home to make dinner before Father arrived. I turned and ran from the park and down the street, past three houses until I reached the smallest one at the end, the green house with the messy yard. I kept one eye on the moving truck as I walked onto my porch, hoping to catch one last glimpse of Kenzie. Seeing that no one was outside, I turned my gaze back to my house, swinging my arms at my sides. A sad sigh escaped my lips as I looked to the place in the driveway where I had hugged my mother only moments ago, the place where I had changed my past and what seemed my future.

I raised my brows, noticing that something was different. I racked my brain in an attempt to remember what the house had been like this morning, before all that had happened, forcing myself to see what was different. I began to talk to myself, listing things that were the same. It was then I noticed that my mother's old car that had sat abandoned for years in the driveway was no longer there, with no sign that it ever had been either, or at least not for a very long time. I looked toward the park, trying to remember what it was I had done. Had Father simply sold it? Had it been stolen? Or was it what I had said to my mother?

I gasped, realizing that everything made sense. If I hadn't known Kenzie in the future, then it made sense that fate already knew I would go back and change my past, therefore changing the path my mother and I had taken, and therefore leaving the car somewhere new.

I blinked a few times, confused. It was then that a sharp bark caught me off guard and I looked to the fence. Rover wagged his tail and stuck his nose through the wood separators. My heart rate surged. I had changed it. I had saved the dog! Another noise pulled my attention away from Rover and to the street where my father's car puttered down the block. I drew in a frantic breath as I ran for the door in my attempt to get inside before he saw me. My feet pounded across the wood, but when I grabbed the handle, I found it was locked. Trying again I became frustrated as I rummaged in my pocket for a key, a key that was no longer there.

It was then that my father pulled into the drive, stopping the engine and falling out of his car, already drunk. Pulling himself off the ground, he slammed the door behind him as he steadied himself, taking a deep breath. I froze, terrified that he would see me and beat me like he often would when I was this late. He stumbled up the path, fumbling with the keys in his hand and mumbling under his breath. A breeze blew toward me and I could smell the whiskey, a smell that had become so normal to me.

He grunted as he looked up, noticing me.

"What do you want boy?" he bellowed, looking at me as though he didn't recognize who I was. He teetered as he stood there, his eyes crazy and lost. "You best get from my property boy, I don't want any trouble!"

I had heard him say this before when the Boy Scouts would come for our Christmas tree, something we never had because we celebrated nothing. I looked down at my feet out of fear, realizing he was so drunk that he had no idea who I was, and I wanted it to stay that way.

"Er... Sorry, sir." I scurried from the door and across the lawn to the sidewalk.

"Damn kids," my father muttered, dropping his lunch pail to the floor and pushing the key into the lock. He looked over his shoulder at me and I looked away, running down the street and out of view.

I shoved my hands into my pockets. Now what? What had I done? I shook my head, finding I was lost. It was true, changing my past had taken my mother and me away from here, making it true that I would not know Kenzie in the future because we would have never been neighbors. It was all connected somehow, but then, where was my mother? Where was home? I looked around as the afternoon light began to fade into evening. I felt the contents that filled my pockets, pulling out a wad of papers and cards that hadn't been there before.

I searched through each, finding nothing but coupons and tickets to movies I was sure I'd never seen but somehow felt I had. There was one card coated in plastic and I pulled it closer, reading the words. "Boston Children's Hospice," was all it read. I felt my heart sink, realizing what it meant.

I thought about my mother then, wondering what had happened, wondering if what I had said had given her the strength to leave, but to where? If this card were true then it meant I was orphaned, but why? Clearly she had taken me, clearly I had another life other than this but I had pulled myself from it, messed with God's plan and left myself no more than a stray.

I thought to go back and see what had happened but my body ached. Searching through my other pocket I pulled out an orange popsicle stick. Shocked, I checked my pants, the same pants I wore this morning and the same pants with a faint orange stain. I exhaled hard, finding that despite the fact I had moved about time, wearing other clothes and living other lives, some things still remained with me.

Not knowing where to go, I made my way back to the park where I climbed into the top section of the jungle gym and leaned against the wall. My stomach grumbled and I began to shake. I thought about Kenzie and the way she had cared for me, understood me without words. I tried to remember the fact that I was still six, still young though my brain had grown considerably.

In a split second I had changed my entire life without knowing it. I was surprised as a wave of relief rushed over me. I was free, free from it all, free from the world and all it made me do. This was my life now, and I was going to conquer it. I rolled my hands into fists and pounded them with happiness against the plastic of the jungle gym, letting out an energized yelp.

After a moment of excitement I finally finished with a contented sigh, leaning back against the blue plastic wall and closing my eyes as the possibilities unrolled in my head. For today, I would settle for a plan, but tomorrow, this life was mine.

Statement from Dr. Ashcroft
Vincent Memorial Hospital, Boston
August 4, 2009
12:23 a.m.

Agent Donnery:
    So did he start right away, changing your life that is?

Dr. Ashcroft:
    (pause) Yes and no, I think it was likely that he spent time with his mother first, trying to save her. He knew I would always be here, naturally, so he had the time. This was when the nightmares started, though, and I began to see him in my dreams. I never realized it was him until much later, as in just a few days ago. I had my hunches, but I thought I was simply manifesting his image because I wished the man was him. Turns out it really was.

Agent Donnery:
    Dreams? What kind of dreams?

Dr. Ashcroft:
    They were more like memories really. Because Jordan changed major portions

of my life, two paths were created. In my dreams I lived the old path, where I remained scarred and became a nurse, and while I was awake, I lived the one I'm still on now.

Agent Donnery:
    So according to his journal here, what came next?

Dr. Ashcroft:
    I honestly don't know because I never had the time to look, but I'm sure we can find out. (pause) Wow I… I do remember this, but I'm surprised that he went there first.

Agent Donnery:
    What happened?

Dr. Ashcroft:
    (pause) I'll tell you my side of it and then his, so that you can see how my dreams and real life mixed, so that you can better understand what it's like to be a part of his world.

Agent Donnery:
    Yes, that would help.

Dr. Ashcroft:
    This isn't the true version of the story, but it's the one I remember. What

you need to understand is that since there were two life paths created for me, he was hopping between both. In this entry, I didn't have the scars.

Agent Donnery:
    But if this came next, why was it you had no scars? Wouldn't he need to change that first?

Dr. Ashcroft:
    Remember, Agent, all of this is going to be backwards. His fate was already sealed. At one point or another, he was going to save me from the accident that burned my face, so that life path was already changed out of anticipation. I guess the best advice I can give you is to listen and try to smooth it all out in the end.

Agent Donnery:
    I'm only shaking my head because this may be one of the strangest things I've encountered to date.

Dr. Ashcroft:
    Really? What about the alien cover-up?

Agent Donnery:
    (laughter) We all know that aliens don't exist, Doctor.

Dr. Ashcroft:

    Perhaps, but I can tell from the smirk on your face that you're lying.

Agent Donnery:

    Believe what you want, Doctor, but right now let's just focus on your phenomenon, shall we?

Dr Ashcroft:

    So you've never seen another Shifter before? Why is that?

Agent Donnery:

    They're too hard to catch. For all I know, I have met one before, though I don't have the sort of dreams you have. There is really nothing we know about them, that's why your situation is so amazing and important. It's our first chance to get inside their world and see what the dangers are.

Dr. Ashcroft:

    I understand.

Agent Donnery:

    Shall we continue?

Dr. Ashcroft:

    Very well.

Told by Dr. Ashcroft,
Stories from the journals of Patient #32185
December 8th, 2002
1:51 p.m.

I looked at the clock and then back at the test, seeing I only had nine minutes left to finish nearly half the problems. I brushed my long, auburn locks from my eyes, finding that the cute haircut I had insisted on was now nothing more than a nuisance. I tapped the pencil against the page, the rubber of the eraser bouncing it back toward me, creating a meditative motion that only left my mind whirling with anything but the task at hand.

I couldn't shake the dream I'd had the night before, and though I tried to erase it, it felt too real to forget. For the last ten years I had been plagued by these dreams, as though I was also living another life when I fell asleep. The lack of rest kept me on edge, and the constant déjà vu was beginning to make me think I was some kind of psychic.

Last night I dreamt that my beautiful face was scarred and mangled, as though I'd been burned. It horrified me to see myself that way, but something about it also felt free and relaxing. Being that I was beautiful made my everyday life here in the real world hard, distracting. The self in my dreams had time to think, time to be alone, and I envied it. Pressing my lips together, I forced air from my lungs as it blew at the edges of the paper.

I needed to pass this test to get into pre-med, and then, eventually, Harvard, but at this point there was no use. My fingers curled into my hair as my forehead slipped toward the desk, makeup smearing across my flawless face, but it didn't matter. Perhaps I should come to school without showering, maybe then there wouldn't be so much pressure to be perfect. I looked at the clock. In six minutes my fate would be sealed and my grade would go down in history. This was the deciding moment of my life: will I be a nurse, or doctor?

My head began to pound as anxiety set in and blood rushed to my cheeks. I looked around at my peers, seeing that some of them had already finished and were lounging in their chairs. My boyfriend, Max, sat across the room, separated from me by the religious teacher that hated the way we looked at each other. Max didn't look too concerned with his work, but it didn't matter for him, either. He had already been recruited to go to Boston College on an Athletic Scholarship in the fall, the same school I had planned to attend for my pre-med.

Max was a decent enough man, even if he was a little controlling and stupid. He lacked any real concept of what it took to live a real life or to work for anything other than looking good. He had been gifted with a talent to play football, not the talent to think or even dream, for that matter. I suppose what it came down to was his looks, and as the head cheerleader, it was my fate to date the quarterback.

The second hand rolled over another minute and I squirmed in my seat as my skirt began to creep up my thighs.

I stared down at the page, trying my best to muster some form of concentration as the words on the test began to blur into a mess of things I could not understand. Where was God when I needed him; fate, luck, anything?

Something outside the classroom window caught my eye and I looked out on the courtyard. The wind blew through a nearby rhododendron and I watched as the breeze took the leaves for a ride, the cold dead flowers holding on for dear life, as I felt I was. The fire alarm began to scream from a box in the corner of the room then and I shut my eyes out of shock, a warm sensation rushing across my body as adrenaline began to pump and relief filled my heart. Apparently, God was listening after all.

The teacher stood, calming the class as everyone looked around with alarmed faces. We stood as we saw other students pass by the window on their way to the field.

"Everybody line up, head to the field. We'll pick up the tests when we get back so leave them where they are, please." He glared at one student that seemed to be attempting to hide his test under his shirt and take it with him.

We all rushed to the door, where I dodged away from Max, trying to ditch him in the rush.

Once on the field, I racked my brain for the answers on the test but as I felt Max grab my ass, I knew it was little use.

"Hey, babe," he leered at me.

I rolled my eyes. "Hey."

I tried to ignore him while we stood, but I doubt he even noticed as he chatted away with his buddies, only concerned with himself. I shifted my weight from one leg to the next, seeing that there was a group of cheerleaders huddled nearby. I thought to join them, but I really didn't want to. Their level of intrigue was rather low, and at the moment I felt the need to talk about something that was more intelligent than their squabbling about popularity and clothes, so I stood alone instead.

After fifteen minutes the teacher ushered us back from the field to the classroom where I knew I would finally meet my doom.

I threw myself back into my chair as Max gave me another pat on the butt. He often did this, ignored me then made up for it with some sort of rude petting, as though that made his ignorance acceptable; such a respectable way to treat a woman.

"You have two more minutes to complete the test because of the disruption. Please continue," the teacher barked, his yellow teeth peeking from below his chapped upper lip.

I felt my stomach sink as I flipped the test back over, bringing my pencil to the page and figuring I'd randomly fill in the remaining multiple choice questions and pray for the best. As I went question to question, however, I was shocked to see they had already been filled in. Had I, in fact, finished? I looked at the margins, seeing they were no longer filled with my mindless doodles though my name still remained at the top of the page in perfect form. I looked around the room with leering eyes, a dark cloud of doubt hanging over me.

"Pencils down." The teacher rose from his desk and

looked at us over his half moon glasses, his eyes cold like a snake.

I placed my pencil onto the desk as a smile grew across my face, deciding that at this point there was little I could do. Besides, my old test was no where in sight and I had to turn in something. I flipped the test over and left it on my desk as I packed my bag, guilt filling my heart as my mind pushed it away. I rolled my eyes as I saw Max approach. The last thing I needed right now was to hear him finish his rant that he had started on the field.

"So, hey, how did you do?" His voice was still arrogant.

I winced, "Save it Max."

My reply felt cold and undeserving, but what else could I do? I was still struggling to understand what had happened and why, and most of all, who had done it.

"Geez, you don't have to be mean."

He turned away from me with a stung ego. It was Friday, and he was in his game jersey and I in my cheerleading uniform; so clichéd.

I had received a lot of flack from my brother for dating such a jock, but it didn't matter. I hated myself, but I'd rather go with the flow than try and run from the life God gave me. I swallowed, telling myself for the hundredth time that I was lucky.

"Sorry, Max, I didn't mean it."

He smiled and leaned into me, hooking his arm around my waist like a chain. I tried my best to sling my bag onto my back but he refused to give me space, sticking his nose into the nook of my neck where he made kissing noises. My muscles tightened, attempting to shrug him away as we walked out into the hall where we met his friends. To my relief he all but forgot about me as he dropped his hand from my waist and they began to wrestle. They threw each other from locker to locker as they laughed like children, slamming one kid in a dark green coat and black hat into the wall, not even bothering to apologize.

I rushed to the kid. "Are you alright?"

He looked at me under the bill of his hat and nodded, turning and dodging away from me with such speed I hardly got the chance to see his face. I watched as he left, something tingling at my memories, wondering if it had been him whom had done this to my test, but how and why? I then turned and grabbed Max by the arm and spun him toward me.

"Would you watch what you're doing? You'll hurt someone," I hissed.

Max shrugged away from me, "What's gotten into you today Kenzie, are you PMS-ing or something?"

He looked at me as though I were nothing more than a spec of dust and my fiery attitude boiled over.

"Screw you," I retorted, turning and storming away from him down the hall, trying to act infuriated.

I tightened my fists around the straps of my backpack. That was my last straw with him, I swear. I grumbled as a little voice inside me tried to retort but I silenced it; this time I was serious. I was never the type to be a pushover, never the type to put up with such crap. I sighed, my guilt taking over as I began to feel bad but I pressed forward anyway, figuring I could apologize later. I was in a rush to get out of here before someone found out what I had done, that I had cheated. The self in my dreams would have never done something like this, and I knew it would eat me alive for the rest of winter break. I tried to think of the fact that I'd be heading to pre-med next year if that test was indeed correct, but on what grounds? A lie?

I pushed open the doors of the hall and stormed out into the parking lot to my car. I saw the kid in the green coat and black hat climb onto a motorcycle I had never seen before, pressing his foot down on the starter as it roared to life. I made a move to run toward him and ask his name but stopped myself, relieved that he didn't notice my attempt as I unlocked my car and stepped inside.

I didn't want to start the engine, afraid that it would draw attention and ruin my voyeuristic game. I turned my head and watched him through the dusty glass of my rear window, wondering who he was and why I felt so strange in his presence. Looking away, I buckled in and put both hands on the steering wheel, taking a deep breath.

For a moment I thought about my dream and the man I'd met there. My mind was twisting to find some resemblance, but the man was nothing but a blurred outline, and though I did not know who he was, I was lost in the mysterious romance of the whole thing.

I shook the thought away, angry that I'd allow myself to think of anyone but Max that way. Still parked in my spot,

I then looked in my rearview and out the back window as I heard the motorcycle engine roar. With poise and a strong sense of independence, the strange boy drove behind my car and out of the lot as my gaze followed him, wondering if he would turn his head so I could see his face, but he never did, and I found myself disappointed.

As he disappeared over the hill I felt my forehead begin to ache, the left side of my face burning as though I'd been slapped, as though the scar from my nightmare was really there. I pulled down the visor and flipped open the mirror, looking at my face and finding nothing was wrong other than the smeared make-up from class. I rummaged through my bag for my powder, cursing the thick leather that hid all the contents so well.

"Hey."

I jumped, letting out a half-hearted scream as Max grabbed the edge of the car window.

"Sorry babe, you know I can't act weak around my friends."

I let out a discontented sigh and flipped the visor back up. "Grow up Max. I doubt they'd see you as a weenie for treating your girlfriend like a human."

He laughed. "I'm the Quarterback, babe. You know I can't show a soft side. I'm supposed to be their leader."

I rolled my eyes and flipped open my compact, dabbing my forehead, "Whatever."

"Will you drive me home?"

He gave me a sweet smile and I felt my guard fall. He

had a way of looking at you that made all your inhibitions melt, like an expert salesman. I paused and tightened my grip on the steering wheel, grabbing my keys and starting the engine.

"Fine." I gave in, so gullible.

He leaned in through the window and kissed me on the cheek. "You're a doll, the best woman in the world."

I laughed to myself, wishing he had even the simplest understanding of who I really was, and not just what I did for him and how I looked. It was amusing to think that in my dreams he actually hated me, taunted me like a bully because I was ugly, a nobody. In my dreams he was also the type that would cheat on his girlfriend. There, he dated my best friend Marcie, not a far cry from someone I could really see him being with, except in the real world, she wasn't the head cheerleader, and if she wasn't the head cheerleader, then they would never date. It was the rules after all; the head cheerleader always dated the Quarterback. It was this dark side of him that I feared was real, but I'd never seen it except in my dreams, so I knew it was just a figment of my imagination; another reason to justify hating him when really he was no more than a sweetheart.

Statement from Dr. Ashcroft,
Vincent Memorial Hospital, Boston
August 4, 2009
12:43 a.m.

Agent Donnery:
     So that's your side of it?

Dr. Ashcroft:
     Yep, that's my side. I wanted to give you the full dynamic, so you'll understand more later in the story when Max and I mature and go to college, then you'll really see why trying to change your past doesn't mean you solve a problem.

Agent Donnery:
     So what does Jordan's side of it say?

Dr. Ashcroft:
     It starts out the same, but then there's a portion here that's different, a portion I had actually dreamt about the very night it happened. It's crazy because what I thought was just a dream is written right here before me. (pause) The next morning I laughed it off, figuring it was my mind's way of coping with the fact I cheated my way into med school.
Agent Donnery:

Well, what does it say was different?

Dr. Ashcroft:
Well there are two endings here, the one I just told you, only from his angle, and then the one that I suppose was what should have really happened if the tests hadn't been swapped out; if he hadn't Shifted my life.

Agent Donnery:
I see. Tell me the bit about what should have happened, the part you dreamt of, but from his angle.

Dr. Ashcroft:
Alright. This feels strange but it's fascinating to think it was real and that he was really there.

I stood near the edge of the school, parking my bike in the lot. It had taken me longer than I'd anticipated getting here, as I forgot that having a bike stored in the future posed a few problems, like old gas. I made a mental note to put some additives in my bag before I left today so that when I came back to this same time tomorrow, I wouldn't have any issues.

I walked down the hill from the lot and onto school grounds. I was not concerned about being caught here because I looked the part of a student in my green jacket and black hat; a part of the grunge crowd no one really wanted to confront anyway. I made my way down the empty halls to Kenzie's classroom where I knew today was her big test, and though she had spent late hours studying last night, her knucklehead of a boyfriend had kept her up with his own issues, distracting her from what she needed to succeed.

When I arrived at her classroom, I made my way around back where a large rhododendron shielded the window, hiding me from their view. I watched her through the leaves, always feeling as though I were no more that a pathetic voyeur, but it was my job. I saw her look up at the clock with a fear in her eyes that I hated to see.

A cold breeze blew then, ruffling the leaves and shriveled

flowers that were left over from summer. Kenzie looked up and out the window. I ducked back, feeling my heart race as her eyes almost met mine through the leaves. I waited a moment before looking back, relieved to see her attention was back on the paper as her head dropped to her hands out of frustration.

"Pencils down."

The teacher rose form his desk and looked at the class over his half moon glasses, his voice muffled by the glass of the window. Kenzie placed her pencil onto the desk, rolling her eyes and looking down at the paper with disappointment. She flipped the test over, leaving it on her desk as she packed her bag. Max approached her from across the room, and I cringed and looked away. The last thing I needed right now was to see him give her another slap on the butt, something all boys seemed to do to their girlfriends but something I felt was obnoxious.

I twisted away and back into the breezeway as I blended in with the crowd. I leaned against a locker for a while and waited, unable to stifle my need to see Kenzie once more as she passed by. I heard her voice as they came out the door, followed by a commotion in the hall as Max met up with his friends and started talking. Before I knew it, they were wrestling, throwing each other about like children and I found myself helplessly in their path as Max threw a large running back at the lockers, squishing me in between.

I winced as my body slammed against the metal, but what was worse was the embarrassment. As Max and his friend continued to fight, unconcerned by the fact they had hit me, I felt a hand grab my arm and I glanced in that direction with alarm, forgetting what it felt like to have someone touch me. For a brief but sweet moment, my eyes met Kenzie's.

"Are you alright?" she asked.

I looked away from her, too ashamed and too scared to let her see me. I shrugged and gave her a nod before dodging away from her and around the corner. I heard her as she said something to Max, and then watched as she stormed away in the opposite direction. Smiling, I realized she had defended me and it felt good to know she still cared. As she disappeared, I quickly turned and ran around the exterior halls toward the lot, figuring it was in my best interest to get out of here and back to the garage where I kept my bike.

In the lot I saw her get into her car, so I kept my gaze low, my face hidden behind the brim of my hat as I climbed on my bike and prayed the separated gas would hold long enough to allow the engine to start. I pressed down hard on the ignition, and to my relief the old pile came to life, purring as it had two years ago when I bought it and stored it for just such an occasion.

I was quick to leave, but in my heart I knew that tomorrow I would see her again, when I came back and changed the fate of her failed test. I knew exactly what I would do, though it seemed like a cheap shot, it was the best thing I could think of at the moment. I would wait a few hours and come back, break into the school and steal a blank test and then tomorrow I would swap hers for the right one. Naturally

I could make it easy on myself and just swap it now, but I couldn't shake the way it felt for her to touch me and a part of me wanted her to know that someone was out there, watching over her.

Statement from Dr. Ashcroft, Vincent Memorial Hospital, Boston
August 4, 2009
12:56 a.m.

Agent Donnery:
    So that was a completely different rendition.

Dr. Ashcroft:
    (pause) Yes, I can't believe that that one test would have changed my life forever.

Agent Donnery:
    Don't worry. Your secret is safe with me. Let's just say it's awful hard for a farm boy from Kansas to pass the C.I.A. test the first time.

Dr. Ashcroft:
    (laughter) We all have our secrets, right?

Agent Donnery:
    So then you still have his side of what happened?

Dr. Ashcroft:
    Yes, right here. Do you care to hear that as well or is it getting too repetitive?

Agent Donnery:
     No, actually I'm intrigued. I'd like
  to know what he was thinking.

Dr. Ashcroft:
     Yeah. (pause) Me too.

Formulated from the Journals of
Patient #32185
December 8th, 2002
01:24 p.m.

I finished forging Kenzie's name, took the finished test from the teacher's desk, and leapt back through time and space as my body heated up like a pot of boiling water. When I opened my eyes, I landed in the lot just down the street where the garage I had rented two years ago was located. I shook away the nauseated feeling from the travel, my body growing used to the feeling after doing it for so long. I arrived at the garage and paused for a moment to breathe and re-group.

I had decided that keeping storage places throughout my life was a great idea, especially considering my condition and the fact that at this point, home was a definite grey area. I opened the rusty garage door that was covered in vines, the same door I had hacked my way through just yesterday. It was tedious at times to have to go through the same dilemmas twice, just as I knew the gas was going to pose a problem yet again, though I had found the time to get the additive. My bike stared at me through the dusty space, the chrome covered in a thick layer of dust as though I hadn't touched it in years. I sighed, thinking of how clean it had just been.

I brushed my hand across the seat and threw my leg over the saddle and sat down. I looked at the gauges and shook the chassis, making sure nothing had changed though I knew it hadn't. The problem with time travel was keeping things straight. Technically, I felt I'd already filled the tank with the old gas from the can, but naturally that hadn't yet happened either because that time no longer existed.

I liked to travel on both paths of Kenzie's life, the one with the scars and the one without, to determine which was better for her. After all the time spent in both, I was beginning to lean toward this life because at least here, the pain only ran on the surface, versus the pain that ran deep in her heart in the world where she had been robbed of all her dreams. She didn't need the option to decide for herself because I knew what was better now, and I knew what was destined for her.

I tilted my head to the side and cracked my neck before placing the bike back on its stand and getting off. I rummaged through the garage for the gas can, already forgetting where I had found it before. Looking at my watch, I saw I was cutting it rather close and Kenzie's class would be out in a little over thirty minutes. If I screwed this up she'd remain in her unhappy life as a nurse, but I didn't want that for her anymore; she deserved better. Besides, I could always just rewind it again and start over, but at times it hurt to do it too many times and it left my body aching for days.

Since that day she saved me, I couldn't forget her. She had become my angel and my reason to live. I remembered the vow I had made to save her from all her sadness, and come Hell or high water, that was what I was going to do. I was given this talent for a reason, and though it's easy to act selfish, it feels good to use it as I have. Besides, I did not need my own life; this was my life.

I finally spotted the gas can in the far corner and gave it a shake, pulling the additive from my pocket and pouring it inside. I gave the can another brisk rattle, figuring it was enough to make it hold for the duration of the task. I opened the tank on the bike and drained the contents of the can into it, breathing in the thick fumes. Satisfied, I let out a contented breath and threw the empty can to the side as I climbed back onto the bike.

Some people would consider my attention to Kenzie's life obsessive, but over the years, I couldn't help but fall in love with her and her angelic way of life. I couldn't let go. I was proud to have been a silent part of every bit of it, right down to the facts of her very happiness. I didn't need her to know me and I didn't need her thanks, because I knew in my heart that if she were in my position, she would have done the same for me.

I pressed down on the clutch and cranked the engine to life. The tense rumbling of the exhaust echoed off the old wooden walls of the garage, fumes pouring from the back in thick clouds of white smoke, choking the air around me. I rolled forward out of the smoke, allowing the engine to have a moment to purify so that it didn't look as though I was riding a beater.

As I leaned against the handlebars, I smirked, remembering the way Kenzie had watched me leave the school lot this afternoon. There was something in her eyes that knew me as though she had remembered being there when she saved me from the bus. I touched my sleeve, feeling the place where her hand had grabbed my arm, reveling in the way it felt to be touched after so many years alone.

If Kenzie had only known that this would be the absolute deciding moment of the rest of her career, I was certain she would have told Max off so she could study. But that was why I was here, to watch over her when she couldn't. Yesterday, or perhaps I mean today, I watched her dreams fall away from her. But on this day, the same day, I would watch her dreams come true. It was the most amazing thing to see, to say I watched the woman I love become the woman she always wanted, ever since she was a little girl.

I rolled the bike forward a little more and let it sit idle while I re-locked the garage. The neighbor was outside and I waved to her as she tended to her roses. She gave me a strange look of disbelief as she watched me, and I was certain it was likely that her and her friends had speculated over this particular garage, wondering if the boy who owned it ever came and what was in it.

I got back on the bike and checked my watch; it was now 1:38 and I was just in time. I revved the engine and tore down the street toward the school, grabbing my black hat out of my pocket and putting it on my head. I didn't bother with a helmet, what was the point? I knew I wouldn't die, and if I did get pulled over by a cop, it wasn't very hard to change that. As far as the world knew, I did not exist. I was stuck somewhere between two places, the past and the future.

I arrived at the school and drove into the parking lot, where I idled past Kenzie's grey Wrangler as a smile stretched across my face. I was so watchful of her that I made sure she got a decent car, not the station wagon she had been destined for. I needed to make sure she drove something safe so that I would at least have peace of mind when I wasn't here to watch her.

I pulled into a spot near the back and parked, shutting off the rattling engine. I drew a heavy breath past my tired lips, wondering how long it had been since I last slept, feeling as though the day had gone on forever. I threw my leg off the bike and grabbed my bag from the back of the seat, hoisting it over my shoulder and walking toward her classroom.

It felt like déjà vu, as it always did, and I let the memory of this day, as it had happened previously, return to me. I knew it was careless of me to let her see me when she got out of class, but I hadn't meant for her brute of a boyfriend to run into me like he did. It was then that I finally noticed the fact that I was sore where Max had thrown my shoulder against the locker. Luckily for me, I was able to erase that embarrassment from my life and no one would ever know that I was the wimp that got slammed by the quarterback.

It was a goal of mine to never let Kenzie see me in her real life. If she ever did, it was only because I knew I was going to be going back to change it, and it would inevitably be erased from her thoughts. There was one time when she was ten, though, before I decided that letting her know about me was a bad idea. It was a quick meeting, a meeting that suggested that despite erasing time, there was still some sort of connection between us. Though we had that one stolen moment, she never remembered me. If she had, I would have changed things but at that age, it's easy for a girl to forget you, especially as you grow into the popular and loved woman that she had become.

It hurt to stay away from her because I knew she could love me, but I also knew that I could never do that to her. I could never allow her to know who I was because the confusion would be overwhelming. Did I feel sorry for myself? No. I figured being here for her was my purpose; like a Guardian Angel. If I could at least help her have a normal life, something I was not destined to have, then that was all that mattered to me.

I looked at my watch again as her classroom came into view down the outdoor breezeway. It was convenient that her high school was set up with outdoor hallways. It made sneaking around easier as well as providing an easy get-away, an advantage I needed. I found my place by the frozen rhododendron once more, taking a deep breath. I was careful to peer around the corner in a way that wouldn't draw attention, like it somehow had yesterday when she looked outside, as though she had felt my presence there watching her.

I smiled as I saw her auburn hair fall in a thick curtain around her as she eased her frustrated hand under her jaw. I looked at my watch, seeing that it was 1:51. Kenzie also looked at the clock on the wall, then let out a sigh and looked out the window just as she had last time. I leaned back against the wall, anticipating her every move. At times I wondered if there was a part of her that recognized me from when she was ten, but I couldn't let myself dwell on the simple pleasure of it, knowing such things could drive a man mad.

I pulled the test from my pocket and unfolded it. I knew it was cheating, but I also knew that Kenzie was a bad test taker. It was unfair to judge her based on a score that was gathered in such a pressured, dull environment. I had seen Kenzie perform in her life as a nurse where she was often more alert and useful than the doctors themselves. She deserved this.

Taking a deep breath, I rounded the corner toward the lockers and found the Emergency Fire Alarm. For as many times as I'd pulled this, you'd think they would have thought to lock down the system. I scanned the halls one last time before lifting the clear plastic cover and pulling it without a second thought, the sirens now filling the halls and echoing off the cement structure. It was then that I casually moved back around the corner by the classroom window and waited as the screaming alarm ushered the entire school toward the football field.

Peeking through the window, I watched as a look of relief crossed Kenzie's face and she set her pencil down. I could hear her teacher's muffled voice through the glass, instructing them to leave the tests on the desk and that they would all be staying after to finish. I watched her rise from her chair, thankful that she would have all the time in the world to think over the answers while she stood on the field, time she would not need because I had them.

I allowed myself the pleasure of watching her move. She had a grace that was intoxicating and legs that went on for miles. Though I had loved her while she was scarred, it was hard to deny the fact of her beauty now. It was not a selfish choice to save her good looks, though a part of me felt guilty for it. I knew as a fact that beautiful people lived happier lives, why not right?

She walked like an angel toward the door, only to be met by her boyfriend and I found myself looking away as I had before. It was painful to see her with him time after time, but at one point in her life it had been something she had wished for and I couldn't deny her that happiness. I looked down at my hands, rough from a life full of running away, ashamed by my meek looks in comparison to Max's effortless grandeur. I pulled the hat further down my forehead and straightened my dark green army coat, justifying my image.

Once everyone had left the room, I waited for them to round the corner before diving in and picking the lock. The teacher was smart to lock the door. Ensuring in the fact that he would know nothing could have possibly been tampered with, except by me. I was quick to grab Kenzie's test and swap it for the finished one I had brought, figuring someone would be by to check that the room was cleared. I shoved the unfinished test back in my pocket and left the room where I walked up the grassy hill and sat by a tree that overlooked the school.

While I waited, I pulled the test from my pocket and scanned her work, smirking at the doodles she'd decorated the edges with. I knew her enough to know that she would not reject the test I had given her, knew enough about her morals that she saw it as a lucky break, not breaking the rules. She always thought she was fortunate; the girl whose life happened in every way she ever wished for, and that was exactly what I wanted.

A few moments later, the students on the field broke off and began making their way back toward class. It was easy to spot Kenzie in the crowd, her hair flowing down her back and her cheerleading sweater like a bright red beacon. I stood and moved in closer, my insatiable need to see her face irrepressible.

I stood back on the path by the rhododendron, watching her from the corner of the window as she flipped over the test. At first she looked confused, flipping through the pages and then rubbing her forehead as though forgetting that she had finished it. She looked over her shoulder toward the teacher, but he seemed enthralled by something he was writing. It was then that her confusion turned to relief and I smiled with her. She flipped over the test and placed the pencil on the page, giving her boyfriend a smug look and crossing her arms against her chest.

With that, I felt content, and I knew her dream career would come true. "I love you," I whispered. It was then that her head shot to the window, and I quickly ducked back. I let out a nervous laugh, relieved she had not seen me.

Standing there with one leg perched against the wall, a vindictive thought crossed my mind as a girl in a black sweatshirt glared at me from across the commons. She watched me as though she knew what I was up to, and I laughed to myself, wondering if this student sensed my sick desire to endure this sort of treatment again, just to feel her touch me once more.

As the bell rang I turned my attention to the classroom door, preparing myself. The already existing bruises tingled, but what I was about to do was harmless and I swore she would never see me again. I had worked hard to accomplish all I had for her, and this was my reward. I deserved it, after all.

Statement from Dr. Ashcroft,
Vincent Memorial Hospital, Boston
August 4, 2009
01:12 a.m.

Agent Donnery:
    So you can remember both sides of the story because of your dreams?

Dr. Ashcroft:
    Yes, some are stronger than others, but reading over the journals is jogging my memory, like reading something you wrote when you were in third grade and then placing it in a time capsule.

Agent Donnery:
    Is that why my colleagues keep giving you MRI's, to make sure it's not damaging your brain?

Dr. Ashcroft:
    I suppose, but it's not. We have so much brain that is left unused, I guess this is why. (laughter) Besides, I guess they want to make sure I'm mentally fit to work, which I am.

Agent Donnery:

So at this point he had already changed your scars it seems. Do you remember that?

Dr. Ashcroft:

The scars are the hardest thing for me to remember because it was so long ago, but I can still feel them at times, just as I did the day of the test in my car. The dreams, too; they're always there, reminding me of this other life I should have lived before Jordan's web of Shifts was created.

When Jordan said he had let me see him only once, he means the day when he came to save me from the scars. (pause) I remember it all the time, always wondering what had happened to that boy from the bus in elementary school. He came out of nowhere and disappeared just as fast. It haunted me for years, just wondering how and why it seemed to connect.

You have to understand that Jordan did not live a normal life from beginning to end. He was all over it, so to speak. Shifting from one place to the next, forgetting time altogether. Maybe one day he'd see himself at eighty, the next at five. Either way, he was able to carry the memories with him, along with certain belongings like his bag and the green coat and black hat, the one thing that eventually drew me toward him. In my dreams, I recognized the things he was wearing and it struck a chord. (laughter) It was as though he was living in a playground, but we were the toys.

Agent Donnery:
    I see. (pause) So tell me about the scars, then. How did he solve that?

Dr. Ashcroft:
    Well, I'll tell you from my angle, what I remember versus what he wrote here. It's the next entry.

"Hi." I was standing at the bus stop, waiting.

A boy stood there with me, a new kid, someone I did not know. He had a black hat and a green coat that was far too large for him, and I figured it had been his father's, or perhaps an older brother. I fumbled with the ruffle of my pink dress, hoping he would answer me.

He gave me a nervous look under the bill of the hat as he kicked a rock on the ground. "Hi."

I looked away toward the road and smiled. "Are you new here?"

His blue eyes met mine, and there was something about them, something curious.

"I, uh…" he paused and adjusted his backpack. "I just moved in down the street." He pointed behind him over his shoulder.

"Oh." I nodded and clasped my hands in front of me.

He looked older than me but not by much, though his aura seemed very mature and I deduced he must be a sixth grader.

"Which house?" I pressed, looking back down the lane.
He kicked another rock. "The green one, at the end." He pointed again.

This time my eyes followed where he was pointing down the lane, toward the green house that had sat abandoned for years. It didn't look as though anyone lived there, but I wasn't about to press the point any further and seem nosey. There had been a family there once, but the mother had left with the boy the day after I moved into the neighborhood and the father ended up drinking himself to death. I always wondered what had happened, made up stories that filled my head with fear.

There were four houses on our lane, all modest homes built in the roaring sixties when baby-boomers were a way of life. There was a park nearby that was shared by five other conjoining lanes, built in the middle, like the nucleus of the whole thing. Each house had a fenced yard with beautiful landscapes, each except the green one, of course.

I cleared my throat. "Do you live there with your mom and dad?"

He nodded quickly, but gave no real reply. It was then that he looked at me and smiled, distracting me away from the conversation and enchanting me with his dark blue eyes.

Changing the subject he then spoke. "So you're a fourth grader, right?"

I smiled back and stood up tall. "Yep."

He nodded. "I remember fourth grade. It was a lot better than sixth."

I blinked back pride, finding I was right about his age and gloating to myself. "Sixth is exciting though, next year you get to go to Junior High." I sighed and tilted my head. I hated school, all I wanted was to grow up and get out.

The bus came over the hill, barreling toward us. We both stood in silence, both aware of the other's presence, and both curious. Having a new kid at school felt exciting and fresh, something I had been waiting for that could give me something to do.

The dogs in the neighborhood began to bark and I watched as the kid looked over his shoulder and back toward his house, smiling at the dog in the neighbor's yard.

"That's Rover," I added, seeing the look on his face, a look of joy as though he wanted his own dog.

"Is that so?" The boy's eyes met mine and I pursed my lips, finding his answer unexpected and strange.

The bus crawled to a rattling stop in front of us as the crossing sign squeaked out from its side. The driver ushered us around the front of the bus where the new boy allowed me to climb up first, offering me a hand. Though I wanted to, I didn't take it, sensing the eyes of a million kids watching me. More teasing was the last thing I needed. I was strange enough as it was.

I walked toward the middle of the bus, feeling everyone's eyes still on me. I kept my gaze on my feet as I moved down the aisle where I sat in an empty row, the same one I sat in by myself everyday. I watched the boy look from one kid to the next, a smug smile on his face as all the girls seemed to swoon.

I looked down into my lap, afraid to stare. At ten, I hardly found boys attractive, but this new kid had something about him that felt warm, though I knew better than to hope.

"Do you mind if I sit with you?" My eyes shot from my lap to his face.

"Er..." I grabbed my things with a nervous hand and pulled them into my arms, making room for him on the seat. "No."

He smiled, and I couldn't help but gawk as he sat down.

"My name is Jordan." He pushed his hand toward me.

"My name is Kenzie," I stuttered, placing my now sweating palm in his and giving it a soft, nervous shake.

He laughed. "You don't have to be so nervous Kenzie. I won't bite."

I let out a nervous laugh. "If you did bite, I hardly think it would matter," I uttered under my breath, touching my face. I could tell he pretended not to hear what I said, but I hadn't really meant to hide it. I was an open book at this point because I no longer cared what people thought of me. No matter what I said, it always came down to the way I looked. My horrid fate was now a cage.

He let out a sharp breath as though content. "So Kenzie, what do you dream about?"

I glanced at him sideways, giving him a strange look. "Um..." I paused as he turned to me with a steady stare, insinuating the fact that he wasn't kidding. I thought hard for a moment, trying to collect my thoughts. No one had ever really asked me this question, let alone a complete stranger, and I wondered for a moment why that was. Perhaps people just figured I didn't have dreams, that I didn't deserve them.

He waited patiently for my reply, tapping his foot against the seat in front of him. The coming bus ride to school was a long one, so we had time. I opened my mouth to speak, only to close it and think further.

Finally, my thoughts gathered and a smile grew on my face. "I want to be a doctor," I said in a plain manner, knowing that was all I'd ever wanted since I was old enough to know what a doctor was. "And I want to be popular," I added under my breath, with a bit of vanity.

He nodded but did not reply, suggesting he wanted to know more.

I took a deep breath and let it all pour out. "I want to change the world, change everything. I've seen so much of the bad side of life. I just wish something could give." I pulled at the strings on my backpack. "I know I will never be the Homecoming Queen, or that girl who dates the quarterback or the one that makes head cheerleader, but I don't mind." I shrugged, watching Jordan's reaction.

There was sadness in his eyes, as though he knew me, as though he had seen into my soul and felt the same pain I had. Something about him felt comforting, like a long lost friend but I couldn't put my finger on it. I looked at his messed up hair, held together by a bit of gel in a fashion that seemed cool and trendy.

He smiled then. "You deserve all that, Kenzie. Don't you

see?"

I frowned and shook my head. "But how does that work? The world is based on superficial things, on vanity. When you look like I do, you see that it's true. Even you…" I paused. "Even you get treated differently because you're…" I swallowed, my cheeks becoming hot. "You're perfect."

A sharp laugh escaped his lips. "Hardly." He hesitated for a moment before grabbing my hand, and I felt my heart stop. "Just because I look perfect," he touched his chest, "Doesn't mean I am, inside."

I frowned as I wondered what he meant, finding the conversation far too advanced for elementary school kids. Was he sick, perhaps? Was he crazy? A million options as to why he was anything but perfect racked my mind, but I came up with nothing other than the fact that he seemed smart.

Since the accident, I had grown up fast and I always outsmarted the other children at every task, ignoring my childish desires and embracing maturity. I was too damaged to get away with acting clumsy and careless. The fact was, I didn't fit in no matter what aspect. I was too smart and too ugly, two things kids my age did not typically relate with.

"How did it happen?" He squeezed my hand, and I felt as though he already knew.

I lowered my gaze. "It was a car accident."

He watched me with steady eyes as the girls across the aisle began to whisper to each other in a way that I knew meant they were talking about me.

"My mother and I…" Tears grew in my eyes but I held

them at bay. "My mother and I got rear-ended by a semi-truck in the city, the tanks exploded and I was stuck. My mother made it out and she managed to grab me, but it was too late and my face had been burned. I was in the hospital for months as they worked to graft the skin." My guard failed as a tear fell from my eye and I was surprised as Jordan wiped it away. "It was never the same." I pulled up the sleeve of my shirt, "Twenty percent of my body was burned but I would give anything if it were the twenty percent that didn't include my face. That alone would change everything."

"When did it happen? What was the date?" He seemed adamant about this question as though it mattered.

I laughed. "Why? You think you can change this? Do you own a time machine, a Delorean?" I continued to laugh, but his face remained straight and my laughter faded. I narrowed my eyes. "Who are you really?"

He laughed then. "I was just curious Kenzie. I just wanted to know you."

I felt awkward, "Well…" I shrugged, "For what it's worth, it was in the summer, August 22nd, three years ago."

He looked toward the ceiling of the bus. "So that was 1991?"

I watched as he repeated the date under his breath, shaking my head and realizing that though he was cute, it was true that he was a little odd.

"So where did it happen?" He was brave to keep pushing for answers like this.

I swallowed, not exactly finding myself excited about

this conversation. "It happened where Southampton meets Massachusetts Avenue, where the packing plants are."

He smiled then and nodded, taking a moment to consider this before changing the subject. "I don't see why you think so little of yourself; I don't see why you can't be the Homecoming Queen and date the cute guys." He smirked, "No matter what, Kenzie, you will always be the person you are inside. Someone will see that one day."

He released my hand, and I discreetly wiped the sweat from my palm on my dress.

"Well, I hope so," I snorted.

As the bus came to a halt outside the school and the noise in the cabin grew loud, I knew our conversation was over. Jordan picked up his bag, and I noticed how out of date and used it was. His clothes and overall style seemed up to date, but the bag threw me off. I gathered my things and slung my backpack over my back, gripping the straps with nervous hands.

Jordan turned to me. "Well, Kenzie, hopefully I will meet you again."

I gave him another strange look. "Sure…"

And with that, he turned and walked off the bus, cutting through the students and heading through the school as though he knew exactly where he was going. Whoever Jordan was, I found my heart would not slow down. Something about him was far more exhilarating than anything I had ever done, anything that had ever happened to me, and I liked it.

Statement from Dr. Ashcroft,
Vincent Memorial Hospital, Boston
August 4, 2009
01:36 a.m.

Agent Donnery:
    Oh, wow, so you really remember that
conversation pretty well.

Dr Ashcroft:
    Yes, I had dreams about it for
years, and then of course, dreams about
what really happened, because I had met
him again in the same situation on the
same bus on the same day, only I was no
longer ugly.

Agent Donnery:
    What's next?

Dr. Ashcroft:
    Well it continues from there, but
this is the part I didn't know about, so
I'll just read what he said.

I cursed to myself as I remembered that I hadn't asked Kenzie what time the accident had happened. I entered the front hall of my old house down the lane, the floor dented and cracked below my feet from the force of my landing, my blood boiling as I waited for it to cool before I pressed forward.

I was still wearing the same clothes from the bus, seeing as I left right away, unable to bear letting her suffer with such unhappiness much longer. My green coat now swam on me and the hat was loose so I took it off my head and shoved it in my bag. I was nine again, my favorite age.

It had taken me a while to get to this specific incident in her life, to save her from her scars. First, I wanted to see what sort of life she had endured on both paths, to make sure I wasn't making a huge mistake by changing this moment, because God knows it would be impossible, not to mention sadistic, to try and change it back in the future.

Pulling at the belt of my now oversized pants I managed to fasten them enough that they could stay up while I walked out the front door of the green house down the lane. I sighed. By now, the house had been abandoned. At eighteen, the house would officially be mine when the trust is released from the bank, but for now, the house was theirs, and I missed it.

The front yard still held a sense of order, and a few tulips left their petals spread across the ground. The blue flowers that lined the drive had now burned out under the hot summer sun of Boston and lay limp across the barren dirt, overgrown and wild. The path looked better than it had three years in the future, and I marveled at its youth, though it was anything but pretty. There was a stone by the driveway where acrylic paint still clung to the surface, spelling out my last name, McKay.

My mother and I had painted it one day while my father was out working odd jobs and spending hours at the bar with his buddies. We had laughed and made a mess. She had been beautiful in her joy. I only wish she could have had a better life, but there was nothing I could do to change that. I was born after they had been married, so I couldn't travel back to before, and until I was old enough to talk, there was little I could say to save her. I often visited those days, just to have her there to hold me before she died.

Though I tried, I could not save her from the cancer; it was too advanced and too aggressive to ever stop, but God knows I did all I could. There had at least been the few years after I had managed to get her out and away from my father. He was too proud to allow her a divorce after we had run away, even on her deathbed. I found it was hard for me to resist the urge to kill him, but I had to. Murder was never a path I wanted to travel down, no matter what my talents of evasion were.

My father was a tyrant. A man deeply tormented by

what could only be described as the devil himself, and to my relief, he died not too long after her. Because of what I had said the day I had saved Rover, my mother had left him when I was four, and that was why her car had been gone that day in the beginning when I had come home to the green house at the end of the lane that was no longer my home; where my father no longer recognized my face or even cared. When we left, my father took to drinking more than in the life where we had stayed, and his liver did not last.

I was all alone now, from age seven on. Luckily I did have my condition, so at times it felt good to see her, to tell her I loved her, even though it made no difference now. I sometimes wondered if she could see me from Heaven, if there even was a Heaven. If so, I wondered what she thought of me, my skill and my curse. Telling her had never been something that had made sense. She had enough to deal with already.

I dragged my feet across the cement by the painted rock, pressing forward as Rover ran to the fence and wagged his tail. He didn't bark anymore, he was so used to seeing me at this point that he'd given up. Though the house wasn't yet mine, that didn't mean I didn't still use it as a crash pad of sorts. There was little the bank could do but let it sit, so everything down to the silverware remained inside. They never noticed, and it was in that fact that I knew they didn't care either. We were twenty busy street blocks away, and too much of an inconvenience to have an agent check in on the house once a month.

As I walked, I pulled my bag from my back. After

discovering my talents, I spent a few years figuring it out, traveling through time and visiting my entire life as it had been intended, before I discovered my abilities. It had been a lovely life, full of happiness, sorrow and pain, but no Kenzie. I saw my death at age eighty three, and my birth, all things you'd expect to see. As I traveled, I found my brain expanded, gaining the knowledge of a life spent in college and the fulfillment of great friends, leaving my heart ready for the loneliness I felt now, and the knowledge to keep it all straight.

I took the bag everywhere with me and it was the last thing I had taken when my mother died, the last bit of that life I still owned. Unzipping the worn canvas, I reached in to search for a knife. There were stacks of papers and journals now, each a depiction of what I saw, and a new one depicting our life, Kenzie's life.

I hadn't had time to formulate a plan to stop the scars from occurring, so I decided the knife was my best bet. Looking up, I saw Kenzie's house just ahead, shaded by a large willow. Each yard was well spaced for the city, and each still as perfect as they had been three years in the future, though the trees and bushes were smaller and more manageable. The fact that Kenzie had ended up being my neighbor felt strange, like an omen. It was fate that I had actually met her at age twenty-five, before I ever met her when she was four. God must have decided then that we were important to each other, and that's why he gave me a second chance at finding her.

I remembered the day in the park, the day I also found out that my father no longer knew who I was, seeing that I'd been handed over into child custody after my mother's death instead of living with him alone, as I had been before all this. I let out a deep breath, finding life was now too complicated to keep track of.

Looking around the neighborhood, I was relieved to see that no one was around to witness what I was about to do; not that it mattered anyway. I walked up the drive, where I knelt behind Kenzie's mother's car. I took a deep breath and peered around the bumper, looking into the front windows, seeing there was no movement. Exhaling, I stood and walked a circle around the car, discreetly piercing the knife through each tire, flattening them as the air squealed through the slits.

The neighborhood dogs began to bark, and I quickly ran around the back of their house toward the kitchen window were I saw her mother look toward the front door, a concerned frown on her face. She wiped her hands with her apron, leaving the pie she was about to place in the oven on the counter. I smiled, finding that though it was wrong, it was also fun to watch.

Kenzie sat at the other end of the counter at age seven with a bowl of cereal, unfazed by her mother's worries, her face still beautiful and her eyes full of happiness and hope for the future. I heard a yelp from the front of the house and saw Kenzie jump, her eyes lifting from her bowl to the front door, her mouth hanging open.

Kenzie's mother stormed in then. "These neighborhood hooligans," she muttered.

"What's wrong, mommy?" Kenzie dropped her spoon

and swallowed a mouthful of Cheerios, placing her doll on the counter and adjusting her doll's dress.

"Oh, nothing, honey," She grabbed the phone from the wall and began dialing. After a pause she opened her mouth. "Hi, doctor LeRoy? We need to cancel our appointment. There's been an incident here. Can we reschedule?"

A smile grew across my face. It had worked. Feeling content, I snuck back out from behind the house and walked down the street toward my own. Walking through the tall weeds and into the backyard, I quickly tried to imagine what the intersection at Southampton and Massachusetts Avenue looked like, getting there just a few moments later as I appeared in the street out of thin air, my arms flailing as they tried to pull through time. I winced as a large semi blew its horn on the street, masking the noise I had made as I crashed through time.

A bum that was resting in the doorway I had ducked into jolted up from his sleep and looked at me with shock, appearing drunk and confused. I gave him a hard stare as the pain in my bones subsided, threatening him in a way that made him shut up and look away. He receded into his grungy sleeping bag, where I heard the clank of glass bottles and tin cans.

I leaned against the building, watching the people pass by. After about an hour, I saw the semi-truck that had caused the accident come down the street, stopping at the light, and then heading on as though nothing had ever happened. I always liked to watch the things I had changed, half out of ego and half to make sure I hadn't harmed someone else by doing so.

Content, I left the streets and ducked into a dark alleyway, headed out of this time and into another, anxious to see Kenzie again. I had put an end to one path of her life, leaving nothing but the life she now lived. It felt good to purge it away, erase the pain and start over. It was time to concentrate on the future now, and make the shift to a better life.

Dr. Ashcroft:

So that's it, that was who slashed our tires. (pause) Did you know my mother was so furious that she called up the local news and had them report that there was a gang out there, vandalizing the neighborhoods?

Agent Donnery:

Really? Now that's funny.

Dr. Ashcroft:

I suppose it is, if not a little drastic and a little too easy perhaps. I can't believe a few flat tires were all it took to change my fate.

Agent Donnery:

So what really happened? What happened in your real life? Where is that part where he let you remember meeting him?

Dr. Ashcroft:

Well, he came back to that same day when I had originally met him at the bus stop, except now I was beautiful. You should know how weird that felt, as though someone had taken tracing paper and copied the life in my dreams, but added onto it. My life felt layered that day, and I see why now.

Agent Donnery:

Well, I can say this at least. It seems Jordan had a thing for busses.

Dr. Ashcroft:

You know, I never saw it that way, but you're right. The first two times I met him, he was on a bus.

Agent Donnery:

Nostalgic man, I suppose.

Dr. Ashcroft:

(laughter)

I was running now, my pink dress fluttering in the wind and my black patent shoes slapping against the cement with little traction. Since my house was right on the corner, there was no point in waiting at the bus stop. Besides, my mother finally allowed me to buy mascara, and I wanted to try it on. My chest was burning as I arrived at the stop, just in time to see the bus barreling over the hill, headed toward the stop.

Slowing as I arrived at the corner, my shoes slipped across the road and I had to flail my arms to balance myself. When I looked up, I noticed for the first time I was not alone. A boy stood there, his back straight and his hands clasped in front of him. He looked at me from the corner of his eye, and I tried my best to stand tall and look somewhat gathered. The bus screeched to a halt and the stop sign squeaked out from under the driver's window as the new boy took the first step toward the bus.

As we walked around the front toward the doors, I watched his stride, noticing how confident and unfazed it seemed. I had never seen him before, but I knew there was a vacant house on our street, and I wondered if he had moved in with his family, or if he had simply come from one of the adjoining neighborhoods, hoping to outsmart the bus.

I hooked my thumbs into the straps of my backpack and prepared myself for the barrage I would receive from my friends on the bus. Another day meant another day of having to act fake, and I hated it. Sometimes I wished people would just leave me alone, sometimes I wished I were ugly. I stopped then, noticing the boy was waiting for me.

"After you." He looked me directly in the eye, allowing me to go first, but I shook my head.

"Oh no, after you." I gestured with my hand out and giggled, noticing he was sort of cute.

He smiled and went up the steps, and I followed after, the driver watching us with a blank stare that suggested he could care less. As we walked down the aisle, my friends stood and waved at me as though competing to see who would win the chance to be my seat mate on the ride to school.

"Kenzie, sit here!" they begged.

I sighed. I hated this part of the morning. I hated being popular, but what could I do? All I really wanted was to sit alone. Sometimes I wished I were invisible.

The new boy took a seat toward the middle, the last empty one. I bit my lip as a strange feeling washed over me, and I looked at the empty spot beside him. My palms were sweating in a way they never had before, and for the first time in a while I began to feel nervous. He didn't look directly at me, but I knew he saw me; every boy always did. I blinked then and looked over my shoulder at the driver watching in the rearview mirror, a sour look on his face and his patience running thin. Taking a deep breath, I walked toward the boy as all my friends pouted at me, sinking back into their seats in defeat.

"May I sit here?" My voice cracked.

The boy let out a snort as he looked out the window, slowly turning to face me with a strange but amused look on his face. "Of course…" His voice trailed off as he moved his tattered bag into his lap and shifted over.

I sat and situated myself a safe distance from him, his green coat engulfing much of the seat but making his body seem large and mature. He looked older than I, but that didn't matter. At ten, I was just discovering the world of boys, and I liked it. He was just the excuse I needed to get away from everyone. I watched him as the bus lurched forward. There was something about him, something I knew but couldn't understand. Goose bumps erupted across my arms, and I was quick to hide them, feeling shy for the first time in my life.

Pressing my lips together and drawing a deep breath through my nose, I pressed my hand toward him and brushed my long auburn hair away from my shoulder with the other. "Hi, I'm Kenzie." My friends gawked at me over the backs of the seats, but I ignored them.

He smiled then, his eyes sparkling in a way I'd never seen from anyone before. "I know."

Statement from Dr. Ashcroft,
Vincent Memorial Hospital, Boston
August 3, 2009
02:01 a.m.

Agent Donnery:
    So he slashed a few tires, and that was it? Sorry to reiterate, but you're right. It seemed too easy.

Dr. Ashcroft:
    Yep.

Agent Donnery:
    And then he was cocky enough to come back and meet you on the bus like that?

Dr. Ashcroft:
    He was still young then, and he hadn't yet decided whether or not he wanted me to know him, or know what he was doing. Eventually, though, it was no longer his choice.

Agent Donnery:
    I still don't understand how the high school test incident could happen first, then the scars.

Dr. Ashcroft:

A timeline is hard to explain and understand, but if you can wrap your head around it then you'll see. He once explained it to me in college. At the time I had thought to myself that it was eerily perfect when it pertained to the memories I had been having, but I said nothing, just as he said nothing to me for all these years.

Jordan already had the intent to change the scars, and fate already knew he would, just as fate can formulate a future for him to travel to. So because fate already knew that he would be going back in time to change the past, then two lifelines were created for me. In one life I had scars and in the other life I didn't, but I only remember the life where I didn't because that was the life he eventually decided for me, and the other one died out.

These are the parallel lives. Jordan Shifted between these two if he needed, in order to determine which things to change and which to keep normal. If you think about it, every time our life offers us a decision, two paths are created from it like a web.

Agent Donnery:

I see. You mean to say that I could go get a cup of coffee right now or not, so fates already created two paths for me: the one that gets coffee and the one that doesn't.

Dr. Ashcroft:

Exactly, but for you, it's still your choice. This is the choice that was stolen from me. I was never given the second option. For Jordan, it was always the decision to get coffee, so to speak.

Agent Donnery:

This may seem unprofessional, but do you want some?

Dr. Ashcroft:

(pause) Sure.

Agent Donnery:
    Better?

Dr. Ashcroft:
    Yes, thank you.

Agent Donnery:
    So tell me about college. How did that
go?

Dr. Ashcroft:
    By then I suppose you could say Jordan
had known me for twelve years, but I
still didn't know I knew him, at least on
this life path. During pre-med at Boston
College, not much happened. I remained
with Max though I knew there were better
things out there, but as a pre-med student
I also didn't have time to date or even
deal with a break up, so I just put our
relationship on autopilot.
    After pre-med, I finally made it
to Harvard as I'd always planned, and I
felt like a new person, free from all the

popularity and expectations of my youth. When I moved across from Boston College to Harvard, my relationship with Max began to crumble, and I don't think he liked it. I knew there were things he did behind my back, but I figured if I was dumping him anyway, what did it really matter?

Besides my personal life, it was here, at Harvard, that I began to have the intense memories and dreams, and when I saw Jordan there for the first time, it triggered something. I know now that he was always watching me, but nothing horrible in my life had arose since the test incident in high school, so there was no need for him to make himself seen, or create a Shift for my life during my time at Boston College.

Agent Donnery:
So your brain made an imprint of him from your dreams, like déjà vu?

Dr. Ashcroft:
Exactly. At this point the dreams were so frequent that he could no longer hide. It felt as though I'd spent a lifetime with Jordan in my dreams, but because things were blurry, I had no idea who he was, and he had no idea I knew about him. I believe this was when things began to get dicey for him, too, and he began to get clumsy.

Told by Dr. Ashcroft
September 31, 2005
5:58 p.m.

"Max, give me a break." I held the phone to my ear. I was so over him, so tired of his childish behavior. I had put up with it through pre-med at Boston College, but now I no longer had the patience.

"You really do think you're better than me, just because you're there." I heard him laugh in the jealous way he always did.

"Max, seriously. You chose football at Boston College and now I've chosen Harvard. Can't you understand my angle on this? That I am doing something I've always wanted?" My flip flops pounded against the pavement as I headed back to my dorm. "Besides, Boston College is right next door! We're not that far away and you'll see me just the same as before. You only have one year left anyway, and you're going to be so busy with pro scouts and training, you won't even notice I'm gone."

"Yeah, well, you haven't even made the effort to come see me this week, not even at practice." He was whining now.

"Max, you know how crazy the first week at Harvard med can be! I don't have the time." I sighed, knowing that was a lie.

"Whatever Kenzie, I've got to go." I could hear the sass

in his voice; the sass of a man that had been pampered his whole life.

"Yeah, fine." I hung up then, refusing to allow him to hang up first. I grumbled as I tossed my phone back into my bag, pulling it up on my shoulder with a feeling of irritation.

This week had been my first at Harvard, and it had been tough on my relationship with Max. Through college, I had stayed with him because what else was there? But now that I was here, I wanted to be free. I took a deep breath and looked up at the ancient trees, smiling and finding the silver lining.

I had been given a blessed life, but I wasn't sure I liked it. Everyone had always expected things from me, always assumed. I was the person who was always meant to be the Homecoming Queen, the cheerleader, and I played the part, but I never felt it was me. Being here was my chance to change all that, to become someone new; someone mysterious and troubled, perhaps?

I arrived back at my dorm where I unlocked the door, looking around the room and seeing my roommate was not yet back. I threw my bag on my bed and slumped into the desk chair in front of the expensive computer the school had supplied for me because of my scholarship. I let out a heavy breath, causing a stack of flyers to flutter on my desk. My mother had wanted me to join any number of clubs while I was here, but I wanted nothing to do with it, so I grabbed the pile of flyers and threw them in the trash.

There was a loud slamming noise as the door to my room shook. I heard Amy curse under her breath and the jingling of keys as she unlocked the door.

"I can't seem to get used to these auto-lock doors," She looked flustered as she walked into the room.

"Hey Amy," I gave her a half-hearted wave. Amy was my roommate, and until this past summer, she was someone I could never imagine being friends with, but now that I knew her, I saw that I wished I had more friends like her from the beginning. She was an English scholar, and hopelessly clumsy, but her insatiable need for fun amazed me. Though she looked like your run of the mill nerd, she was far from it. It seemed as though she had two sides, the one she went to class with, and the one she went to college parties with.

There was no lack of things to do at Harvard, and I was surprised to find that most nights there was always a party. Amy loved to go out, whether to the local pub for a beer or the craziest party the boxing team could throw. I never understood why she hid herself away until the moon rose, but it made sense. Amy was gorgeous, but during the day she draped her body with frumpy cotton and covered her face with large glasses. At night, the change was astounding, as though she were a werewolf.

The first day when I met her, I was a little surprised. I had pictured her as someone different over the phone. It was that night when she pulled out her "evening wear" that I realized she had a dark side. She was one year older than me so she took it upon herself to be the leader and introduced me to the hidden world behind the Ivy League exterior of Harvard. So far it had been a whirlwind, but I liked it. I never told Max that I had already met far superior men, but I had promised him I'd try to make it work, though in reality I was no longer sure I even wanted to.

Harvard men were different, they had a sense of fun about them but they were also smart. I trusted them to be gentlemen and they always bought me a drink, even if I wasn't going to give them the time of day to deserve one. Max, on the other hand, still needed to grow up, but I knew that there was a possibility with him that someday he could, but I wasn't about to sit around and wait either. I had stuck with him only because I thought it was worth giving him a chance, but that chance had been long exhausted.

I watched Amy move about the room as I marveled at her posture. If there was anything she was an expert at, it was the art of attracting men. She was always the promiscuous one, always the flirt. I was never like that; I had morals but that didn't mean I judged her, either. No matter what her fetish, I didn't care, just as long as she made a good friend.

"Whew!" Amy threw herself onto her bed and pulled her glasses off her head and rubbed her makeup-free eyes. "So the rugby team is having a party tonight over at the rugby house. Are you in?"

I smiled. "Of course I'm in."

She sat up and looked at me with narrowed eyes. "Good."

I laughed. "Tell me something, Amy. How does anyone even recognize you enough to inform you of all these parties?"

She chuckled like an old lady and waved me away, "They don't, I just overhear." She blinked a few times. "I like it this way. I'm such a mystery to them. Where do I live? What's my real name? All these things are important to me, because I don't need my slumming past coming back for me in the future when I'm sitting in a chair next to Barbara Walters discussing my bestselling novel about the morals of women."

I let out a sharp laugh, finding her words both abrasive and truthful.

"But you, my dear, you are going to be a doctor. The slummier the better." She winked at me and removed her top layer, one of what looked like five, that helped squish her chest like a pancake. There were two closets on both sides of the room which was perfect for her, one for Jekyll and the other for Hyde.

"So, how is your ass of a boyfriend today?" She threw open her 'daytime closet' and hung her clothes, stripping down to her underwear before opening her 'evening closet.'

"Shut up, Amy. He's not that much of an ass." I didn't know why I was defending him, but I guess it was my nature to retaliate.

She gave me a narrowed look over her shoulder, her tattoos now showing, "Honey, from how he sounds, he's one beer and a date rape away from a degree in prison."

I laughed. "So are you there, Honey."

She squealed. "I am not! I'm a woman. Women get away with *murder*."

"Sure, Amy." I rolled my eyes at her back.

She grumbled and pulled a shirt from her closet. I tilted my head. Or perhaps it was a dress? I watched her pull it over her head, finally deducing that somehow it was a dress, though it frightened me to put it in that sort of category. She dove back into her closet and pulled out a pair of heels that were taller than I'd ever seen, and bright red.

Amy didn't trust Max, even though she barely knew anything about him. I wanted to believe he was faithful, but I knew how he had always been. He had two sides, just like Amy did: the one he showed me and the one he hung out with his friends with.

"So, let's go get some food before leaving. I'd hate to throw up later when I drink too much."

I laughed. "It's frightening how your brain works. You only eat to prevent alcohol poisoning."

She tilted her head as her mouth twisted into a smile. "Well, what else would I eat for? Food is overrated unless used to keep the party going!"

I shook my head. "Whatever, Amy. Let me just get changed and we can leave. I don't want to look like the nerd next to you."

Statement from Dr. Ashcroft,
Vincent Memorial Hospital, Boston
August 3, 2009
02:21 a.m.

Dr. Ashcroft:
    Later that night, after a few pieces
of campus pizza and a martini, we grabbed
a cab and drove to the rugby house. I
remember that the house was crowded with
people from all over, not just Harvard.

Agent Donnery:
    I see. I never heard this side of it
before.

Dr. Ashcroft:
    Naturally you wouldn't. Jordan had no
idea I was there, he'd been elsewhere at
the time I decided to go. But here is
where he begins to write about it.

Agent Donnery:
    And fate threw you a curve ball.

Dr. Ashcroft:
    Yes.

We arrived at the house and tried to find a place to park.

"Stupid drunks, it's not even nine yet." Amy slammed her hands against the steering wheel.

"Here!" I jumped and pointed at a spot between an old Camaro and a black Tahoe.

"I hate parallel parking," Amy whined.

"Come on, it's not that hard." I guided her forward and then back into the tight spot, and she followed my directions to a tee.

"There." Amy let out a contented sigh of relief and grabbed her heels from the back seat, strapping them on her feet as her tiny dress rode up her thighs, revealing her bright pink thong strap.

"Geez, Amy." I shielded my eyes and turned away.

"What!" She laughed. "Oh come on, you prude, at least I'm wearing them! Let's go."

We both crawled out of the car as I stumbled onto the curve, the effects of the double martini already pulling at my center of balance.

Trees lined the street, and I found myself wary of them, as though someone was there watching us. I nudged Amy to hurry as her heels sank into the damp grass.

"This is tricky," she added, trying to look composed though she really looked like an idiot, or at least a hooker, but I loved her anyway.

She put one hand on my shoulder and used me like a crutch as her heels sank into the grass. I couldn't help but laugh at her concentrated face, as though she were in some sort of competition against the lawn to win her heels back. Her struggles were fitting for an entrance at a Rugby party, considering they made competing against the lawn an official sport, just not in the hopes of winning a pair of red pumps, or so I hope.

We knocked on the door once before letting ourselves in, figuring there was no way anyone could hear the sounds above the loud music that made my soul shake. Before we even breached the threshold, a handsome jock in a pair of jeans and no shirt handed us a keg cup and pointed us in the direction of what I supposed was the kitchen. Amy thanked him and gave him a pat on the chest, trailing her finger between his pecks and down his stomach, smacking her lips.

Amy then grabbed my hand and led me through the crowd as she commanded the attention of what seemed every man in the room. She didn't acknowledge any of them but rather held her head in the air and batted her eyes in some sort of mating ritual.

"Hey there, gorgeous." A man shamelessly stared at

Amy's chest and grabbed her ass before staring at me next. "And hey to you, too." He winked at me and I tried my best to hold back the eye roll. What a pig!

"Hi," I said back, giving him a half-hearted smile that told him to go away. I wasn't drunk enough to find those lines attractive.

As we walked, I began to wonder what Max's parties were like, and if he acted the same way. Despite the fact that I acted as though I didn't care when women stared at him, a part of me still felt jealous just because he was mine to a degree, even if it wasn't a very strong one.

Once in the kitchen, we filled our cups and chugged them, wincing and breathing heavily as the beer stung our throats. I was at least relieved to find that the beer had been premium, not the watered down beer spritzers I had been subjected to at Boston College. It was a crime people even brewed beer that bad, but there was a market, and that market was cheap college kids.

I took a few sips as the foam settled, and assessed the situation in the room. There was an equal ratio of jocks to girls, and I felt comfortable knowing that it wasn't as though they were preying on a few gorgeous women, because they all looked like super models. I stood tall, knowing that I was also beautiful, but perhaps not as beautiful as some.

As I drained my last sip of beer, my head tilting toward the ceiling, I felt someone come up behind me and grab my waist.

"Do you want to dance?"

I dropped the cup from my lips and turned around with a look of shock on my face. I hadn't really expected to get picked up while I was here. More or less, I was expecting that my job was watching to make sure Amy stayed out of trouble.

My eyes stared into those of a tall, brawny man with brown hair, and I smiled. "Sure." I put the cup down by the keg and left it, feeling as though I'd had enough to hold my buzz.

I glanced back at Amy and saw that she was already playing tonsil hockey with another brawny man with dirty blonde hair and arms strong enough to snap her in half. His hand was half way up her thigh and under her dress, and I laughed at the fact it had taken her only moments to find suitable entertainment for the night. I figured she was in good hands for now, and I'd come check on her after the dance. It wasn't as though she was really going to go anywhere seeing as she had the man pinned against the wall in the corner. It was clear that she had things under control.

The guy next to me leaned in close to my ear, "My name is Jack." His breath smelled like whiskey and it tickled my skin as I wrinkled my nose, thinking his name fit the smell of his breath.

I turned my attention back to him. "Well hello, Jack," I paused. "My name is Heather." It was best to use fake names.

He led me from the kitchen into the main room where the music was blaring over the speakers that were nestled into every corner. He moved his body close to mine, and we began to dance. I looked over his shoulder and around the room, the beer making my body even more fluid than it already was. There were couples cramming the space, all dancing in a way that made me feel awkward. I turned and looked to my left as Jack put his chin on my shoulder, acting like someone that had been dating me for years instead of someone I'd just met.

I swallowed hard and rolled my eyes, thinking that I didn't belong here. Looking back toward the door we had come in through, and my inevitable escape, it was then that I spotted someone watching us from across room. I narrowed my eyes to look at him, seeing that it was a face I couldn't recognize yet had known, as though it were the face of a famous actor. When our eyes met, he quickly turned away and disappeared around the corner, a look of frustration on his face like you'd see from a jealous boyfriend.

I furrowed my brow as my rhythm slowed and I became distracted, my mind searching to place the face with a name, something familiar, like a professor or childhood friend.

"Hey, baby." Jack put his hand on my lower back and pulled me closer. "What's wrong?" He trailed his nose across my cheek.

I giggled to save face, but my insides curdled. "Nothing." I allowed my pace to pick back up, erasing the thoughts of the man from my mind.

He smiled against my neck. "Good."

When the song stopped, Jack gave me a polite peck on the cheek and stepped back as though the music gave him the right to act forward, but now that it was over he had to be a gentleman. Though he had a creepy vibe, my gut told me he was safe and I could trust him. I was not the Amy type, who would jump in bed with anything that moved, and tonight was no exception, but it was always fun to play along to a point.

"Can I get you another beer?" He ran his hand down the arm of my white long sleeved v-neck, his eyes wandering to my chest which had been enhanced by one of Amy's water bras.

I nodded as he grabbed my hand and led me to the side of the room, where he sat me in a blue velvet chair that looked like it was straight from the sixties.

"I'll be right back." His smile was adorable. "So don't run off with someone new." He touched my auburn hair, allowing it to lace through his fingers.

I laughed and gave him a coy look.

He disappeared around the corner then, and I looked around the room with curious eyes, wondering where the man with the familiar face had gone. If I could only get a clear look at him, I was certain I'd know where I knew him from. I had a knack for remembering a face and an insatiable need to figure it out if I didn't.

I watched everyone dance, peeking my head around each body in the hopes of finding him. Sighing as I began to give up, I looked toward the kitchen where Amy had been but she was gone, replaced by a new couple and Jack, who was filling a keg cup. He looked back toward me and gave me a wink so I winked back, letting him know I was still here and still thinking of him, though that was hardly the case.

I let out a sharp breath and looked back toward the room, thinking about Max and now looking for Amy. I wasn't being fair to him. I should just bite the bullet and break it off so that the feeling of guilt would no longer trap me. Max was an old crutch that I needed to get rid of; I wanted to feel free again. I sighed. I felt as though I had been trying to justify our relationship, our coming breakup, and our failures all day, and it was beginning to get obsessively repetitive. I needed to stop. It was then that I felt a hand on my shoulder, and I jumped, looking up as my eyes met Jack's.

"Here you are, Heather." He pressed a red keg cup toward me, and I took it as he offered me his hand.

I placed my palm in his and he pulled me up out of the chair. "I'm impressed you remembered my name." I was leaning close to his ear, the music blaring.

"Of course." He placed his hand on my lower back and led me back into the crowd, where we danced some more, my drink sloshing onto the floor.

Looking around I began to get concerned about where Amy was. I was a worrier, and I couldn't help it. She was someone to worry about. A guilty feeling washed over me then, and I couldn't help but feel something was wrong. I took a deep breath as my heart began to race, ignoring the fact that Jack's hand was now on my ass. I took a sip of my beer to cool off, the bubbles scratching their way down my dry throat.

Jack began kissing my neck, and for a moment I forgot what I was worried about, my skin tingling as I shut my eyes.

He trailed his hand up my back, and I shivered, feeling the way his touch seemed to make my whole body go numb. I tilted my head against his shoulder and opened my eyes again, looking across the room toward the entryway where stairs led up to the second floor. Jack ran his hand through my hair and I giggled and blinked, feeling rather woozy.

I watched the people enter and leave the room, my thoughts of Amy and the strange man trailing away from me on a river of thoughts, all the while feeling the music become a part of my movements as it lulled me into a trance. Jack whispered in my ear, but I couldn't understand what he was saying so I just nodded, leaning against him for support. I took another sip of my beer, spilling it some more, and I cursed my clumsy grip.

"Whoops," I laughed, stepping back and brushing the beer from my jeans. When I looked up, I looked back to the hall where the strange man had returned, walking up the stairs in a manner that looked frantic. I shook my head as Jack put his hands on my shoulders to steady me, a sly look on his face as my stomach dropped, and I realized what was happening.

"Are you alright?" he drawled.

I looked down at my beer and rolled my eyes. How stupid of me! I dropped the cup on the ground as it sloshed all over the floor, not caring about the consequences it caused. I looked back at Jack, now wishing I had the strength to deck him, furious that he would have the gall to spike my beer. I looked back at the stairs as I stumbled, and Jack caught me. Despite the danger I was in, the insatiable need to follow the strange man was pulling me like a magnet, and I knew that Jack's strength could help.

"I'm fine," I lied, grabbing Jack's hand and pulling him toward the entry. I heard him laugh behind me, his thoughts obviously changing from that of the gentleman to that of an arrogant pig.

"Where are we going?" he asked, grabbing my ass and smiling.

I rolled my eyes, finding it hard to walk as I encouraged Jack to brace me. For whatever reason, I was not worried about me but rather whatever the man in the hall was doing, and where he was going. Somehow, I felt as though my problem wasn't the biggest issue at hand, and an undeniable feeling of fear and anxiety washed over me as I reached the steps. I was climbing with difficulty but Jack helped, though I knew his intentions were anything but chivalrous, as the groping became rude. At the top of the stairs, I looked down the hall as my legs threatened to buckle, my clouded gaze meeting those of the man in the green coat, his eyes blue like a stormy ocean.

He quickly looked away as though disgusted by my actions, but too involved in his own task to do anything about it. Jack grabbed my waist and leaned me against the wall, his mouth attacking mine as he gave me a sloppy kiss. I tightened my jaw in frustration, my eyes still trying to watch the man but finding my efforts now thwarted. I tried to push Jack away from me, stealing another glance at the man. He was staring at a shut door in the hall with a pensive look on his face. It seemed as though he was on a mission somehow, as though he knew me but was too distracted to entertain a friendly gesture.

Jack pushed against me, almost hurting me now and shoving his tongue down my throat. With an annoyed grumble, I mustered all the strength I could manage and channeled it to my arms so I could finally push him off me, throwing him into the wall on the other side of the hall with a strength I had learned serving in the cheerleader army. I stumbled then, and Jack laughed, trying to belittle me into submission, but I was smarter than that.

"Heather," he said with a voice that now had turned almost evil.

I was staring at Jack, but I could see the man in the green coat now turn his attention on us from the corner of his eye. I began to wonder why he wasn't helping me as he shook the knob on a door halfway down the hall, finding it locked. I could swear he had fear in his eye now, sweat coating his brow. It was as though I could feel his heart beating in my own chest, and it was then that I knew there was something going on behind that door that I needed to see.

A group of guys were standing in the hall. "Feisty one you got there," they teased.

"Heather, it's okay," Jack hoisted his large body off the floor and walked back toward me. He grabbed my arms to steady me away from the wall before leading me down the hall toward the man, just the direction I needed to go.

My lids were heavy and I found it hard to stay awake,

but I kept my eyes fixed, hoping it could sober me. It was hard to know exactly what was happening, but I remained focused. I needed to remember this.

The man became frantic over the lock as he saw us approach, as though he was running out of time. Just as we were about to walk behind him, the man lunged back and finally kicked open the locked door, clearly tired of playing games.

"Hey, man, what's your problem?" Jack's voice echoed in my right ear as I slumped against his shoulder.

I saw the man look at Jack with hate in his eyes. Without a second thought he then pulled his arm back and punched my captor on the broad side of his cheek as his other arm caught me. Jack fell to the ground like a sack of potatoes, no longer conscious.

"Hold on, Kenzie," I heard the man say into my ear.

I looked at him with surprise, but his determined gaze was fixed on the room he had just opened. Breathing deep, I found his scent familiar, like something I had smelled before, but I still couldn't put my finger on it. I looked up at him and followed his gaze as my chest gripped with anxiety, recognizing the red fabric of Amy's dress on the floor. I then saw her limp body on the bed as a tall athletic man loomed over her with nothing but his boxers on and a look of hunger in his eyes. I craned my blurred vision as I recognized the pattern on the boxers, the same pattern I had bought for Max on his birthday.

"Max?" my voice was slurred as I tried to say his name.

The man on the bed looked at me with horrified eyes, and then looked at the man that had saved me from Jack. A sudden fury replaced the fear in Max's eyes. "What did you do to her, jerk? Leave Kenzie alone!" He stood as I felt the man's hand tighten around my arm, his feet bracing us. It was then that Max rose from the bed and lunged at us. My savior was quick to turn me away, his free arm swinging from behind him and punching Max square in the jaw.

Max fell to the ground with a grunt, as the man holding me shook the pain from his hand before diving in and grabbing Amy. My mind was racing as I tried to stay conscious, tried to understand what Max had been doing and why he was here. The man holding me had known my name before Max had said it, and I wondered what it meant. Amy was unconscious in her underwear and I finally understood exactly what was going on. Feeling sick, I leaned over and threw up, as the man holding me released his grip and rubbed my back before lifting me again, and taking us back out into the hall where I felt him work to carry us both from the house. I fell in and out of consciousness as we left, unsure of what was happening around me or if we had made it out safe. When I finally felt the cool air on my hot skin, I let myself fall asleep, knowing that, for whatever reason, I was safe enough to let go.

Statement from Dr. Ashcroft,
Vincent Memorial Hospital, Boston
August 4, 2009
02:37 p.m.

Dr. Ashcroft:

That feeling was so strange, as though he were my best friend. For all I knew, he could have been another bad guy, taking us both away to God knows where, but something inside me knew that wasn't the case. I realize now what his scent reminded me of. When I was young, my friends and I would sneak down to the green house at the end of the lane and break in. It was abandoned and no more than a stupid dare, but that was the smell, like lilac and dust, a smell that had been layered on my memory by fear and adrenaline. I could never forget it, even now.

Agent Donnery:

I see. So your senses knew before you did.

Dr. Ashcroft:

Yes. I don't know why it took me so long to put it all together. It seems so obvious now.

Agent Donnery:

(pause) Moving back to the incident, though. So you found out Amy had been drugged and was about to be raped, but he had saved both of you?

Dr. Ashcroft:

(laughter) Don't look so solemn, Agent Donnery. It was my boyfriend that was about to rape her. I was happy to find out then, and not later. That's one Shift I was glad he made.

Agent Donnery:

And it was Jordan that saved you both?

Dr. Ashcroft:

Yes, it was his way of saving me from the life that could have followed, but as you can tell, this was his first major screw up. After this, there was no hiding. He had to let me know him.

Agent Donnery:

But, don't you suppose he tried to go back and change it?

Dr. Ashcroft:

He did, but the incident kept happening as though God was determined to make a point. One way or another, I was going to be raped, so he had to make a change not just for me, but for himself.

Agent Donnery:
    How did he stop it?

Dr. Ashcroft:
    The only way to stop it was what I
remembered, for him to stop hiding from
me. This is why I had such an overwhelming
reaction to him downstairs at the party.
He had tried to erase the incident from
my mind so many times that his image was
seared into my memories and the fear in
me was triggered far before the incident
happened, as though I knew beyond a doubt
that something was going to happen.

Agent Donnery:
    So this here is his side of the
story?

Dr. Ashcroft:
    (pause) Yes.

I landed on the grass outside of the Rugby house for the last time, coughing violently as I buckled over. The pain in my side was unbearable, and I felt my insides twist as I threw up. I fell to my knees as my hands cupped my stomach. I lay on the ground and rolled onto my back, lifting my shirt. Half my side was bruised a deep purple, my stomach pulsing with a sharp twang. Another cough escaped my lips, laced with a bit of blood, and I wiped it away, staining the sleeve of my jacket. I rested my head on the grass as I closed my eyes and took a deep breath, trying to force my body to calm down.

I looked up over the hill toward the house as I heard a group of people approach. Seeing Max and his other Boston College football buddies walking up to the door made my blood boil, cooking me from the inside out with both hate and sickness. My breath came fast as I tried to calm down. Why wasn't this working? Why couldn't I change this?

As I tried to stand I felt every one of my joints seize. This was my last chance; I could not go back and risk doing this to my body again. By now I knew what I had to do, and besides, what other choice did I have? I always knew that eventually this day would come, like anyone with an addiction. I just wish it were under better circumstances, but it was finally my turn to have something not work to my advantage.

I lifted myself off the grass and braced my body against a tree as I saw Amy's car pull up to the spot on the street. I could hear them bicker through the thin aluminum, her brake lights flickering as Amy tried to parallel park. I focused on my breathing then, stuffing the pain away. Blinking back the tears that blurred my vision, I watched them park, the hum of the engine ceasing. Both doors clicked open, and they slowly got out, my heart breaking as I saw Kenzie, beautiful and innocent.

Kenzie looked around with a concerned look on her face, and I ducked back, waiting for them to pass and make their way to the front door. I heard a single knock on the mahogany and the familiar sounds of the party as they entered, followed by a click as the noise was hushed by the shut door. I let out a long, focused breath, pushing myself away from the tree and ascending the hill toward the side of the house, where there was a separate entrance.

In my other failed attempts, I had already tried making it in the front door, but considering my overall appearance, they never allowed me, so I'd resorted to finding another way inside. Jocks weren't all that smart, after all; there was always a way in. I found the path that led toward the backyard, pushing through the thick groves of ivy and finding the door, giving it a heavy tug, wincing as I felt the blood in my side swell.

I entered through what used to be a laundry room, back when someone other than the rugby team had lived here. There were beer cans all over the floor and a single bulb hung from the ceiling, swinging as the door hit it. Across from me was another door, and I cleared the ground enough to grab the handle and open it, running one hand through my hair as I tried my best to look somewhat presentable. This was my moment to finally meet her after all, and this time it was going to count.

I cleared my throat and entered the crowd unnoticed, finding myself at the base of the stairs for what felt like the fifth time. I looked across the room and into the living room, spotting Kenzie's auburn hair as she danced with Garret Brown from the rugby team, or Jack, as he had so eloquently named himself. I felt my insides curdle at the sight, disgust filling my soul just knowing what he planned to do to her. I waited there for a moment, feeling exposed as I urged her to see me so that I could bait her into following me upstairs, where she could see for herself what was happening.

As I stood there, I felt my stomach turn over and I placed a cool hand on my side, the need to throw up overcoming me as she finally looked over with a look of confusion and shock. I was anxiously tapping my foot now to distract me from the sickness in my side, but it was doing little to help. When Garret turned her on the dance floor, I was quick to dodge back into the laundry room, throwing up in the giant sink, my feet crumpling the aluminum cans, sweat coating my brow. I watched as blood stained the sides of the basin, and I took a deep breath, hoping I wasn't blowing this last chance, and praying that I could at least live long enough to get her out of here.

After a moment, my stomach settled and I stood, feeling a renewed sense of purpose and exited back out into the hall. I found Kenzie in the crowd, noticing that she already had another beer in hand. I was hoping I would be able to prevent her from being drugged, to make my job easier, but I could see God was taunting me at this point, teaching me a lesson for defying His divine plan in the first place. She took a hefty sip from her glass, and I cringed.

Moving to plan B, I found there was little I could do but draw her out of the room as I had planned, so I waited for her to notice me again. I saw her spill her drink and her laughter resonated in my heart, the sound not unlike an angel, and her voice echoing as though it was the only one in the room. She brushed the beer from her pants and then slumped against Garret, my heart leaping as her gaze lifted from the ground, locking on mine.

I quickly looked away as I saw her gasp, and I knew then that I had caught her attention; now it was a matter of reeling her in. I looked up toward the bedrooms, focusing on the task of Amy and Max, leaping up the stairs as I skipped full steps. As I reached the door, I leaned against the wall to catch my breath, my head spinning as adrenaline forced blood through my deteriorating veins. I turned my head back where I saw Kenzie breach the stairway, and we locked gazes. The look in her eyes was full of truth, the truth that she recognized me though I had tried so hard to erase it. Garret grabbed her and pressed her against the wall, and despite my attempts to remain calm, my jaw locked and I looked away in disgust, shaking the lock on the bedroom door instead.

I didn't want to burst into the room just yet; this had to be timed perfectly if it was all going to come out the right way; me being the hero, that is, and not that asshole, Max. As I tried to ignore Kenzie and Garret, I thought about the humility of what was happening and the way this was taking me down off my pedestal of playing God. This was my fault, after all; a result of what I had changed, and that was why the guilt in me ran so deep, as though I'd committed murder, though that was the very thing I was trying to change.

After all my careful planning, Max had ended up being the wrong choice for Kenzie. I should have been able to see it, but I was so infatuated with her dreams that I didn't recognize the signs. I looked back at the handle of the bedroom door, my patience wearing thin. I just knew that if I burst in now, Max fully clothed, he would play it off as though he'd found Amy that way and saved her. Kenzie would believe him, too, because she had seen Amy downstairs with the blonde guy, not Max, and despite the voice inside her that did not trust him, she was weak when it came to him.

I heard a commotion and looked back to where Kenzie was, seeing her shove Garret away from her, slamming him against the opposite wall. I narrowed my eyes, angry as I heard him laugh at her, his ego like that of the devil, too weak to get a girl by any other means than drugging her at a party. He grabbed her arm as though she were a bought commodity, and walked toward us and I knew that was my cue. I lunged back against the wall and kicked in the bedroom door with all the strength I could muster from my dying body, the door breaking at the hinges as splinters flew around me.

"Hey man, what's your problem?" Garret's voice was beside me now, and I turned to look at him, Kenzie's head leaning against his left shoulder, her eyes heavy but open. I felt my teeth clench together and I pulled my arm back, my patience too thin to bother with negotiation. I felt the force of all my blood rush to my fist as I hit him square on the jaw, knocking him out with one blow as I tried to catch Kenzie with my free arm.

She slumped onto me, and I winced again, my side aching as though the bleeding had now breached the surface of my skin. "Hold on Kenzie," I whispered to her, revealing for the first time the fact that I knew her.

She looked at me, but I looked into the room instead, focusing on the last thing I had to do before I could get out of here. Max was looming over Amy's unconscious body, the look on his face making the anger in me far worse than ever before. With Kenzie at my side, I lunged at Max, throwing a punch to his face and knocking him out before grabbing Amy and dragging her from the room.

In the hall, everyone was staring at me but by this point they were all too ashamed of themselves to do anything, each filled with the guilt of what they allowed to happen in their house. There was blood everywhere, but I knew it wasn't Kenzie's or Amy's, or even Max and Garret; it was mine.

I was able to get them outside where I fumbled for Amy's keys in the pocket of Kenzie's pants. She was unconscious now, too, making this difficult. As I finally sifted through the obscenely large collection of keys, I managed to get the car unlocked and I propped open the back door, the party roaring behind us as though nothing had happened.

I laid Amy across the backseat, covering her with a blanket that had been wadded on the floor. Luckily for me both girls were relatively thin, but their long legs were impossible to manage. Next, I opened the passenger door and placed Kenzie in the front as she moaned; her body still aware as she went through the motions of buckling in, a tremendous relief to me, as my side was now numb.

I then shut both doors just as a group of angry looking rugby players burst out the front door, drunk and looking for a fight. I walked casually to the driver's side and got in, roaring her car to life as I jetted out of the spot and down the street. I prayed the jocks were too drunk to remember me, that this was the last time I'd have to face them. The last thing I needed right now was to be followed and beat up, especially in this condition, one kick to the side would send my organs flying.

After tonight, I knew I was stuck at age twenty-three. I sighed, finding it felt ominous, as though my life had come to a sudden halt. I shifted gears and looked at Kenzie asleep beside me as a feeling of comfort replaced my disappointment. If there was anyone I would want to spend living a normal life with, however, it would have always been her. I knew this indulgence of mine was going to be hard to break, but I was done with it. I needed to accept the natural order of life and be human for once.

I saw the dorms come into view up ahead. I had no idea what she would say when she woke and no idea what she would think of me, but I had to make the best of it. It was obvious that something had happened to her after all these years, something I had done to her, which I could not explain. I knew she would have so many questions, but I could never tell her; she never needs to know.

Statement from Dr. Ashcroft,
Vincent Memorial Hospital, Boston
August 4, 2009
02:42 a.m.

Agent Donnery:
    He was already sick then?

Dr. Ashcroft:
    Yes, I suppose he was, though he told
me the bleeding was from a fight with the
Rugby players after I had passed out. I
remember what the bruise looked like. It
was horrible, but he acted as though he
didn't care, as though it was nothing more
than a flesh wound.

Agent Donnery:
    I bet it hurt a lot worse than that.
(pause) So he referred to his Shifting as
though it were a sort of addiction, like
smoking or alcohol.

Dr. Ashcroft:
    If you knew you could go back and
change things about your life, you'd be
addicted, too, Agent Donnery.

Agent Donnery:
    (laughter) Of course I would, I'd change
just about everything, get a higher salary
perhaps. But I'm off subject (pause). So

after that night he stopped traveling, am
I correct?

Dr. Ashcroft:

He knew something was wrong with him,
and he knew he needed to take the time to
heal. I can imagine it was hard for him
to remain in one place as he did, in one
time, but at least it was the right time
and he was his true age.

Agent Donnery:

So he healed, and you two got to know
each other more?

Dr. Ashcroft:

Yes, but I knew him based on lies,
based on the man he claimed to be. He only
let me in half way. It was so unfair that
he knew everything about me and that I
could talk to him about everything my life
entailed, but he couldn't. Well almost.

Agent Donnery:

Almost? What did you keep from him
that he did not already know about? It's
important we learn all about his life.

Dr. Ashcroft:

It's important for me, too, Agent. He
was the man I loved, the man with a dark
secret I never knew. I guess now I can
see that he did know everything about me,

but it was at least nice to hope I had
a secret and my secret was the man in my
dreams.

Told by Dr. Ashcroft,
Stories from the journals of Patient #32185
October 1, 2005
12:48 p.m.

I woke as though I had fallen on a rock, bringing my hand to my head and feeling the cold sweat that covered me. I opened my eyes as they met the familiar pattern of my dorm room sheets, and I felt relieved. It must have been just another dream. I tried to think back, tried to remember what had happened, but most of it was blurry, and I felt as though my head was not yet a part of my body.

I heard a page turn and I slowly twisted my neck to face the direction of the noise, expecting to find Amy, but my eyes instead found a man. I jumped, letting out a shrill scream as I sat up straight, covering my body with my blankets. Had I literally imagined him from my dreams to here? Or had those events in fact happened? I brought my hand to my mouth to muffle my yelp as the man looked at me with calm blue eyes, his chair situated in the middle of the room. Amy let out a snort and rolled over on her bunk, still asleep. I didn't bother to look at Amy as my eyes stayed fixed on the man's, too afraid that he'd disappear, or worse, kill me.

The man made no sudden movements, blinking once with a soft smile lighting across his lips. After the initial shock subsided, I continued to stare into the eyes of the man, a feeling of calm resonating from his soul, giving me the feeling that I was safe though my conscience fought to deny that.

"Who are you?" I barked. My mind began to remember the previous night as I looked at his green coat, memories and thoughts pouring through my already throbbing head like a movie in fast forward.

He placed the book on my desk, and leaned back in the chair. "Do you remember anything from last night?" His voice was melodic and soft, his lips moving with such articulation that I found myself in a trance.

I let out a sharp breath. "I…" I struggled to put the events together, remembering that I saw Max somehow, and Amy, and then him. Things were still mixing together in my head; contradicting thoughts that made me question what was real. "I'm not sure," I finally replied.

He took a deep breath. "You were drugged at a party. So was your friend." He pointed toward Amy over my shoulder.

Thoughts began to click into order, and I extracted those that were just a dream. "So that actually happened?" I brought my hand to my head and began to rub it, finding that looking at the man made it hurt, as though he had broken in and rearranged all the furniture.

"Yes. I found your friend here first, then you." He searched my face as though he expected me to fill in the rest of the story.

I leaned back against the wall, my covers tucked tightly under my chin. "Yes, and Max…" I paused and he nodded as though he knew who he was beyond what had happened last night. "You know Max?" I gave him a strange look.

He quickly shook his head, "Oh no. No, I don't know Max, but you said his name, that's all."

I nodded back. "Right, yes." I felt my heart break then, realizing the gut feeling I'd always had about Max was true. He was a lying scumbag from the beginning, and I felt like a fool for playing along. I shuddered, the feeling of disgust making vomit well in my throat.

"So, I guess I should get going." He stood. "I'd hate to see what happens when she wakes up," he turned toward Amy, and lifted one brow in a humored fashion. "She seems feisty."

I laughed as he forced a smile to come to my face, though my body felt weak and useless, a deep depression lingering somewhere in the distance.

"I wanted to make sure you were okay before I left. I can see now you will recover." He clapped his hands together with a contented nod. "I have some appointments I need to get to..." his voice trailed away as he touched his side in a manner that suggested he was favoring it, and I deduced that it was a probable wound left over from last night.

I continued to smile at him, thankful to have such a curious savior. He smiled back, watching me in a way that told me he thought I was attractive. I found that I accepted the look from him instead of repulsing it as I should have, given my situation. Was I really so flighty that I would be attracted to this stranger just hours after realizing Max and I were over? I took note of his features, his eyes like storm clouds and his brows raised and innocent, like a lost child. He looked away then, as the awkward silence grew between us.

"Wait," I leaned toward him. "I still don't know your name."

He reached down toward his feet where he plucked a tattered bag from the floor, wincing a bit from soreness. He threw the bag onto his back. "If you guess it, then I'll tell you." He gave me a teasing smile.

I pouted. "Well, that seems unfair." Memories from last night were finally returning, and I remembered the way he had said my name as he had punched the man that drugged me. "Wait a minute…" I furrowed my brow, reliving the way his breath fell across my ear as he had spoke to me, telling me everything was alright. "How did you know my name?"

I saw the corners of his smile fade ever so slightly, suggesting there was something he was not telling me, but then the smile quickly returned. "From class."

I crossed my arms against my chest. "Alright then, which class?" My nose was in the air, as a part of me was convinced he was lying.

"Biology 101," he challenged.

I snorted. "Yeah right, there must be hundreds of people in that class. There is no way you'd know me.

He pointed to my laptop bag. "It's not like you hide it."

My heart sank. He was right. My mother had insisted on giving me a bag with my full name and information sewn right on the front of it, just in case it got lost. I looked down at my bag. Right there in a bright green, two inches tall for everyone to know and see was all the info he would need about me, right down to my phone number. I sighed, my cheeks blushing. "I wasn't the one that got that put on there, if that makes this any less embarrassing."

He laughed again, his thin green coat accentuating his muscular chest.

I looked away, the embarrassment growing as I realized I was flirting, not to mention gawking. Max had had a nice body, too, but he didn't have the personality to match. "Anyway…" I paused. "So if you won't tell me your name, then I guess that's goodbye."

He began to tap his foot. "Oh come on, humor me. It's not like I have much else to do today." He glanced back at Amy. "We have time before she wakes. Guess my name."

I clasped my hands together on my lap and leaned back against the wall. "Ok, fine. I'll guess but…" I narrowed my eyes. "If I guess in the first five, you have to take me out for coffee."

A half smile cut across his tanned face, a face that didn't seem to fit at Harvard, and I began to wonder what his studies were and how it was possible that we had the same class.

"I accept your offer then." He shifted his weight.

Grinning, I felt my heart leap. "Good." I gave him a sharp nod.

Bringing one hand to my face, I scratched my head in a dramatic fashion, analyzing his overall physique in an attempt to figure what name would best fit his personality based on looks alone. It was always a belief of mine that certain names depicted a certain person. Like take Amy, for instance. To me it seemed all Amys had a hot streak just as she did, so therefore there had to be a science to this. I tilted my head from side to side, craning my neck in order to dramatize the effect. The best part about this little game was that we could eye each other openly, the attraction between us palpable.

A warm feeling began to fill my stomach, much as it had last night when I had seen him from across the party. I remembered how intrigued I was, and how frantic I suddenly felt, as though I needed to talk to him immediately, but about what? I looked away, feeling a lingering disturbance about the way I felt I knew him, though I could never remember meeting him; rather like an itch I couldn't scratch.

His smile faded as he kept his gaze on me, the tension between us growing as though I'd fallen into a trance. He drew his bag down his shoulder and placed it back on the desk chair before tucking his hands in his pockets. He took a slow step toward me, but I didn't move. I took in every inch of his face, from his messy brown hair to his stubble, a few days overdue. He continued toward me and sat on the edge of my bed, his hands remaining in his pockets, as though telling me he was merely allowing me to look more closely.

An image began to form in my mind then, like chalk that was slowly being drawn across a blackboard. "I think I have it," I whispered, breaking the silence, the air around us thick like the hottest summer in Boston.

His smile returned. "Are you so sure of yourself that you think you know on your first guess?"

I knew he was trying to make me doubt my decision,

but the image in my mind was still blaring at me, still too strong to ignore or change. "Yes." I gave him a curt nod.

"Well then, what is it?" he pressed, watching me.

I looked back toward where he'd placed his tattered bag back on the floor, finding it familiar, like everything else he owned. "I don't know why, but I feel like I already know you. Are you sure we've never officially met somewhere? At a party?"

He laughed. "Well I don't really party, so I doubt that, but…" he paused. "Then if you've met me, what was it I told you my name was?" He said it matter-of-factly, as though finding it interesting that I assumed so much.

"I think your name is…" I narrowed my vision, trying to make sure what had been written across my thoughts was right. "Jordan."

A slow exhale left his lips, but he did not smile as I expected, and for a moment I began to feel afraid, as though I had said something wrong, like the name of a deceased relative.

"What made you guess that?" He tilted his head.

I shrugged as my smile faded. "I don't know, it just fits somehow." Relief washed over me as I saw his face relax, and then he smiled.

"Well, I guess its coffee then." He looked into his lap, tracing his fingers across his palm, having taken his hands out of his pockets.

I clapped my hands together. "No way! I was right?"

He laughed as he watched me jump with excitement.

Amy moaned then, and I slunk back, regretting my reaction as I saw Jordan stand and walk toward his bag. "I better go," he whispered, plucking it off the floor and fastening it to his back once more. "But I'll see you soon, Kenzie."

I didn't want him to go but I did nothing to stop him. His gaze remained locked on mine as he walked toward the door in silence, like a shadow.

"Wait!" I threw the covers off my lap and leapt to the floor, Amy stirring now. Without a second thought I ran toward him and threw my hands around his neck, giving him a kiss on his warm cheek, his stubble tickling my lips. "Thank you," I whispered, letting my lips graze his ear, wondering what I was doing and why I didn't find my actions strange.

He brought one hand up to the center of my back and pressed against it, like a man that had never been hugged before.

I stepped back and crossed my arms against my chest. "Sorry for that, I just felt so overwhelmed by the whole thing. Thank you."

His face looked shocked, like a boy being kissed for the first time. "I, uh…" His voice cracked, so he cleared his throat, "Uh, anytime." He smiled one last time, his cheeks now flushed as he turned away from me and grabbed the handle. He kept his gaze locked on his feet out of embarrassment as he slid out, just in time for Amy to pop upright in bed, sweat coating her brow and her skin ash white.

"What the hell happened?"

Agent Donnery:
You guessed his name right away?

Dr. Ashcroft:
Of course I did. It makes sense now why it had seemed so obvious then, and why I had felt so strongly toward him. The day we first met had left a lasting impression on my heart, if not my memory. It is my belief as a doctor that a heart can remember as well, as though it has a mind of its own. I've had a lot of time to think about this in the past week.

Agent Donnery:
I see. I can certainly believe that. The heart is a powerful thing. (pause) Do you think that your guess got him thinking about all he had done for you? Do you think he knew at that point that you actually remembered these things? And what about you? Didn't you pick up on the signs?

Dr. Ashcroft:
It did get me thinking a lot, but there was no explanation that made enough sense

so I dropped it. As for Jordan, I'm sure he knew something was happening between us beyond what he had anticipated. Besides, he had understood the fact that if I saw him at the party that I would follow, because of the remnants he'd left behind in my heart and memory. He used that to his advantage though he didn't understand how or why it had worked.

Agent Donnery:
    I guess that's what happens. There is always going to be some un-named variable, something no one could predict. He was a Shifter, after all, and Shifters don't exactly pass this information around.

Dr. Ashcroft:
    Yes, exactly. He was finding this out as he went along. He had no warning or set of rules.

Agent Donnery:
    Neither did you.

Dr. Ashcroft:
    And even still, I don't know much about him, so if it's alright with you, I'd like to move on to what's next.

Agent Donnery:
    We've got all night, so by all means, go ahead.

I lifted my hand to my cheek, touching the spot where Kenzie had kissed me as I walked down the hall to the stairs that led to the lower parking lot. My heart was beating faster now than it did when I traveled, and I brought one hand to my chest, trying to calm it as it stung with pain, still too damaged to handle the excitement. I took a deep breath and exhaled as I pulled back my jacket and lifted the hem of my black thermal shirt, exposing my side. The bruising there was better than it had been last night, but blood still seeped from my pores as though my stomach had become a sponge. The shirt was sodden as well, but luckily for me, it was too dark to show the stains.

It was clear the pain was getting worse with each travel I made through time, each whisking my blood in a manner that was causing every organ in my body to seize, especially what seemed to be my kidneys. If I had understood what was happening to my body earlier, I would have been a little more careful, but I didn't have that knowledge. It wasn't as though there was a manual for what I was doing that I could pick up at the local book store.

I hadn't been lying when I said I was enrolled in Kenzie's

same biology course. It had occurred to me that learning more about the human nervous system and science could help explain what was happening to me, and how I could possibly manage to travel through time. So far, nothing made sense but my mind could not accept that it was magic. There had to be another reason, a scientific or psychological one.

As I made it outside, fat drops of rain began to fall but I hardly noticed. Amy's car sat by the curb, and I wished there was some way I could get back to my bike without having to walk the twelve blocks; not when all I wanted was a shower and a nap. I knew I could not risk skipping the time between now and then, and wasting a travel, knowing that it could be the one that finally kills me.

Growing up, I had wondered about the consequences of what I was doing but ignored it, instead opting for a free life where there was no retribution, no rules, and no death. Now, however, it was becoming obvious that my future was growing shorter with each travel I made through time. When I first decided to go all the way to the end, to my death, I was old and grey, the way God had intended me to be. I'll admit that going into the future to see my day of reckoning was astonishing, and I'll never forget the way it felt to be teetering on the brink of death like that. It was an amazing thing to be able to understand at such a young age.

Admittedly, it scared me, and after that I didn't go back to revisit the experience until years later, after all the gallivanting around to save Kenzie. When the urge to see my death finally did return to me, I went there. Only it was much different, and I was much younger when I died than I had been before. I shuddered. Just the thought of going back now makes my blood curdle, because I fear my death is even closer, possibly tomorrow, for all I know. I figure it is better not to have the knowledge, better to believe that life will always go on. But despite all the worry it has welled deep inside me, I had to do what I did to stop the damage last night's events would have caused on our lives. I had to save her from him, and I had to stop the pregnancy.

I stepped gingerly off a curb and onto a path that led under a row of maple trees. The rain hit each leaf with a dull splash, lulling my mind away from death and back to the life I still had ahead of me. My choice to stop my travels would be my saving grace. I could heal, I had to.

I finally made it to the church parking lot where I had parked my bike what felt like days ago, though in reality it was only yesterday. Eleven times I had tried to stop the rape from happening, eleven days spent planning and re-planning, seeing the same sun and the same gust of wind lace its way through every branch. The important thing now was that I had succeeded, and that was all that mattered. I had stopped what could have ruined Kenzie's spirit for the rest of her life, so there was no shame in that. She did not possess the strength to handle raising a bastard child, a child that reminded her everyday of the man that had hurt her, and the man that had stolen her pride and happiness.

I sighed. Beyond Kenzie, the world held little interest for me anymore. Things were so predictable to me, that having someone like Kenzie felt refreshing and new, as though I was finally being rewarded after years of hard work and diligence; after time spent sacrificing my own life for another. She was unpredictable and wild, much like today when she kissed me, taking me by surprise when she guessed my name. I'm not sure what it was that possessed her to know these things, to feel my presence every time I was around, but she did. I had left an impression on her life, and no matter how hard I tried to stay out of it, she still felt the connection between us that had been so clear that day when we first met.

I thought about that fact as I pulled my bag from my back and threw it on my bike, strapping it down and grabbing the helmet I never used from the seat. I laughed to myself, seeing that all that time spent living without rules still led to the day I'd have to exercise caution and be like everyone else.

"Nice bike."

I jumped and turned around as I saw a girl about eighteen standing behind me. She wore a black hooded sweatshirt far too large for her frame, and a pair of old jeans. Her hood was pulled over her head and draped just above her eyes, which were a bright turquoise that glowed against her pale skin.

She smiled.

"Oh, uh… Thanks." I looked at the helmet as I flipped it onto my head and secured the strap.

"Looks old," she added, pressing the conversation.

I threw my leg over the saddle and sat down, kicking up the stand as I turned to look at her. She had her hands shoved into the front pocket of her sweatshirt, her lips parted as she let a calm breath escape her lungs. She blinked a few times, her movements slow, as though in a dream.

"It is old," I replied, trying to brush her off.

She nodded, looking as though my cold comment had broken her heart. She slowly pulled one hand from her pocket. "Here, this fell out of your bag a ways back. I figured you'd need it for something." She shrugged and took one step toward me, handing me my knife as she leaned in as far as she could. The knife glittered in her hand, the same knife I had used to slash the tires on Kenzie's mom's car.

"Oh." I paused as I took it from her hand, her skin cold as ice as our fingers touched. "Er... thanks." I looked at her sideways, noticing the way she seemed to recoil.

She was quick to tuck her hands back into the pocket of her sweatshirt, as though she were freezing though the temperature outside was unseasonably warm; wet, but warm. She avoided direct eye contact as she smiled again. "Well, I'll let you go. I need to get back as well."

"Yeah. Sure. Well, thanks again, though." I looked down at my feet and stepped down on the starter as the engine roared to life. I shook my head in disbelief, ashamed at myself for losing such an important object so carelessly, and thankful the girl had found it. Looking up, I saw the girl was already halfway down the street toward downtown, her pace quick, as though I'd scared her off. Without a second thought, I pulled out onto the street and headed back to the green house at the end of the lane, my mind still racing from the events of the day and the pain in my side.

Statement from Dr. Ashcroft,
Vincent Memorial Hospital, Boston
August 4, 2009
03:10 a.m.

Agent Donnery:
    So that was it. He was stuck with
you.

Dr. Ashcroft:
    I hardly consider it an imposition,
sir.

Agent Donnery:
    Does your stomach still hurt? I see
you're rubbing it.

Dr. Ashcroft:
    Yes, just knowing that there was a
child that was destined for me hurts, but
Jordan was right. I would have never wanted
to live with that child. I know it sounds
selfish, but what woman does? (pause) I'm
sorry, it's just… shocking.

Agent Donnery:
    I understand. I could never imagine
being in your position. First all this,
then finding you had a child destined for
you as well?

Dr. Ashcroft:

Yes, I (pause) it's very difficult, but I told myself to be prepared for anything that I may find here. Perhaps, though, this news was the worst.

Agent Donnery:

I'm sorry for the tears. It's just sad to think that child never got the chance to live.

Dr. Ashcroft:

If you believe in God, as I do (pause) excuse me, you've got me crying now (pause). As I was saying, if you believe in God, then you would believe that the child still does live. I think that its soul found another more suitable situation to live in, just not as my child.

Agent Donnery:

So for lack of a better phrase, it was sort of like terminating a pregnancy.

Dr. Ashcroft:

If that makes it easier for you to relate to, then, yes, like abortion.

Agent Donnery:

(pause) Let me change the subject. So how is it that Jordan came across his money? Surely he cannot work a normal job, and it's not like his parents could have left him much more than the house.

Dr. Ashcroft:
    Agent, I see now that when you know what will happen as Jordan did, it's not very hard to find a way to become rich. He never took much, just enough to live on, but knowing now that he was cheating makes it seem like a cop-out. He was good at hiding it from me and good at making it seem as though he was just a lucky guy making a living.

Agent Donnery:
    Let me guess. Vegas, right?

Dr. Ashcroft:
    (laughter) Sort of. More like Kentucky.

Agent Donnery:
    Kentucky? What's in Kentucky?

Dr. Ashcroft:
    The greatest sport in the history of man, Agent...

I leaned against the wall around the corner, realizing the gravity of what I was about to do, and wondering if I could pull it off without any trouble. I had come here for one reason and one reason only: the money. Besides, corporate CEO's and bankers cheated all the time; why not me? It wasn't like I was going to clean them out; just take enough to live on until next year when I would do it again.

I knew that technically I was not twenty-one, though my body looked it at this moment, but I needed the money if I was going to live the easy life and concentrate on being the superhero. Besides, I could never understand why superheroes didn't just get paid by the government so that they wouldn't have to count on large trust funds like Batman, or live in poverty like Spiderman did. If that were the case, I'd have been the first to sign up.

A lady in the largest hat I'd ever seen walked by, and I did all I could not to laugh at her. It was absurd what people did when drinking massive amounts of whiskey laced with mint, and I wondered what all the hoopla was about, but I liked it. It was a longtime dream of mine to come here one day, but now it seemed one day was easier to come by since I could easily travel into the future to get it.

Only moments ago, I was sitting in the green house at the end of the lane watching the old TV my father left behind, abandoned with little more than a few channels that I was able to pick up on the antennas. I was ten, laying down to watch the Kentucky Derby in 1992 after a day peeking through the windows and watching Kenzie ride her bike with her friends.

My father was a big fan of horse racing, and the Triple Crown races were the crème de la crème. I couldn't help but fall in love with it as well. Laying there on the floor eating stale crackers and wearing old jeans, it had finally dawned on me that I had the power to live a better life, and that's what brought me here to 2003, so that I could make my dues.

Sure, I'm cheating time, traveling forward to take money from the future, only then to bring it back. I laughed, wondering how I could manage to pass off money printed in 2003 and hoping no one would notice, I mean, who ever did anyway? Money was money; by the time they figured it out it would be too late anyway. I pulled my bag from my back and set it on the floor as a lady glared at me from across the room. She was dressed in a bright yellow sun dress and a yellow hat that had daisies on it, while I wore the old green jacket and torn jeans, looking like a bum.

I fished through my bag and pulled out the cashier's check I had withdrawn from the bank, my entire inheritance of roughly ten thousand dollars. I stood then and threw the bag over my back, standing tall in my attempt to act the age

I looked, though I still felt like a child. The woman in yellow continued to glare at me, her cheeks red from the liquor and the noises outside deafening as the horses entered the track. Didn't she know it was rude to stare?

"Last bets please!" The speakers shook on the walls, and I looked away from the woman and walked up to the counter.

"Your bet, sir?" I slid the cashier's check toward him along with my shiny fake I.D.

"On Funny Cide please," I kept my eyes down, my hands pressed against the counter to keep them from shaking with excitement.

"12-1 odds sir, are you sure? Empire Maker is a guaranteed win and the odds are 5-2, that's pretty good for a safe bet." He held the check in his hand, tempting me.

I smiled then, finding the humor in the situation. "I don't like safe bets," I winked at him.

The clerk let a humored chuckle pass his lips. "First timer," he whispered under his breath, shaking his head as he opened the register and printed my ticket.

I watched him with confidence, the smile on my face growing.

"Well, here you are, sir. Best of luck." He slammed the register shut in a manner that was meant to be threatening. "And thank you for your money."

"No, thank you, and I'll see you in a few moments," I gave him another wink, the clerk's smile now stretching from ear to ear.

I then took my ticket and walked through the complex, finally finding a spot where I could see the track. Despite the fact that I had watched the race already, it felt new now that there was ten thousand dollars on the table.

"Mint Julep, sir?" A vendor walked up behind me.

I eyed the cups he had before him, the smell triggering the memory of my father. I had never tried it, not even one drop, because I refused to be like him but what part of me would ever let that happen? I tilted my head, then nodded and dug through my pocket for some loose bills. What did it matter if I had just one? Besides, I was celebrating.

"Here you go." I pulled a twenty from my pocket and handed it to him as he handed me the change and a drink.

I took one sip and cringed, but as the flavor lingered, it seemed to change, as though my taste buds were suddenly catching up to my physical age. After the second sip I was in love, the feeling numbing the tingle that still lingered in my blood as a result of the travel here. An old man stood beside me, his ticket clutched in his hand as though it was the last thing on earth he owned.

He noticed me watching him as the trumpet began to play. "There's nothing in the world that supplies a greater thrill than this, son," he chuckled and shrugged. "Well, that is except the love of a woman."

I laughed then, nodding in agreement.

"What did you bet on, son?" His old eyes kept flickering to mine, his tanned skin and dusty white suit showing his age, but also his social class.

"Funny Cide, sir," I replied, showing him the ticket.

The man gave me a slow nod with a knowing smile. "Good choice son, good choice."

I found his company relaxing. "And you, sir?"

He smiled. "The same." He held the ticket toward me, and I noticed the amount he paid: one-hundred thousand.

I let out a sharp breath. "Wow, hefty bet there."

He turned and looked me in the eyes. "I've lost all I've ever loved. What else is there to live for? All I want is to do something reckless before I die. I want to risk it all for once." His eyes twinkled.

I nodded, seeing his future was about to change. "Well, sir, here's to us." I raised my glass toward him, and we bumped cups, taking a sip as the trumpet began to play.

I placed my hands on the banister, gripping it with such excitement I hardly noticed as they went numb. There was a loud clank and a roar from the crowd as the horses raced out of the gates, tackling each other for the lead spot on the rail, running as horses were intended to do, free and wild. As anticipated, Empire Maker was in the lead a quarter of the way around the track, but the gelding was lazy with the rail as Funny Cide sat in third, inching his way up. The crowd around us was cheering wildly with their tickets in the air, suggesting that a good portion had bet on Empire Maker to win and I smiled with secret delight.

I looked sideways at the man as the horses came into the final stretch, Funny Cide hugging the rail as he blew past the horse behind Empire maker, taking advantage of the inside track the gelding was failing to protect. The man's face was alive, as though he were twenty-one again, watching the race for the first time. Looking back I saw Funny Cide was advancing at a rapid pace, now only half a length behind Empire Maker, clicking at his heels; the horse finally tiring from being in the lead for so long.

I put my hand on the man's back and whispered in his ear, "Congratulations." Before I even saw the end of the race, I walked away, the room now silent as I heard the excited cry of one old man whom had found his thrill in life. From today on, his fate had created a new path for him, a path where he would finally live again, and it felt good to have been the one there to see it.

Statement from Dr. Ashcroft,
Vincent Memorial Hospital, Boston
August 4, 2009
03:29 a.m.

Agent Donnery:

That's funny, we've gotten reports over time about money from the future but I blew it off, figuring the reason would eventually surface. I guess now is that time. (pause) Wow, though, quite an experience. So a form of investing, I guess. What happened when he could no longer Shift? Where did he get his money then?

Dr. Ashcroft:

He'd take me to the races in college from time to time (pause). He had told me he wanted to turn over a new leaf and get an honest job one day, but the money we had already was enough to invest in a bank and live off the interest, quite comfortably.

Agent Donnery:

I thought you said he never took too much?

Dr. Ashcroft:

He didn't, it was the time he took me in college and I bet on a total loser horse that we really won. It was as though the horse knew. What was great about that day was that it was as much of a surprise to me as it was to Jordan, because it was after he stopped Shifting.

Agent Donnery:

So it was an honest win, instead of cheating.

Dr Ashcroft:

Exactly, so I don't feel bad about it because I know it was pure luck, as though there was a real Guardian Angel watching over us, and not just Jordan.

Agent Donnery:

So what happened next?

Dr. Ashcroft:

This was where I get a little lost. After the Rugby party, I soon saw that things were not yet over, and though I put everything behind me, Max eventually had to have his say. The events of these few days still haunt me; naturally they would. Now that I've seen all this though, I'm surprised Jordan had the guts to do what he did next. I'm surprised he lived. I'll tell you what I remember happening.

"I found you." I placed one hand on his back, leaning in and hovering just next to his ear.

I could see the corners of his mouth curl into a smile, but he didn't look back. "It seems you have."

I laughed. "I can see now why you knew me from class, from up here you can see everyone, but it's close to impossible to see you." I threw by leg over the back of the seat, moving into the row Jordan was in, and taking the spot next to him.

"I like it that way; keeps me invisible." He put his pencil down onto the paper in front of him.

I looked at the doodles he had made across the page. "What is that?"

There was a web of connecting lines running parallel to each other, each ending in a dot or an X. I was certain it wasn't something I had seen in Biology, or at least I hoped not, because I hadn't taken notes. He made a motion to close his notebook, but I placed my hand on his forearm.

"No really, it looks interesting." I looked more closely. "It almost seems like art."

A half smile lit across his face under the bill of his black hat, the same hat he wore at the party, and the same hat he wore when I woke up the next day. "It sort of is art. That's a good way to put it."

"Looks complicated," I added.

"It's my way of keeping things organized, so to speak." He rubbed the palms of his hands on his jeans, and I could see he was nervous.

"Dynamic form of filing I'd say. How does it work?" I pressed for more, hoping to strike up a good conversation to prove to him I was an interesting person.

He looked at me, his mouth still curled at the edges before looking back to the page. "This here," he pointed to one branched line that ended in a dot, "is a place, like a coffee house, that I've been to and think would be a good choice to go to again." He looked me in the eye. "Theoretically of course. And this here," he pointed to an X, "this is a coffee house that had really bad service. Never go there again." He shook his head with a grave expression that didn't seem to warrant a bad coffee house.

I wrinkled my brow. "But then, what does this mean?" I pointed to the arrow at the front of all the bracketing.

"That's the coffee place we are going to go to when I hold up my end of the bargain and take you out for a cup." He smirked, revealing a more confident side.

I laughed. "Whatever, Jordan." I gave him a playful tap on the shoulder. "What is it really?"

He shrugged. "I know, absurd analogy but I thought it would work." He thought for a moment. "Really, though, it's my way of keeping things in order, like decisions I make and where those decisions take me. It's sort of like the philosophy and science of a timeline," he paused and I saw his face light up. "My major is philosophy and physics so..."

My eyebrows shot in the air. "It seems as though you just figured that out, Jordan."

He laughed. "Well, you could say that."

"Wow, double major at Harvard, huh? That would cost a fortune for the poor sap that's giving you the scholarship."

He laughed. "I wish, but I pay for it all on my own."

I thought about that fact for a moment, looking at his coat and bag and wondering why he couldn't afford new ones, and figuring there was an underlying reason I did not yet know. I brought my attention back to the drawing. "So, you mean each of these is a parallel life of sorts? So say, if I made the decision right now to get up and leave, that would create a new bracket." I pointed to one ending in an X. "That branches off from the main path. Only I won't do that, so it ends in an X." He nodded, and I tilted my head, looking at the ones ending in a dot. "I don't get the ones with a dot, though, because if I went there, there would be no way back unless Stephen Hawking finally figured out how to ride black holes and travel through time."

He laughed. "And that's highly unlikely right?"

It was as though he was testing me. "Well, I'm no science geek like you, but anything is possible. Especially if Stephen Hawking says it is. That man is a genius." He continued to laugh and I reveled in his smile, something he seemed to be new at, as though life held little that amused him prior to now.

"Kenzie, you never cease to amaze," he shook his head.

"Well, you've only known me a day. There's a lot more to be amazed at." I winked at him.

Naturally, I hadn't yet talked to Max about the fact that we were clearly no longer together, and I never will, but what had happened trumped any formalities I owed to him for a formal break up anyway. That went without saying, so I was single. I still just couldn't believe I hadn't seen it in Max sooner.

"Yeah, I've known you just one day," he said it as though it were a joke.

I narrowed my eyes at him. "Yeah, but..." I paused, thinking about what I was about to say and refraining, figuring it would make me seem like a stalker for following him around the party like a gawking idiot, all because I thought he looked like the man in my dreams.

The professor made his dramatic entrance and the lights dimmed as slides lit up the screen. I reached down into my bag and pulled out my notebook and a pencil, placing it on the desk as I already began to feel the boredom of the lesson tug at my bones.

"So, we're still on for that coffee I take it?" I leaned in and whispered in Jordan's ear, daring myself to get close enough that my breath tickled his hair. I liked the thrill of new love. It was something I had missed, something I had felt I didn't deserve.

He turned and looked at me, his face half lit by the light of the projection, his dark blue eyes illuminated. "Of course," he smiled as the wrinkles around his mouth were magnified by the contrast of the room. "How about this afternoon, around four?"

I smiled. "It's a date." I looked toward the screen, but I could see him watching me from the corner of my eye, his face alive as though he'd never had a date before. He touched the bill of his hat and looked back at the screen a moment later, sliding down in the seat. His large frame seemed awkward inside the confines of the chair, his knees touching the seat in front of him.

I placed my hand under my chin and leaned against the desk, allowing myself the pleasure of dreaming about Jordan, my senses heightened to every sound he made as I begged my mind to remember them. I desperately wanted to tell him about my dreams and the way I had thought I'd seen him there. It was as though I had actually lived the parallel lives in his timeline with him, but it was absurd to think that of a complete stranger.

I focused on my dreams as the slide flipped to a new one. Though I could never make out the face of the man I saw there, the man that always seemed so curious about my life, there was still something with Jordan that clicked. I always figured they were dreams about my angel, or dreams my mind wanted to believe about the man I would someday fall in love with. Whatever the reason, something about Jordan reminded me of that man and it was a feeling I couldn't shake.

I always felt in my heart that one day the reason behind the dreams would be revealed to me, and at that party, I felt it finally had. Perhaps the dreams were God's way of warning me about what had happened, and what still could.

A figure in a black sweatshirt stood from the opposite corner of the dark room and walked toward the door. The professor, being as arrogant as he was, stopped his lecture and looked up at the figure. "Excuse me, why do you find it so pertinent to disrupt my class?"

I craned my view to look at the figure, but they kept themselves well hidden.

"Sorry," a girl's voice echoed across the crowd, and I found myself surprised by the tone, as though someone had struck a tuning fork that was stuck in my ear. I cringed and shut my eyes to the sound, opening them as I felt Jordan move in his seat. She left then, as though the professor had scared her off, her hands empty as though she had come here merely to observe.

The professor shook his head as the door to the lecture hall closed, and I looked at Jordan, who was still looking toward the door, his face frozen.

"Jordan, it's like you've seen a ghost," I squeezed his leg, and he snapped out of it, looking me in the eye.

"Oh, sorry, it was just distracting is all." He looked back down at his paper.

I crinkled my brow, finding his behavior suddenly strange and distant. When I looked back to the screen, I saw him flip the page in his notebook back to the bracket he had been working on. He erased an X and replaced it with a dot in a manner that was meant to be discreet, but I caught it anyway. I wondered what it meant, and why that event had changed it. There was something about the girl that had also resonated with him, as it had with me, as though he'd known her, or perhaps he was really an undercover CIA agent and she was his perp. I could at least assume, right?

I laughed to myself, finding my daydreaming refreshing in an otherwise dull situation. For the duration of class, Jordan remained silent, and though I made it obvious that I wanted to talk more, he didn't fall for my attempts, so after a while I merely dozed off into dreaming. When the lights finally came back up, I stretched and looked around, finding I was not the only one that had found the lesson less than stellar, as half the class began to yawn.

Jordan stood and placed his bag on the seat, stuffing his notebook inside. "Well, Kenzie, I've got to run, but I'll see you at four?"

I also stood, hooking my computer bag over my shoulder. "Looking forward to it."

We stood there for one awkward moment before Jordan finally spoke. "Well, ok, see ya." He turned, and walked in the opposite direction down the aisle.

I allowed myself to watch him, his gate quick and frantic as though he was always in a rush, but a handsome rush at that.

Statement from Dr. Ashcroft,
Vincent Memorial Hospital, Boston
August 4, 2009
03:41 a.m.

Dr. Ashcroft:
So that is where my side of the story ends, but I see here that his picks up where I left off.

Agent Donnery:
Perfect then.

Dr. Ashcroft:
I know, this is beginning to become fun.

Exiting class, I looked around, trying to find the girl, feeling as though she were still nearby, lingering. I had known it was her the minute she opened her mouth to speak, the voice resonating the same way it had yesterday in the church parking lot. I had never seen her before, and I wondered who she was and why she seemed to be showing up in my life out of nowhere, and with such frequency.

The feeling I had now was a feeling all too familiar with me; the same thing I had done to Kenzie for years. There had to be something I did that night at the party that had brought this girl here, perhaps a slight wave I had made. For a long time I've worried about the effects I had on other lives and not just Kenzie's, like the truck driver that never hit Kenzie's car, or the person who lost their scholarship to Harvard when Kenzie passed her high school test.

The class came out behind me and interrupted my thoughts. I was quick to walk around the building, unable to afford having Kenzie there to see me looking around like a terrified idiot. I walked toward the bushes that were against a large tree, watching everyone passing through the courtyard. I brought my hand to my mouth and chewed on my nails as I waited, finding it narrowed my vision and kept me focused.

It was then that I spotted the girl about a hundred yards to the left up the path, watching Kenzie over her shoulder as she walked away in the opposite direction. I took off toward the girl, taking note of the look on her face as she continued to watch Kenzie. The girl was walking fast but my stride was faster so I gained ground, now just behind her. "Excuse me."

Her head snapped around and she halted as though she had seen death, taken by surprise.

"What do you want?" she hissed, her voice even and annoyed, as though I'd ruined something she was in the middle of. She shook her head with disgust as she turned and tried to walk away.

"Well, that's what I was here to ask you." I put my hand on her shoulder and twisted her around, her hood shielding her face, as always.

She rolled her eyes. "I'm on my way to my next class. What are you doing?" She had a sense of sassiness about her, but I could see her looking at me with awe, as though it was torturing her to treat me this way.

"Why are you following me?" My face was like stone.

She let out a slow, steady breath that felt cold as it landed across my face. "I'm not following you. You're crazy. Just leave me alone."

I furrowed my brow. She was trying to make it seem as though I were mad, but I sensed a guilt about her, as though she knew she had in fact been watching us for a reason.

"What's your name?" I barked.

Her eyes met mine, and I found myself shocked by the turquoise color a second time, illuminated under her dark hood. "Molly." She gave me an irritated exhale. "There, are you happy now?" She crossed her arms against her chest, the sleeves of her sweatshirt covering her hands.

The name made my heart sink; it had been my mother's name. "Okay, Molly, I'll bite." I shifted my weight, though she had my mother's name she did not have the same hazel eyes, "I'm Jordan."

She nodded. "Yeah, so?"

I could see I had her in an uncomfortable situation, with her hand stuck in the cookie jar, so to speak. "Why did you give me my knife back when you seem so..." I paused. "So rude."

She rolled her eyes. "You need it."

"I need it?"

She shifted her weight. "I mean it was yours, and I'm not a thief." I could tell she was flustered and annoyed, perhaps on the brink of causing a scene just to get away.

I backed off, figuring I had interrogated her to the point that there was little more she would tell me. "Well, yeah, sorry."

"Can I go now?" She looked up at me, her skin like porcelain.

I stared at her for a moment, trying my best to remember her face but there was nothing. "Yeah." I adjusted my bag on my back.

She let out a long breath. "Just..." She began to walk

away. "Just don't be late, okay?"

I pressed my brows together as she stormed off. "Wait…" I took one step to go after her, but I stopped as a feeling of fear overcame me, and I looked back in the direction Kenzie had gone. I felt my stomach clench as I broke out into a cold sweat. The air around me stood still, as though a bell jar had been placed over my head, silencing every sound. Something felt wrong, very wrong, and the sudden need to find Kenzie now overwhelmed me.

Looking back in the direction in which the girl had walked off, I saw she was already gone. Disregarding Molly's sudden absence, I took off then in the direction Kenzie had gone, pushing through the crowds of students and finding my way back to her dorm. On the way there, I noticed people staring at me as though I were crazy, but to me it seemed as though they were telling me to run faster. I rounded the block, her dorm just ahead now. I ran up the steps to the outside door, and I leaned my hand against the wall and took a deep breath. Tapping my foot, I waited outside until someone exited the building, catching the door before it shut, charging in. By now my heart was pounding and my body was drenched in sweat as the strange feeling of fear grew.

I sprinted up the two flights of stairs to the third floor. Kenzie's room was just down the hall. I slowed my pace, trying not to draw too much attention to myself too soon, and hoping there was no real reason behind my fear. Coming to her door I grabbed the handle, but it was locked. I stood there for a moment, but heard nothing and I began to wonder if I was finally losing my mind, along with my health. Exhaling, I leaned against the wall and let my back trail down the frame of the door until I was sitting on the ground.

It was then that I heard a muffled squeal and it heightened my senses as I pressed my ear to the door. There was a deep voice on the other side, followed by more squeals and frantic breathing. I brought my hand back to the handle, testing it to be sure it was locked, not wanting to make too much commotion in case whoever it was would do more harm.

I pulled my bag in front of me and fished through the contents, finding the knife and flipping it open. Placing the bag on the ground, I knelt down to the lock on the door and wedged the knife into the keyhole. Pulling my hand back and preparing myself for the pain, I punched the heel of my palm on the butt end of the knife, slicing it into the keyhole so that the lock broke and the door swung open.

Kenzie squealed as she saw me, her mouth covered by Max's hand, his other hand holding a gun that was pointed at Amy as she sat bleeding from her head in the corner. Kenzie's eyes were watering from the pain, her arms already showing bruises. My stomach sank at the sight, realizing now that the threat was never over; that I would never be at peace.

"You, again." Max's voice sounded low and drunk; nothing like it had for the years I'd known him as Kenzie's boyfriend.

"Max, what are you doing?" I put my hands up as the gun in his hand shook, Amy cowering even further into the corner.

"Stay out of this, man. This is no longer your fight." Max's arm was around Kenzie's neck as she looked at me, her eyes wide with fear and her face red. He brought his mouth to her ear. "Your boyfriend won't save you this time, you slut."

The lump in my throat rose further into my mouth, the words he said stinging my heart.

"Max, please, we weren't going to go to the cops," Kenzie whispered with what little breath she could muster.

"Ha!" His laughter filled the room as a girl in the hall looked in.

I turned around and saw her before she ducked back, the look in her eyes suggesting she was going to run and get the cops, which was good.

"You think you can cheat on me, and then try and ruin my football career as well? Well, you're wrong, honey." Max shook Kenzie in his arms, his teeth clenching. "All those years I allowed you to be in my spotlight, and this is how you re-pay me? By humiliating me in front of all my friends?"

"Max, there was no harm done. As far as I know, nothing happened and everyone was fine." I was trying to make it seem as though he could still walk away from this, though at this point there was no way I'd ever let him.

He pointed the gun at me now and I blinked, figuring if anyone had to die, I'd rather it be me. He whispered into Kenzie's ear again. "It's your friend's fault, Kenzie." He eyed Amy with a cheap glare. "She was all over me. What else was I to do? She was asking for it as though I'd be doing her a favor."

I saw Amy begin to sob and shake, the gun migrating back to her.

"There's no one blaming you, Max." I inched closer, but he brought the gun back toward me.

"I'm not falling for that, man. You stay where you are."

Kenzie was muttering under her breath, but I couldn't make out what she was saying.

I heard the distant sounds of sirens, and my heart leapt. Max heard it, too, as his face seemed to become further distraught and annoyed, the tension growing.

"The last thing I need is for some stupid girl to ruin my whole career," his voice cracked as though he was about to cry. "All this time I nurtured you." He jerked Kenzie in his arms, his mental stability flipping from one extreme to the next. "And this is how you repay me?" He pointed toward me, depression lacing his face. "Falling in love with some vagrant?"

I watched as he inched himself toward the window, the sound of cops entering the building and the reflection of lights outside. He pulled back the shade and threw Kenzie to the side where her body slammed against her desk chair. She fell limp to the floor, but I could see she hadn't been knocked out.

"Max it's over. Just think about your choices." I took another step into the room, edging closer as he looked outside, the gun still raised in his hand.

"No, it's not over." I watched as he opened the window, two stories above the street. "I always get away, I'm a *star*."

I couldn't help but roll my eyes as a cool fresh breeze

filled the air. New sounds drifted toward me as I heard the cops coming down the hall, their voices calculated and poised for attack. Startled, Max looked back at me and through the door, then turned and dropped the gun to the floor with a weighted clank before climbing onto the sill.

"I'll be back for you, Kenzie," he glared down at her. "You owe me," he added with an evil nod, and with that he jumped.

I ran to the sill as two cops came in with their guns up, watching as he landed in the bushes below, now fighting his way out as cops surrounded him faster than he could manage to get away. He was screaming and yelling, like a delusional child, and I shook my head, wondering how I could have missed this for so long.

They cuffed Max and took him to the car. I turned and ran to Kenzie as one of the cops took care of Amy, the other leaving the room to check the rest of the floor.

"Are you alright?" I whispered in her ear, helping her up off the ground.

She nodded with pursed lips, fighting back tears in her own stubborn way, though it did little to hide the fact she was terrified. "I knew this was going to happen. I dreamt about it, but I didn't know it would be so soon." Her breath was shaking as it passed her lips, shock setting in as I comforted her. "I'm sorry," she shook her head with guilt, guilt that was also pulsing through me.

"It's okay, Kenzie. Take a deep breath. It's over." I took a deep breath as well, relieved that it had ended without any serious damage. I cursed myself for being so careless, for wasting all my talent leaping around for so long instead of saving it to save her.

"How did you know to come?" Kenzie looked at me as I cradled her in my lap.

It hadn't dawned on me until now that the only reason I did come was because of Molly. Kenzie continued to watch me as confusion prickled through my veins. How had Molly known? The sudden questions that streamed through my head only further solidified the fact that Molly was different, that Molly was up to something. But what? Kenzie touched my face, still searching for an answer.

I swallowed. "An angel told me."

She let out a contented sigh. "You always save me Jordan. You're my angel." I could tell she was weary now, her words almost accusing me of the fact that she had known I had saved her all her life.

She gave me the best smile she could muster as I brushed the hair from her face. "I will always protect you."

Another cop entered the room and came up to me. "Did you see what happened, sir?"

I nodded as I stood with Kenzie, taking her to her bed.

"Is it alright if I collect a statement from you?" The cop reached behind him and pulled out his ledger.

I nodded. "Of course."

Statement from Dr. Ashcroft,
Vincent Memorial Hospital, Boston
August 4, 2009
03:53 a.m.

Dr. Ashcroft:
    (pause) That girl...

Agent Donnery:
    Had you ever noticed the girl before Doctor?

Dr. Ashcroft:
    Yes, in class that day just like every other student did. But like I said, when she spoke, something about her voice resonated with me.

Agent Donnery:
    This is the second account he's written of her, and then also you. Excuse me for noticing, but it seems there was a connection. Do you think she had a roll?

Dr. Ashcroft:
    (pause) I suppose now that I know of her and what Jordan knew of her, yes. (pause) I always thought that perhaps he just found her attractive that day in

Biology and that my reaction was just a fluke to the fact that I had expected the voice behind the hood to be male. But how would she know about what was happening to me? Was she like him, too, you think? It would explain how he was there to save me without Shifting to the future to know it. Molly tipped him off.

Agent Donnery:
    (pause) Seems so. It seems as though this girl helped him in a major way.

Dr. Ashcroft:
    It explains the dream as well, because in the dream I had dreamt that I had been hurt, but when I wasn't, I didn't see that it was him there to Shift it as usual. This time I saw a girl, and it must have been Molly.

Agent Donnery:
    Tell me about the dreams. Did you ever mention them to Jordan?

Dr. Ashcroft:
    I did tell him, because I wanted to know how he would react. Like I said, I saw a man in my dreams that was a lot like him, and the memories of the boy from the bus, though vague, still remained somehow. For some strange reason I always hoped he'd say that he'd had the dreams

too. I guess it worked out to be a little
more than dreams for him, though. It was
his life.

Told by Dr. Ashcroft,
Stories from the journals of Patient #32185
October 2, 2005
04:27 p.m.

"Are you ready to finally get that coffee?" Jordan gave me a smile, and I couldn't help but feel it lift my spirits.

"Yes, I'm beyond ready. Starving too." I put my hand on my stomach, my arms dappled with bruises where Max's hand had held me. "Let me just grab a sweater." I ducked back into my room as the cops disappeared around the corner down the hall, finally done with all their questioning and evidence-gathering.

"Sure, take your time," he lingered at the door. "Perhaps then we'll forgo coffee and just get dinner. We can go down to that sports bar."

I laughed. "The sports bar is the best you can do? I almost died Jordan. I want something amazing."

He smirked and chuckled. "How did I know you'd say that?" He paused. "I just didn't want to make it seem like too much of a date, especially when your ex-boyfriend just tried to kill you and your roommate. It seemed presumptuous."

I pursed my lips. "Screw him. I want a date." I gave him a wink. My number one priority at this moment was to put it all behind me, and that was exactly what I was going to do.

"Well, then, I guess it's Aujourd'hui, then," he said it as

though he knew French.

I raised my eyebrows. "You want to take me there? I was thinking a step above bar food, not complete French, but I'll take what I can get." I smiled. It had been a dream of mine to go to Aujourd'hui just once, but I never had the money.

"I may be a bit under-dressed but…"

"Wait," I walked over to Amy's closet. Amy had gone to the hospital with the cops, the cut on her face in need of stitches. "She has men's clothing in here, I swear."

He tilted his head and gave me a strange look. "How did I guess."

I laughed, making light of the situation. "Don't think she's going to acquire much more now. She may turn into a nun after today."

I opened the door on the right hand side, the party side, fishing through toward the back where shirts and slacks were draped in laundry bags. Amy had a thing for keeping men's clothing as a sort of souvenir, though I never quite understood what the men wore home.

"What size are you?" I looked him up and down, and I swear I saw him blush.

"A 34 should be fine."

I fished through each, finding the extensive collection somehow appalling. "Here," I pulled a black suit and held it before him, "This will work fine."

He took it and pulled off the plastic, "Are you sure it's clean?"

A loud laugh escaped my lips. "Let's hope."

He lifted one brow. "You know, I've never really worn a suit before."

I pressed my brows together, "Never? Not even for your entrance interview for Harvard? Then what about to Aujourd'hui?"

He shrugged. "I guess I got into Harvard on charisma alone. And as far as Aujourd'hui goes, it doesn't matter when you only go at closing and you're alone. There's no one to impress other than tired waiters and burnt out chefs."

"I see. Well, there's a first for everything, isn't there?" I started to close Amy's closet, but then an idea came to mind. My dress selection was rather bland, and in the spirit of the night, I felt like pretending to be someone else. I opened the door once more, fishing through her evening wear until I finally found a black dress with capped sleeves, the only tasteful one in the bunch. I looked at my bruises and then back at the dress, finally deciding that I really didn't care. I had makeup, after all. I pulled the dress from the rack before fumbling through her shoes, finding a pair of black heels to match.

I blew a few thick strands of hair from my face as I stood, looking at Jordan.

"Er… where should I dress?" He was standing in the middle of the room like a lost boy.

"Oh, just dress here. I don't care. Nothing I haven't seen before." I waved him away, trying to make him comfortable, though I doubted there was little I could do.

He continued to stare with a nervous look on his face.

"Here, I'll turn around if that makes it easier." I faced the wall as I began to undress, relieved to get out of these clothes. I could sense the fact that he hadn't turned around as fast as I had, and there had been a moment there where I felt him watching me, and I smirked.

I stripped down to my underwear and pulled the dress from the hanger, pulling it up over my hips, as it fit snug. I looked over my shoulder, catching him in his boxers as he pulled on the pants. He didn't notice me so I continued to stare, watching as his muscles flexed, his arms fighting with the pants.

His skin was tanned and dappled with freckles, his hair curling ever so slightly as it lay against the nape of his neck. My gaze trailed down his back where I narrowed my eyes to look closer, admiration now replaced with alarm. There was a bruise across his side that swallowed his abdomen from his belly button to the base of his spine, as though he'd been beat to the ground and kicked repeatedly. Perhaps he'd gotten it at the party after I passed out, though his face seemed unscathed. Things had gotten so hectic in the past few days that I never found the time to talk to him about what had really happened.

"What is that from?" I turned, revealing the fact I had been looking as I walked up to him. He covered himself with his hands, the pants now buttoned though he seemed shy as though any inch of skin was like being naked. I, on the other hand, had no reason to be shy.

"Oh, nothing." He put his hand on the bruise though it

hardly hid anything.

I traced the tips of my fingers from his elbows to his hands, pulling them away, "Is it from the party? Did they attack you?"

He looked down at me, his eyes locked on mine as though he hadn't been paying attention to what I was saying. He nodded.

I ran my hand across the bruise as he winced away, my touch tickling his skin. "Does it hurt in your gut?" I was analyzing him in a medical manner, making sure there wasn't any internal bleeding.

"My gut?"

"Yeah, your gut." I gave him a stern stare.

He shook his head.

"Are you sure? You haven't spit up any blood or anything?"

He shook his head again, but I doubted he was telling the truth; men rarely did. I drew my hand away from his stomach.

He blinked and turned away to grab his shirt, pulling it over his shoulders as he buttoned it, ending the conversation. I took it as his way of telling me to stay out of his business, but if he thought I was going to ignore it all together, he was wrong. He played with the collar, not sure what to do.

"Here." I walked up to him and unbuttoned the top button, ruffling the collar to give him a relaxed yet sophisticated look since I didn't have a tie for him, but I liked it that way. From my desk I grabbed some of my own hair gel and rubbed it in my hands, running my fingers through his hair as he closed his eyes, as though he had rarely been touched by another person.

"Have you had a girlfriend before?" I grabbed his chin and made him look at me so that I could inspect my work.

His eyes searched mine. "No."

I smiled, holding back a laugh as I sensed it may come across as rude. "Never?" I was a little surprised. I figured someone as handsome as him would have had at least one.

He shook his head. "It never worked out for me to have one. I, uh…" he paused. "…traveled a lot as a kid." He put his hands in his pockets.

I nodded, feeling brave. "A mother?" It was clear he lacked a sort of tenderness, something only a mother could teach their son.

He looked away from me. "No."

I felt my heart sink with sadness, wondering what life was like without a mother. "I see."

I dropped the subject as I grabbed a bottle of cover-up and began smearing it on my arm, walking to the mirror to give him some space. Jordan watched me as I reached to get the back of my shoulder, straining my arm. In the reflection of the mirror, I saw him grab the bottle off the desk, putting some on his hand and walking up behind me.

"Here, let me help." I felt his eyes on me as though an artist at work, taking in every inch of my beauty as his cold palms met my skin, making me shiver.

He stepped back and smiled as he inspected my back,

rubbing the rest of the cover-up on a towel that hung near the door. "There, all gone."

There was an awkward moment of silence before I spoke. "Well, are you ready?"

He nodded and grabbed the coat from my bed and hooked it under his arm, making sure to keep his hands safely tucked in his pockets as we left the room and made our way to the parking lot. Once in the car, it was easy to get to the restaurant, suggesting Aujourd'hui was more than just a place he went from time to time, but a frequent hang out.

"You come here a lot, don't you?" I looked at him as he shut off Amy's car. We took the car figuring she wouldn't care, especially considering all Jordan had done for her.

"Yes." He jingled the keys in his hand.

"So the scruffy hero has a sophisticated hideout."

He shrugged. "Small luxuries, is all. When your life is like mine, it's nice to know you always have a place to go, where things are played in a orderly fashion."

I felt sadness for Jordan. Such loneliness. There was a guarded air around him, something I had sensed from the beginning, as though his life didn't matter nor didn't count, as though there was no one but him in his world, both body and soul. I was envious of his secret life, and I felt now that I wanted to be in it as well; the only two souls on this planet.

I unbuckled and got out of the car and I walked up beside him, hooking my arm in his as he looked down at me. I did not look back, letting him know with that simple gesture that I was here; that he was not alone. We walked to the restaurant in silence, the sounds of the city acting as our sole entertainment. When we got to the door I finally spoke. "Excuse me for saying this, but I feel sort of funny being here."

"Why is that?"

I shrugged. "It's just so fancy."

He looked at me. "It's only fancy if you think of it that way. Think of it as though you're at home, that everything in the restaurant is something you've missed. Besides, I thought you wanted to eat someplace fancy." There was a hint of reproach to his voice.

I felt bad for a moment, as though I'd gotten him all dressed up for nothing. I shook my head. "No, I do! I'm just not used to it like you clearly are."

He looked down at his clothes. "Well, I'm not used to this, if it makes you feel any better. Bit uncomfortable, really. Never thought I'd see the day."

I let out a sharp breath. "What! You look great. Like a secret agent that's taking the night off to take his female conquest to dinner."

He snorted. "Okay, I'll buy that. Is this a game to you, or something?"

I gave that question some thought. "I like to pretend sometimes, makes things seem interesting."

He nodded. "So, then, let's pretend. I'll be the agent, you can be the female conquest, as you say."

I gave him a sharp nod of compliance. "Deal."

"You certainly are a different kind of girl, aren't you?"

He opened the door for me.

I walked into the lobby and sent him a sly look over my shoulder. "Actually, for the most part, I don't act this way. I just feel like you're different, that you won't laugh or think I'm being childish."

He looked down at his feet with a smirk on his face. "I'm likely the last person to think those things about you."

I thought about the man in my dreams then, as his eyes met mine, the fog of it clearing as though trying to replace it with Jordan.

The low music of the restaurant muffled the sounds of the city outside. "Well hello, Jordan." The blonde hostess was looking at him with shining eyes. She clearly had a crush. "You seem different." She looked at him sideways, eyeing me as well.

"Hello, Meghan." Jordan cleared his throat and gave me an innocent look, as though telling me her flirtation was not his fault.

The waitress glared at me once more before turning around to grab two menus from the rack. "Two tonight?"

I leaned close to his ear. "And you've never had a girlfriend, even when women like her look at you like that?"

He gave me a nudge and a glare, looking back at the waitress. "Yes Meghan, two."

She gave him a smile, as though complimenting the fact that he was finally bringing a date, even though that date wasn't her. "Right this way."

She sat us at a table that was out of the way toward the

back, a table he clearly seemed to own. We both sat and I tried my best to remain polite, though it was hard for me. Growing up, I was used to pizza parlor dinners and home cooking, hardly ever fancy restaurants. It was then I decided to test his theory, treating each thing around me as though a part of my home, and things became easier and I relaxed.

I watched the waitress walk away. "So, how do you make your money?" The question was blunt, but I was burning with curiosity.

He let a sharp breath pass his lips as I watched his mouth curl. "Investing."

I nodded, finding his answer vague and unassuming, an obvious cover up for a real reason that was surely unsavory. I chuckled under my breath. "So tell me, are you involved in the mafia, or anything like the mafia, because I don't really think I want to be a part of that."

He laughed. "I thought I was a secret agent?"

I tilted my head and glared at him. "I'm serious, Jordan. My own safety always comes first."

He gave me a mocking look. "And that it does, obviously."

I made a face at him.

His smile faded. "No mafias, nothing illegal, ok?" He paused for a moment, "More like betting, much like the stock market."

I could see through his veil of secrecy. "That all sounds good, but I still don't buy it. I want the truth. If you tell me the truth, I'll tell you something about myself that will even the playing field. Promise."

He nodded. "Alright then…"

I cut him off. "I knew it. You were lying."

He chuckled. "Not quite. I do invest, but not in your typical way. I have a knack for placing bets, if that makes sense. When I was twenty-one, I took all the money my parents had left me and bet it on the Kentucky Derby, and won a couple grand. After that it became a hobby, and now here I am."

"Seriously?" I leaned toward him in disbelief. "See now, that is a lot more interesting than saying you invest."

He looked me in the eyes. "Does that make me more appealing?"

I smiled. "Actually, yes. I like interesting. In my opinion, the weirder the better."

"Really?" He gave me a look that suggested he was thinking of many more things I may enjoy, and I reveled in the mystery of it. He lifted an eyebrow and tilted his head, "So then tell me something that's weird about you. It's only fair."

The first thing that came to mind when he said that was the dreams. "Well, I dream a lot. A lot more than normal people, it seems. Really sucks actually; I can never sleep."

His face was suddenly still. "Really. How do you mean?"

"Well, as soon as I fall asleep, it's like I flip to some other life of mine. I always told myself I had a vivid imagination," I laughed. "Perhaps one day I'll make a movie of it so that explaining it is easier." I rolled my eyes and sat back. "I used to take something to try and make them stop, but it was no use. After years and years of it, I no longer mind. It's almost become something I look forward to, something that is unique about me."

"Hmm." He looked at his water glass. "What sort of dreams?"

I sighed. "You really want to hear all this?"

He sat up straight. "Yes, I'm actually quite intrigued."

I shrugged and put my napkin in my lap as he had, following his lead. "Nothing spectacular. It's as though I wake up in this alternative life. I have friends, make friends, go to work, just typical life stuff. I always thought that dreams were supposed to be wild and unexpected, with flying and so on, but they never were for me." I laughed at the absurdity of it, but his face remained solemn.

He scratched his head in thought. "Really?"

"Really, I swear." I put my hand in the air with a flat palm. "Scout's honor."

He laughed before his face again turned serious. "What about today after the Max incident? You told me you had dreamt that, too?" He placed his hands on the table in front of him as I saw the waiter come around the corner.

"Are you ready to order?" He smiled politely, but under it all I could see he hated his job.

I exhaled. "Gosh, I didn't even look."

Jordan looked at the waiter as though they were buddies. "I'll just have what I always do. Get her the quail. I believe that will work?"

He looked at me then, and a bit of disappointment

washed over me. It was true I would have loved the quail and would have picked it on my own, but I also wanted the option to choose for myself first. "Sure." My voice was laced with hurt.

"What? You don't want the quail?" Jordan shrugged.

"No, I do! It's just weird that you can choose like that and know what I want, secret agent." I said the last part under my breath.

Jordan looked at the waiter, and he nodded, returning to the kitchen.

I crossed my arms over my lap, sitting up straight. "So, it's your turn again."

"My turn?" He pointed at himself. "I was enjoying talking about you."

"Nope, fair is fair." I brought my finger up and pointed at his face. "I want to know about that bruise."

I saw him sink into his chair. "It's just a bruise, is all. It will go away in ten to fourteen days."

I laughed. "Are you making fun of my medical abilities?"

A smirk lit up his face. "Just keeping it light is all; letting us acclimate to each other without digging up too much dirt."

I thought about what dirt he could possibly have. "You've got a lot of secrets Jordan, I can tell."

"Really, is it obvious?" He winked at me.

"Whatever. You're avoiding my question. What's with the bruise?"

He sat up. "Like you thought, it's just from the other night at the party."

I thought about the party and all the big rugby players, feeling his pain. "Ouch, that must have hurt." I gave him a sympathetic face.

The waiter came back then with a bottle of wine, uncorking it at the table, which I admit was a bit awkward. He placed two glasses before us, and poured a little. Jordan took the glass and smelled it, then took a sip and I played along, finding it exciting. In one gulp it was gone, and Jordan looked at me over the rim of the glass with amusement, placing it back on the table.

He nodded at the waiter and he poured us a full glass and left. "So, it's your turn, Kenzie."

Anxiety washed over me. This felt like truth or dare, "Yeah, and?"

"Tell me something." He took another sip of wine in a manner that was so masculine, it just added to the suave effect of his suit.

I felt the need to spice up the conversation. "Well, I like you."

His eyebrows went up, and he smirked. "No offense, but that's obvious."

"Wow, for someone that can act as shy as you do, that was rather cocky."

"Well, you wear your emotions on your sleeve, so…" He sat up, and I could see the topic did indeed fluster him a bit.

"I don't know, there's something about you that I knew I

liked from the beginning. You were different." I eyed him.

"Well, what do you want me to say?"

I felt annoyed. "I want you to tell me what you think of me."

He pursed his lips. "You're intriguing, and you always seem to find trouble," he winked.

"Well, you're always in the right place at the right time, like you know it's going to happen." I thought about that fact, knowing how weird it was. "Why is that?"

He let out a sharp exhale. "Luck."

I laughed. "Come on, luck has nothing to do with it. I think it's fate."

Our dinners came then, and the smells were all I needed to distract me from the subject at hand. I rolled my eyes at his typical male pick, steak and potatoes. He cut into the meat and ate a bite, the silence between us growing.

"Fate's a strong word, you know," he broke the silence after he'd swallowed.

I nodded. "Why is that?"

He smirked. "Because it's subjective."

"Subjective? How can fate be subjective?" I took a bite of my own food and nearly swooned. It was delicious.

"Fate is what you make it. You've heard that before right?" He looked at me.

"Yes, and I do believe that to a degree, but human nature is also human nature, and it can sometimes interfere. And besides, how can you be so certain that fate doesn't know you may change your mind about certain things already?

Maybe when you think you're making something happen, fate already wanted that."

He looked at me sideways. "That's a profound point. But then how can human nature interfere?"

I thought about it for a moment. "Love, anger, emotion. If fate is subjective, then there is always emotion there to try and trump it, sort of like devil's advocate. What I'm saying is that in the end, fate always prevails because you can't ignore emotion, and you can't change everything. Whether it takes a day or years, fate always gets even."

He nodded. "That's interesting. I suppose I never looked at it that way."

I nodded and our conversation fell to silence for the rest of the meal. At the end of the night, I was full and happy, nearly forgetting about all that had happened that day, or even this week. Jordan drove me back to my dorm, where we parked outside.

"What should I do with the suit?" Jordan was looking at himself.

I shrugged. "Keep it. You'll need it."

He shut off the car and gave me a nod.

"How will you get back to wherever you live?" I looked around, realizing I had no clue where it was that Jordan lived.

He pointed to a motorcycle across the lot. "That's mine."

I gawked. "Really? I've never known someone with a bike."

He was playing with his hands. "Well, you know, it's practical." He grabbed the handle then and got out of the car.

I let out a sharp breath of disappointment. Clearly he had never done this before.

"Well goodnight, Kenzie." He looked at me over the top of the car.

"Wait!" I walked around the hood and came right up to him.

There was a scared look in his eye. "For what?"

I glared at him. "You're from another planet, aren't you?"

He laughed. "No, why?"

I put my hands on his shoulders. His eyes never left mine. I thought to say something, but I figured it would ruin the moment, so I leaned into him instead, bringing one hand up onto the back of his head and pulling him toward me. He did not blink as my lips met his, giving him the softest kiss I could manage without scaring him away. I pulled back and saw him blush, his eyes catching what little light there was in the dark parking lot.

"Wow," he swallowed.

I giggled. "Just wanted to see what it was like, is all."

He put his hands in his pockets. "Well…"

I stopped him. "Thanks for dinner, Jordan. See you tomorrow?" I knew that he was struggling to find something to say, so I figured I'd help him out.

He nodded. "Yeah, tomorrow."

I smiled then and trotted off toward the dorm, looking

back when I got to the door, only to see that he was still standing in the same spot, watching me. I gave a little wave and unlocked the door, entering the hall and going straight to my room to tell Amy.

Statement from Dr. Ashcroft,
Vincent Memorial Hospital, Boston
August 4, 2009
04:07 a.m.

Agent Donnery:
     So you told him about the dreams, but he told you nothing about the fact that he had caused them?

Dr. Ashcroft:
     No, not at the time, but it made sense. If he had told me right away, it would have freaked me out, to say the least. I was certain I had actually scared him because my story seemed crazy. (laughter) Apparently not. I don't think he ever knew that the dreams would happen, so I'm sure he felt guilt for it.

Agent Donnery:
     So then I'm guessing this is when you started dating, right?

Dr. Ashcroft:
     Actually, no. I never understood what really happened, but I did see that girl again, the one from class. A part of me thought she had something to do with it, like I said. Perhaps they were seeing each

other. (pause) I'm actually hoping some
of these papers may shed some light on
things, something he hasn't yet told me.

Agent Donnery:
    Here, there's one dated a few days
after the incident. Shall we read this?

Dr. Ashcroft:
    Of course. Please.

Walking to class two days later, I found that I was more excited than usual to see Kenzie and I knew it was because now it was different; now she actually knew who I was and the conversations between us were no longer in my head, but real. What I couldn't forget, however, were the things she told me about her dreams and the parallel life that was still hers.

It had never occurred to me that all this was doing something to her memory beyond her hunches about knowing me somehow. If I had known what it was doing to her perhaps I would have let it be, but so far, my actions did little than steal her dreams from her, leaving her instead with a sort of double life that turned over every night like Jekyll and Hyde.

I watched my feet as they hit the pavement, droning onward in a meditative fashion. I wondered what that would be like to fall asleep in one life and wake up in the other, and how on earth she ever kept it all straight. I suppose there was something that told her this was the life she was really living, but, what if it wasn't? What if she just told me that and she really didn't know which life was real?

I shook my head, my thoughts becoming deep and confusing. This was the real life she lived now, and all the past was just a memory. Besides, if I should worry about anyone keeping it straight, it should be me. It was hard enough to know what day it was, let alone year, but the truth was I just knew and that was it. My brain had adapted to this way of life much like hers had, and regardless what had happened, we were still alive and that was all that truly mattered.

I looked up at the trees, the breeze picking at the leaves as they desperately tried to cling to their branches, much like me. It had only been four days since I stopped traveling, but already I was growing tired of the routine. I put my hand on my side. The bruising was beginning to lighten up, and the aching pain was ebbing. I was relieved, at best, no longer fearing that I had finally done it and killed myself.

"Hey!" A girl's familiar voice crept up from behind me, causing chills to run up my spine.

I stopped cold in my tracks, turning slowly as I looked into the turquoise eyes I dreaded. I pursed my lips. "Oh, you."

Molly was standing there, her hood up over her head, as always. "Good to hear you're excited to see me."

"Who are you? And what's with the hood? Is it supposed to scare me?" I shoved my hands in my pockets, the cool fall air stinging my fingers along with the sudden chill Molly had brought with her presence.

She tilted her head and glared. "I wear what I want, got it?"

I let out a sharp breath. "Alright, alright, I got it." I lifted my hands along with my coat, refusing to take them out of my pockets, just as Molly had.

"So, yesterday went well I take it?" Her voice was all business as she walked past me and continued up the hill.

I followed her, drawn in by her comment. "How did you know about all that, Molly?"

"How do you know what you do? You didn't think you were a happy accident, did you?" She looked at my side, knowing the bruising that was there, "Obviously a careless one, though."

"You're like me?" I caught up to her, grabbing her arm and twisting her to face me, her eyes so clear they were hard to look at.

She snorted. "Hardly."

"You are like me, aren't you? That's why you knew all that, that's why when I see you, something happens in my head." I was surprised, but not as surprised as I had anticipated. When I first started leaping, I had wondered if there were more people like me that had it figured out.

"Yes, I'm like you, a Shifter." She blinked and looked at a group of students nearby.

"A Shifter?" I was shocked that there was even an official name.

"Yeah, except I don't delight in microwaving my body at every whim. I'm careful." Her voice had sass, just as it always did.

My jaw tightened. "Seriously, do you have to be so rude? Lighten up a little."

Her mouth was so pale and there was no visible hint of

happiness anywhere about it. "Life is serious, Jordan."

I rolled my eyes. "I know that, but if you take it too seriously, you'll never get out alive," I retorted.

She rolled her eyes. "No one gets out alive."

I let out a sharp breath, stung by her negativity. "Alright, I get it." I looked at her sideways. "Geez."

We walked for a moment in silence before she spoke again. "Listen Jordan, you're hurt and I can help."

I laughed. "I don't need help."

She kicked a stone on the ground. "Trust me, you do."

I touched my side and rubbed it, finding she was right. "What's in it for you? Why does it matter that Kenzie is alright?"

She laughed and I looked at her, the corners of her mouth finally giving. "I don't care about Kenzie. I care about our kind, the Shifters. I just know that you're dumb enough to fall for the Romeo and Juliet of your little love story, and right now you should concentrate on healing."

Another disgruntled snort escaped my lips. "I will not fall for that."

She looked at me sideways past the rim of her hood. "Yeah, right."

"What's so wrong with that?" I shrugged. "Love is a wonderful thing."

"Yeah sure, one sided relationships with someone who has no real idea of who you are is a real blast." She let out one mocking laugh.

I locked my jaw. "Whatever."

Molly paused for a moment. "Jordan, have you ever cared about yourself? Have you ever lived life just for you? Made a friend or had fun?" She rolled her eyes. "Other than at the race track."

Her words stung, but only because she was right. I had never allowed myself the fun and pleasure of living. I had no friends, two college degrees, and an obsession with Kenzie's life. In the normal world, I'd be considered in the running for the next serial murder suspect. "So what?"

"I'm just saying, perhaps you'd live longer if you had a little fun, lived a little of the real life like you have the last few days. We can't Shift around like you have so frequently. We're not cut out for that. After all, we're still human." She was watching the ground in front of her. "Each Shift you make, you burn through your life as though it were fuel, think of it that way. You're like an S.U.V."

"Have you seen me die?" I lingered on the idea, my curiosity piqued.

"Maybe, but it depends on you, depends on the choices you make between now and then. If you're smart, than that time will grow. If not." She brought her hand out of her pocket and slid it across her throat.

"Real nice, Molly. That really makes me feel much better about all this." I swallowed hard, thinking of death and how horrible it feels. I saw the biology building up ahead and knew our conversation was coming to an end. "So, what do I do now, if you seem to know so much better than me?"

She sighed. "Just be friends with Kenzie. No dating."

"What? Why?" I felt as though she were my mother telling me what to do.

"Think about it, Jordan. Even in the real world, a relationship born from the situations she was just in will never last. A friendship, on the other hand, will. Trust me on this one. One day you will get your chance, but right now she needs a friend, and so do you. She'll understand. She's not as flighty as you think. Just remember who she was before you Shifted the living daylights out of her life, and you'll know what I mean." We stopped and she looked at me, a strand of her hair trying to fall from her hood, but she pressed it back before it even got a chance.

"I suppose you're right. I guess you know." My face was frank. The things she told me were advice because she knew what paths lay ahead, because she had been there. "Well, where are you going to go?"

"Back to my life." She shrugged.

I reveled in her reply, wondering what it was like to have a life. "How soon will you be back?"

"Not too soon. You won't need me for a while. Just work on being friends." She dropped her hands from her pockets, her sleeves hanging to her fingers.

"What can I tell her?" I paused. "I mean, she's already told me so much about her dreams, about her other life."

Molly smiled. "You can tell her things, just don't tell her about what you do." Her face became stern. "I'm serious. That is just as detrimental as all else."

I furrowed my brow, but saw the reality of it.

"She'll freak out, trust me. I know that right now she just needs someone that's always going to be there. You can't dump a friend, so it's a guaranteed way not to screw it up." I saw her give me a look as though she'd expected me to mess it all up.

"What about you? What is your life like?" I had so many questions and stories to tell, but no one to relate to until now.

"Good. There are some things I wish I had, but I'm working on it. I have friends, at least." She gave me another small smile.

I looked at her face closely, "How old are you right now? About eighteen, right?"

I saw her smile. "Yeah, just. Finally an adult, I suppose, though what's the point in getting excited when you've been there?" She gave me a look of understanding.

I laughed. "Tell me about it. Things certainly lack luster in that respect."

She watched a group of students walk into the biology building, "She'll be here soon, so..."

"Well, I better go, then." I looked at my watch.

Molly nodded, her face solemn once again. "Have a good time, Jordan. Try to think of yourself. Heal. I'll see you soon." She reached out and touched my arm.

Her touch felt electric, cold and soft. She was different than me, but I didn't understand how. All I knew was that she, too, could Shift, and that alone was a comfort. "Thanks, Molly, for helping me." I felt nervous. "I'm not normally the type to ask for help, but then again, no one has ever offered to give me any, so..."

She nodded. "I know Jordan, but now you do. So next time, just look for me before you leap, got it?"

I felt my mouth curl into a smile, "Sounds like a deal."

She walked away then, and I saw Kenzie out of the corner of my eye, walking up the path. When I looked back in the direction where Molly had walked, I found she was already gone.

"Who was that?" Kenzie reached me faster than I'd thought with her long stride, and I turned to face her.

"A girl looking for her class," I blinked.

She pursed her lips. "She doesn't look like she belongs here, that's for sure." She tilted her head, "Shall we?"

I nodded. "Yep, time to be bored I suppose."

Statement from Dr. Ashcroft,
Vincent Memorial Hospital, Boston
August 4, 2009
04:18 a.m.

Agent Donnery:
    Heavy stuff.

Dr. Ashcroft:
    Yes, but wait, there's more I want to add. This totally makes sense now…

Agent Donnery:
    Then by all means, don't let me interrupt.

"Hey Kenzie, I was just thinking." Jordan was fidgeting with the bottle of make-up from my desk. He had seemed a little distant all day, shell shocked perhaps, by the fact that I had kissed him.

"What were you thinking?" I smiled, lathering on the charm and wondering why it wasn't working.

"I just... I've never had friends you know, and well, I was hoping that perhaps we could just keep things like that for a while." He looked at me with sorry eyes.

I took a slow, discreet breath. "Yeah." I paused, disliking the idea but figuring I'd take what I could get. "That's fine. I understand." I forced a smile.

He nodded. "I think that considering the situation and all, it seems like a good idea. I think we could both use someone to talk to, someone that won't end up growing apart because of love, or whatever."

I could see the way he flinched when he said the word love. I knew so little about him, and I felt as though there were a lot of underlying issues at hand. There had to be another reason why he was saying this. There was no denying the way he looked at me.

"Jordan, tell me about your childhood. What was that like for you?" I dove right in, figuring I hated suspense.

He gave me a surprised look. "It was…" He paused. "I was an orphan for most of it. That probably sums it up."

I leaned into my pillow with my long legs sprawled out in front of me, and I hooked my hands behind my head. Jordan sat rigid in my chair, unwilling to relax, though I'd tried to put him at ease. I exhaled as I mourned his continual sad stories.

"I don't know what to say to that…" I looked at his face, wondering what it was like to be like him. "I'm sorry."

He smiled. "Don't be, it was no one's fault that I had to grow up alone. It was what it was and…" He paused again. "And nothing would have changed that."

"Did your parents die?" It was another curt question, but a necessary one.

"Yes, first my mother from cancer, then my father to alcohol and liver failure." He didn't seem at all phased to say it, and I felt relieved.

"Wow. So you really are all alone." I cursed myself as soon as the words left my lips, and I instantly wished I'd had more of a filter.

He laughed. "Gee, thanks for pointing that out."

I sat up. "No, I didn't mean it like that. I was thinking out loud. I'm sorry. I just thought, perhaps being friends does make a lot of sense." I could see that perhaps his decision was more about him now than me, and I felt relieved to know that it wasn't something I had done wrong.

Jordan changed the subject. "Any word about Max?"

I let out a sharp chuckle. "Institutionalized."

"Really? Good. That guy was weird. I feel bad that you spent half your life with him." His eyes sank as though he felt guilty.

I swung my legs over the edge of the bed. "Jordan, it's not your fault." I laughed. "You need to learn to lighten up a little. Breathe."

Amy walked in then. "Oh hey Superman. What's up?"

Jordan smirked. "Hi, Amy. How are things?"

"Refreshing." She took a big dramatic breath of air. "Do you smell that?"

I rolled my eyes. "Smell what, Amy?"

"The makings of a great memoir." She gave us a sly smile.

Jordan lifted one brow. "I thought your thing was to write a book about the morals of women?"

Amy laughed. "Ha! I think I'm better off chastising myself into a story, total bestseller material."

"Real nice, Amy." Jordan tapped his finger on the chair, and I saw him begin to relax.

I could be friends with him. This would work. I knew he wasn't about to run off and be with another girl. He didn't have the guts. Besides, as his best friend, I would be the first to know.

"Well, I better get going," Amy sighed.

I pressed my brows together in frustration. "Where are

you going?" I looked at her frumpy clothes and bruised face.

"The library," came her curt reply.

"Really? So, you have changed." I pointed at her with pride.

She shrugged. "I've had enough date rape drugs and guns for one year. The library is safe."

"Good for you, Amy." Jordan smiled, as though proud of himself for getting her to turn a new leaf.

She left then, and the room fell back to silence. Jordan stood and walked over to Amy's bed, finally lying down to relax.

"So, where do you live?" I had never asked and I began to wonder.

I could hear him breathing as he looked up at the ceiling. "I have a house."

"A house?"

He nodded. "Yeah, a house. Maybe I'll take you there one day."

"Soon?"

He traced his finger along a crack in the ceiling. "Sure, Kenzie, soon."

I shook my head, thinking that each time he opened his mouth, something surprising came out. Though I felt as though I could love this man, did love him, this was the smart decision. With all his secrets, it did make me worry that there could be more, less savory ones, in the wings. I could tell that he was relieved he didn't have to jump into anything serious. And after all he'd done for me, I could wait.

Statement from Dr. Ashcroft,
Vincent Memorial Hospital, Boston
August 4, 2009
04:26 a.m.

Agent Donnery:
    So he listened to Molly, and you became friends, though it's clear now that both of you really wanted more.

Dr. Ashcroft:
    (pause) Sorry, I'm just surprised, but yes. And just as we thought, Molly was like him somehow.

Agent Donnery:
    There are certainly more like Jordan. Hearing about Molly confirms that for us.

Dr. Ashcroft:
    It seems your work is not yet over, Agent.

Agent Donnery:
    So, tell me the truth (pause). You really never knew about any of this?

Dr. Ashcroft:
    No, he never told me about Molly. I guess he didn't want me to know about her.

Perhaps he thought I'd be jealous, as I already was, because they seemed to have a connection that was stronger than ours, though I didn't even know her. It was just something I sensed.

Agent Donnery:
    Did you see her again?

Dr. Ashcroft:
    No, I… no.

Agent Donnery:
    Are you sure?

Dr. Ashcroft:
    Yes, I'm sure. I've never seen her again.

Agent Donnery:
    Okay then, I trust you.

Dr. Ashcroft:
    (pause) I remember asking myself why he didn't want to date me when it was so obvious we had chemistry.

Agent Donnery:
    Again, he did it to save you.

Dr. Ashcroft:
    I know that now, but at first I never understood. For years it was like that, and

we remained friends. Eventually, though, we could no longer bear it.

Agent Donnery:
    He was the one to make the next move, then?

Dr. Ashcroft:
    Yes. Flipping through these papers, I see that for quite some time he just wrote about everyday life, nothing more than a journal. But here, this one, I remember this day.

Agent Donnery:
    What day was that?

Dr. Ashcroft:
    Graduation. Let me explain.

Told by Dr. Ashcroft,
Stories from the journals of Patient #32185
May 5, 2007
04:27 p.m.

"Jordan! We're finally getting out of here. We're finally free!" Kenzie jumped up and down in the hall.

I watched her, laughing. "Yes we are, Kenzie. Finally." For her, it was just two years, but to me it had felt like decades.

We were in the living room of my house, though not the green house down the lane. After I told her that I had a house, I couldn't bring myself to take her back there, to let her know that the person there had been me. Instead, I bought the quaint row house that I had owned in the other life, the house she had brought me to when she had found me on the bus. It seemed fitting.

She threw herself down on the couch opposite me in the living room, the space set up in the same fashion it had been in the past. It was a bit strange, but like it had been before, it was exactly the way I wanted it.

"Jordan there's something about this place I love," she sighed and smiled, her cap and gown still on her head in celebration.

I looked at her sideways, wondering if along with the dreams she had also developed a way to read my thoughts. "Really, why is that?" I prodded.

She sat up. "I never told you this because I figured you'd think I was crazy, but we've been friends for two years now, so I trust you."

"You know I would never think you're crazy." I tilted my head. "Just tell me."

"Well," she paused and looked around. "I feel like I've dreamt about this place before, even before you ever brought me here."

My heart rate picked up. We often talked about her dreaming, but this one was the first that really hit home for me. Often many of her dreams were snippets of her other life I had never even seen, but this dream was the one dream I dreaded most, the one dream that had started it all.

"It was night and I was on a bus where I found this injured man. He was lost and sick, and I think I brought him here," she looked around. "Does this mean I'm psychic, you think?" She began to laugh.

I shrugged. "Perhaps it does."

She stood then. "Yes, and you know me, I talk too much so I divulged my whole life to this vagrant, this man." She walked around the coffee table and sat next to me.

"So, do you remember it as being a happy place? The town home, I mean," I dove deeper still.

Kenzie nodded. "Yep, I do. I think about it every time I'm here. I think about the way it makes me feel, as though it was the beginning of something great."

"And what about the man?" I cursed myself the moment the words left my lips. I had never indulged her constant referral to this man in her dreams. I didn't want her to put the pieces together, though I feared she already thought it.

"He was tall and handsome, terribly injured, but I remember thinking about life with him and falling in love," she laughed. "To tell you the truth, I actually think I had been married to Max in that life. I remember this horrible husband I had in the dream. It would make sense, wouldn't it? If my dreams act as a place for me to store bad memories, then he would be there."

I nodded. "It does make sense."

She watched me, her green eyes locked on my face. I avoided making eye contact as I always did, knowing all she wanted was to corner me, fall in love with me.

"He reminds me of you a little," her breathing was steady. "I never told you that, but you never asked, either."

I nodded, feeling my stomach churn, not knowing what to say.

"Jordan," she touched my arm.

I made the mistake of looking at her, her eyes catching mine. She smiled, her hair in knots where the graduation cap had been pinned down only to be torn from her head at the end of the ceremony.

"What now?" Her eyes looked lost.

"I suppose you go out and save lives," I gave her an unassuming answer though I suspected her question was not about her career.

Her face was solemn, and I felt my heart continue to race though I couldn't understand why. We had been friends for so long that I had grown comfortable with her, but right now felt awkward again, as though being with her like this was finally too much to handle. She began fussing with her graduation gown, finally lifting it over her head and tossing it on the ground.

She leaned back then and let out one deep breath, letting it pass her lips with a controlled elegance as though putting all her hard work behind her. My arms were tingling and I shifted in my seat. I had never seen her more beautiful than I had in this moment. For so many years I was used to seeing her live her life from an outside perspective, but for the last few, I had been invited in.

"Well, I guess it's time I get a real job right?" I tried to break the silence.

She laughed. "Yeah, I suppose so." She jumped suddenly. "Hey, you should take me to Kentucky once. I know you haven't been in a long while, but it would be a good way to celebrate the fact that you're putting all that behind you and moving on. Your last hurrah."

I tilted my head. "Yeah? You'd want to go?" I had never asked her, thinking she wouldn't care to watch horses fight their way around a track all in the name of money.

"Of course I would. Who do you think I am?" She gave me a playful slap on the arm, but I caught her hand before she was able to take it back.

She was giggling, so I gave her a yank and pulled her toward me. As her laughter finally faded, she looked me in the eyes, her breath falling across my face in warm, sweet waves.

I took a few quick breaths as I tried to resist kissing her, but it did little to help as I felt my arms erupt with goose bumps, her scent surrounding me like a drug. I leaned toward her to test the water, pleased that she didn't flinch or look away and change the subject, as we normally would. Her vivid eyes searched mine, as though she knew my secret and the raw reality of what I was. I mustered the courage as I ran my hand across her cheek and through her hair, resting it on the nape of her neck and lacing my fingers across her back. With a gentle force, I pulled her toward me, pressing my lips to hers in a way I had dreamt of for far too long. At first she seemed surprised by my forward behavior, politely resisting out of respect, but as I continued to coax her to give in, she finally leaned into the kiss, almost trapping me against the couch.

I ran my hand across her collarbone and down her arm as my lips curled around hers, her skin becoming warm. I opened my eyes and looked at her, suddenly feeling guilt wash over me as I realized my life was still a lie to her. I wrapped both hands around her shoulders, wanting so bad to feel the beauty of the moment, but my mind refused to give me peace. I cursed myself and pulled away, slinking out from under her and onto the floor where I took a deep breath.

"Sorry, I didn't mean to do that." I propped myself up off the floor with my trembling arms.

She frowned. "Why are you sorry, Jordan? I liked it, I wanted it." She looked down at me as I lay on the rug, my knees bent and my gaze resting on the floor in front of me.

"We shouldn't, Kenzie. I don't want to ruin the friendship

we have." In my head, I saw Molly and remembered what she said. Over the past couple years, I had manifested her advice into a sort of warning. I was worried about what she knew, worried that if Kenzie and I were together, something horrible was going to happen.

Kenzie grumbled and got up off the couch, her cheeks reddened. "I'm sick of this, Jordan. I don't think I can be friends with you anymore because I love you. How about that?"

I blinked and sat up. "You do?"

She was pacing the room, her eyes wild. "Are you really that dense? I've loved you since the day I met you, but you seemed so alone and afraid then, and so I couldn't force you into a relationship when you didn't want one. But now I can't bear it anymore."

I stood. "I didn't know it was that hard on you, Kenzie."

She shook her head in annoyance and walked over to me with clenched fists. "Is that all you can say? I pour my heart out, and that's it? Jordan, we can't be friends anymore." She was furious, and I knew there was little I could do to calm her down. She whisked her graduation gown off the floor and stormed to the kitchen, where she grabbed her bag.

"Kenzie, don't go." I took one step toward her.

She spun and looked at me with fury in her eyes. "Jordan, deal with it."

She walked toward the door and grabbed the handle. I felt an intense need flood my body as I lunged forward, crossing the room in three strides and grabbing her arm as she opened the door. I twisted her to face me. "Kenzie, please." I brought my hands to her face, cupping her cheeks. Her furious breath laced around my face and lips, fogging my thoughts as her hair fell between my fingers in fiery waves.

I could see her green eyes begin to well with tears as she tried to look away, but I forced her to accept the moment as I forced myself to be the man she needed.

"Kenzie, I love you."

She began to cry, and I felt her entire body relax into mine. She put her head on my shoulder, locking her arms around my torso. After a moment, she stepped back but before she could speak, I kissed her again, but this time with more practice and more meaning. I felt her wrap her hands around my back and sides, a feeling I longed for but had quelled out of fear.

We fell against the door and it slammed shut. Kenzie pushed her hand against my chest, holding me at bay as she looked at me once more, testing me with her eyes. With soft but frantic hands, she then pulled my shirt over my head, jumping right in. Since the day she had seen my bruises, I hadn't let her anywhere near me without a shirt on, but her touch now felt as so right, that I couldn't imagine how I'd lasted this long. It was crazy to deny the feelings we had, and I was tired of waiting. She ran her hands across my chest and down my back, placing them where a faint bruise still remained.

"Jordan..." Her face became concerned and she knelt to look at it. She ran her hand across the shadowed bruise as I shied away from her touch. I swallowed hard, my heart racing. She looked up, but did not bother me with a question, her eyes understanding as though she knew the bruise was from something else, something beyond her comprehension.

She stood and touched my face, and I wrapped my arms around her. I held her so tight that I could feel her heart beat against mine. The heart I had protected for so long. She kissed the inside of my neck, causing all my inhibitions to falter, and it was then that I gave up trying to save her, and instead gave in to what I wanted.

Statement from Dr. Ashcroft,
Vincent Memorial Hospital, Boston
August 4, 2009
04:44 a.m.

Agent Donnery:

He gave in then, didn't he? I mean, stopped trying to be friends.

Dr. Ashcroft:

(laughter) That's a personal question there, Agent, but yes. I suppose he thought he was healthier, and that he could handle it, but…

Agent Donnery:

Now he's here.

Dr. Ashcroft:

Yes.

Agent Donnery:

And so are you.

Dr. Ashcroft:

Yes, I am aware I am also in a hospital bed because of all this, though it's strange to be on the other side of things as a doctor. I suppose it's not so bad.

Agent Donnery:
     Yeah, I bet this is hard. You probably just want to doctor yourself.

Dr. Ashcroft:
     I am okay with being here, I just wish I had known sooner, this never would have happened. I would have been okay, and so would he.

Agent Donnery:
     But we'll get to that part right?

Dr Ashcroft:
     Right, first comes other things.

Agent Donnery:
     Right (pause). Anyway, so after that day, you became a couple, then. Correct?

Dr. Ashcroft:
     Yes, and I started a career, and we started living together, as well. Look here, this is the part where he takes me to a horse race for the first time.

Agent Donnery:
     First and last right?

Dr. Ashcroft:
     (laughter) Yes, you're right.

"I like that one." Kenzie pointed at a horse I had seen before.

"Him?" I cringed, seeing already that this was a bad idea. "You know, Big Brown is not a bad bet either."

"Nope." She was frank and to the point, her mind already made. "That one."

"Da' Tara? Really? But he's the last place pick." I was trying to make her change her mind in the nicest way possible.

"Yeah, so? I like him." She gave me a stern look. "You've always told me about the time you picked the loser and won remember? This is my chance."

I laughed and put my arm around her neck to give her a hug. "That's true."

"What are you going to bet on him?" She looked up at me.

We walked from the paddocks back to the main concourse at the Belmont in New York. "I'm not really sure." I took out my checkbook and began to write something that made sense. For the first time, I had no clue which horse would be the winner and it felt strange, like walking blind in a dark room.

"Bet a lot. Come on, it's my first time and I want it to be exciting." She seized my arm, looking down at my hand that held the checkbook.

My stomach wrenched into a knot. It wasn't that I didn't trust her choice. It was that her choice was the last place pick. "Alright, I will."

I wrote the check and handed it to her and her eyes got wide. "Twenty thousand dollars! Really?"

"Kenzie, quiet. You say that and people will clamor to make the same bet as us, thinking we have some sort of inside info," I whispered under my breath.

"Oh." She brought her hand to her mouth to silence herself.

I grinned, finding her innocence cute. "You go pay. I'll go get us something to drink." After writing a check like that, I needed one.

"You're going to let me pay? But I don't know what to do." Her eyes looked lost.

"You can do it, Kenzie. Seriously. If you can extract a toy truck from a boy's esophagus, you can do anything." I nudged her on the arm.

She gave me a proud smile. Kenzie had landed a job at the Vincent Memorial Hospital where she quickly became a favorite with everyone, not that I was surprised. She was always happy and always smiling, so naturally people were drawn to her. Everyone saw what I had that day on the bus, the love at first sight and the beauty deep inside.

I watched her walk away before turning to find the

restrooms, then the bar. I rounded a corner and saw the sign overhead, but as I looked down, my heart sank and I lost the need to pee. I halted for a moment, wishing I could turn around and slink away, but finding at this point, there was no getting out of it.

I let out a low growl. "I don't know if I should be happy to see you or not." I shoved my hands into the pockets of my suit pants.

She looked at me from under her same hood. "What are you doing?"

I shrugged. "What do you mean? It's just a bet. It's not like I know who's going to win."

Molly's jaw clenched. "I don't mean the betting…" she paused. "Though you should trust Kenzie on her choice." She tilted her head, giving the thought consideration as I did.

I laughed. "Well, that certainly takes a load off my mind." My laughter faded as I saw Molly didn't find it amusing.

"You know why I'm here, and you know what I mean when I ask what you're doing." She pointed to my pocket.

"What?" I pretended not to know what she was talking about.

"Jordan, don't play dumb," she glared at me. "It's not that I'm against it, but here I was living my own little life and find that when I come to check on you, you're about to get engaged?"

I shrugged.

"I thought I told you to just be friends with her." She crossed her arms against her chest.

"Well, it didn't work out. I tried, really I did," I frowned as she rolled her eyes and struggled not to smile. She hadn't changed at all since that last time I'd seen her, right down to her clothes, as though she hadn't aged in the last three years.

"I guess this is it then." She looked at me with her electric eyes.

"This is what?" I was a little short with her, but I was tired of the games.

"Where it all begins." She raised her eyebrows.

I exhaled sharply, "Where what begins?"

She had a smug look on her face now. "I don't think telling you is the right thing. It could be a detriment..." she trailed off.

"Molly, it's really hard to believe you when you're like this." I dropped my hands to my sides and analyzed her with a critical eye. "Why don't you age?" I began to turn the attention on her.

She blinked a few times, as though she were trying to make up an excuse in her head. Her lips pursed as she found her answer. "It's part of why we're different, Jordan, that's all."

I nodded, finding there was little else to say to her. "What's with the hood, then. Does it make you feel sneaky or something?"

She laughed. "Thanks, Jordan. You really know how to compliment a girl."

I smiled. "At least you laugh from time to time. Seriously, what happened to you?" I was joking when I said it, but Molly's smile faded.

"Life, Jordan, just as it has for you." She shifted her weight.

"Sorry, I didn't realize that was a sore subject." I relaxed a little, letting down my guard. "So, does this mean I'll be seeing you more?"

She shrugged, but I could tell my earlier question was still bothering her, "Maybe a little sooner than three years, yes."

We stopped talking for a moment, and things got awkward. I wanted to know what she knew and what was about to happen, but considering she seemed calm about it, I didn't figure it was pressing.

"Well, I better get going." I broke the silence. "Thanks for dropping in, though." I tried to smile at her, but found it hard.

She looked up at me. "Yeah, I better get going as well. Take care, Jordan." She turned to walk away but halted herself, twisting back to face me. "Just remember that in life, sometimes bad things happen for a reason, perhaps even for something good."

Her words were eerie but true, and I bowed my head. She nodded and I took it as my cue to leave, so I pushed past her and went into the restroom, finally getting my chance to pee. When I came back out, she was gone, though I still felt her presence watching me from somewhere nearby. I scanned the crowd but did not see the familiar sweatshirt. I felt my heart sink. A hand grabbed my arm and I jumped, turning around and coming face to face with Kenzie.

"Oh, there you are. Did you fall in? The race is about to start!" She was jumping up and down with excitement. I laughed, forgetting Molly as I took her hand and we walked to the rail where we stood as the horses rattled in the gate, anxious to run as they loved to do.

The trumpet played and Kenzie was beaming. It was nice to see her so happy, perhaps the happiest I had ever seen her in all her life; or rather, lives. I saw then that this was truly meant to be, that we were destined to be here in this life together, at this moment.

The gun went off and the gates opened. The horses leapt onto the track, mud flying in their wake. To my surprise, I saw Big Brown at the back, slow out of the gate. I chuckled to myself as Da' Tara sped for the lead, thinking of Molly and the fact that this win was pure luck for the first time in my life.

I reached into my pocket where I felt for the ring, rolling it around in my fingers. I took a deep breath and pulled it out as the horses rounded the track, my gaze now stolen by its beauty and its meaning. I wanted to do this before the excitement of winning. I wanted to make sure she knew that it was for love, not money. I nudged Kenzie as the ring sat in my palm, grabbing her hand. I let go then, leaving the ring behind as a strange look crossed her face. I watched her in amusement as her brow crinkled.

The horses had made it half a mile now, but she pulled her attention away from them and to the ring, all life dissolving around us and leaving only the sound of our hearts beating. She gazed at it in her hand for what felt a long while, her face frozen and her eyes reflecting the light from the diamond.

She looked at me. "Really?"

I nodded. "Really."

The crowd around us came screaming back, the sound now deafening as a smile grew on Kenzie's face. A voice boomed over the speakers, announcing the winner, "Da'Tara wins the two thousand and eight Belmont Stakes."

Her face did not flinch when she heard it, instead she remained focused on the ring, plucking it from her hand and placing it on her finger. Her eyes welled with tears.

"I love you, Kenzie, always have and always will." I touched her cheek where a tear began to fall.

"Always, Jordan," and she kissed me, pulling back moments later with a big smile on her face. "And we won!"

I laughed as the joy in her bubbled over and she jumped up and down in circles, the spectators beside us watching her as though she had gone stark mad. I glanced past her where I saw the crowd part, and Molly stood along the rail, her arm leaning against it in a relaxed pose. Though her eyes were hidden under her hood, she could not hide the fact that she was smiling. I smiled back, giving her a wink before she turned and walked away.

"Jordan," Kenzie stopped bouncing and touched my arm. "How much did we win exactly?" She looked confused but cute.

My mouth felt dry at the thought, afraid to say it. "Almost a million dollars," I grinned.

"Are you serious?" She started jumping up and down

again, her eyes even wider than before.

I nodded with a cool look on my face, trying my best to stay calm though it felt good to finally live. I had to admit, her choice on a horse with 38/1 odds was no longer anything to frown about. And after all, it was a good present for the future, a future that was still a lie, but by now it was a lie I felt I could live with.

Statement from Dr. Ashcroft,
Vincent Memorial Hospital, Boston
August 4, 2009
04:59 a.m.

Agent Donnery:
    There she was again, though.

Dr. Ashcroft:
    (pause) Sorry, Agent. I'm just
shocked.

Agent Donnery:
    Something horrible was about to
happen, wasn't it? Was it this? You in the
hospital, and Jordan…

Dr. Ashcroft:
    Yes. Yes, I believe so.

Agent Donnery:
    But he did nothing to try and find out
what it was from Molly?

Dr. Ashcroft:
    I often caught him sitting in the
library in deep thought, but when I asked
him about it, he blew it off. I suppose
he was worried about the outcome, worried
he would die if he tried to Shift to the

future to see. As far as I know, Molly
never told him, she never came back, but
then again, I didn't even know about Molly
to begin with.

Agent Donnery:
    Of course. So then, what was it that
made him finally decide to Shift?

Dr. Ashcroft:
    I think you know, Agent.

Agent Donnery:
    Well, I can see that, but where was
Molly in all this? Why didn't she stop
it?

Dr. Ashcroft:
    I honestly don't know. After reading
all this, you'd think she would have tried,
especially when she wanted to save him and
their kind. Why invest the time, then let
him die?

Agent Donnery:
    And you haven't seen her at all?

Dr. Ashcroft:
    (pause) No.

Agent Donnery:
    Tell me then, what happened next?

Dr. Ashcroft:

We got married in the summer, too anxious to wait much longer. It was a beautiful day; rainy, but still beautiful. After that, we settled into a routine. He never did go get a job, though. He never wanted one. I always felt he was waiting for the right thing to come along, something that fulfilled him in a manner that would bring joy to his life, much like my work as a doctor did. Besides, since the race, we really didn't need to work. I just continued because I loved it, and he respected that. For me, it was fun.

Agent Donnery:

So he sat at home all day?

Dr. Ashcroft:

(laughter) Hardly. He was always doing something. Always tinkering with his bikes or going to the nearby park. He liked to run and play tennis as well.

Agent Donnery:

What about the bruise on his stomach. What did you think?

Dr. Ashcroft:

Honestly? I just figured he had a residual scar, tissue that had been so damaged that it remained grey and dark. It's not unheard of. He told me that it was from that night at the Rugby House. So, I never thought otherwise. If I had known he had literally micro-waved his organs to the point that they were holding on by a thread, I certainly would have never let him drink as he did.

Agent Donnery:
    Certainly that did little to help the healing.

Dr. Ashcroft:
    No, it didn't, but it's not like he drank much, not when his father had the alcoholic gene. He typically only had one drink a day, unless it was a bad day.

Agent Donnery:
    What were his bad days like?

Dr. Ashcroft:
    Just depressing. He would recede into the study and sit for hours. About once a year it happened, right around the anniversary of his mother's death, which I understood.

Agent Donnery:
    Did your parents love him?

Dr. Ashcroft:

Like their son. They still do. I haven't told them about Jordan's secrets yet because I figure it would scare them. Besides, they have enough to worry about right now, considering the circumstances.

Agent Donnery:

So what next? What happened?

Dr. Ashcroft:

He got restless.

Stories from the journals
of Patient #32185
December 15, 2008
02:38 p.m.

"There you are. Have you seen how much snow here is outside?" I took a few steps into the room and halted.

He looked up from the book he was reading. "Oh yeah, look at that."

I sighed, sensing he was in another mood. "Are you doing alright?"

He looked at me, his face drawn. "Yeah, sure."

He always tried to hide it from me, but I knew. "No you're not. What's going on?" I sat in the leather chair beside his as he closed his book and placed it on his lap.

"Do you still dream like you did in college?" He breathed slowly.

I shrugged, wondering where the question came from. "Sure, from time to time, but a lot less now than before, and I no longer have dreams about events that could have happened, the déjà vu stuff. It's all repeats now, and that's all."

He nodded. "Well, that's good." He ran a hand through his hair. "Do you ever wish you could still see those things, though? I mean, do you miss that other life of yours?"

I looked back at the book he was reading, noting it was

The Time Machine by H.G. Wells. "Is that why?" I pointed to the book. "I doubt my dreams had to do with time travel."

He shook his head. "No, that's not it." He flipped the book over and stashed it away. "I was just wondering if you missed your dreams, that other life you told me about."

I tilted my head and looked toward the stacks of books on the wall. "Sure, at times, but I also enjoy getting a good night's sleep." I leaned forward in my chair and put one hand on his knee. "That life was never real. I figure it was my mind's way of coping with the popular life I was subjected to growing up, and once all that ended in college, so did the dreaming."

He looked at me. "You didn't like your childhood?"

I shrugged. "It's not that I didn't like it, it's just that it was a burden at times. But it was a burden for the Kenzie in my dreams as well. She had other issues to face that caused equal pain. She just seemed freer, that's all."

He let out a long, sorrowful breath, and picked up The Time Machine once more. "I was just thinking about how he tried to save his fiancé so many times, but no matter what, she still ended up dead. She was meant to die."

"Well, sure. You can't change fate, Jordan. It is what it is, one way or another. Like I said, the person in my dreams suffered in a different way. She suffered for her looks, her bad luck, and her failed career. I suffered for my looks in the same way, but opposite, and though I love my career, it has its pressures and a certain honor that I have to uphold." I leaned back in the leather as it creaked in protest. "Jordan, life is what it is, people die and people suffer."

He nodded. "It's true, there was never anything I could do to try and save my mother. No matter what, she was meant to die."

This week was the anniversary of her death, and I feared this week more than any other every year. Losing her had taken something out of him, something I could never understand. "I know you may wish that you could go and change things, Jordan, but it won't. Saving her won't make things better. I need you here with me now, and she wants that for you as well."

His jaw tightened.

I looked away from him, figuring I'd said enough.

"No, it's just, I…" he paused and sat forward. "I've lived a unique life, Kenzie."

"Of course you have, Jordan. I know…"

He cut me off. "But you don't know, Kenzie, and it kills me. You don't know how beautiful you were as a child, how amazing and innocent, you don't know how cared for you were."

I nodded with wide eyes. "But I do, Jordan. I know I had a wonderful family, and I know that it kills you that God did not grant you the same, but you cannot blame me for that. You cannot compare our lives in the hopes of finding answers."

He leaned forward and grabbed my hand. "Kenzie, I know that. That's not what I'm trying to say. I chose my childhood. I know the life I lived, and I wouldn't change it, not anymore."

I frowned. "Jordan, I'm trying to understand, but I

can't..."

"Kenzie, do you remember the day when your family moved into the house they live in now?" His eyes were intense.

"A little, sure, why?" I was confused.

"Do you remember going to the park that day?"

His words shocked me as they jogged my memory. "Yeah, sure I do, but how do you know that?"

"I was there, Kenzie. I was the boy in the park." He shook my hand, his eyes full of a storm I had all but forgotten.

"That was you? You were the boy? But..." The thought began to gain strength in my head. "But where did you go? How did you know that was me?" My eyes searched his but the storm had faded, and the window to his soul had closed.

He sighed and sat back. "I lived down your lane, but I moved out soon after."

I pursed my lips, trying to remember which house and which memory was real. "The green house down the lane? The abandoned one where the sad old man had lived?"

"Was he sad?" His eyes seemed to gloss over.

I shrugged. "Yeah, sure. At first he seemed angry, but after a while he grew sad and lonely. Stopped working, stopped caring for anything, really. He didn't live long, though." And that's when it hit me. "He was your father, wasn't he?" A rush of shock sent a cooling wave across my body, and I shivered, seeing the old man's face.

He nodded. "Yes, he was."

I had nothing to say then as sadness fell over me, the

room now filling with thick emotion. The eyes of the old man should have given it away, but how was I to remember such a seemingly infinitesimal moment with such clarity? My friends would tease and taunt the old man, but I remember I'd always felt grief for him, as though we were connected. Now to find that we had been connected by the future.

"I still own that house, you know." I saw a tear fall from his eye as I looked at him.

I could understand why he never told me about his family, so I wasn't angry, just surprised that they had been so close to my own life. Exhaling, I tried to wrap my head around the thought of owning a house, and not just any house, but that house. "We do?"

He nodded. "Yes."

I waited a moment before saying anything more. "Do you ever go back there?"

He continued to nod. "All the time."

I thought for a moment about the fate of it all, and how he'd saved me so many times since. Was that a coincidence? Were we really so star crossed that all our past had been fate? I thought about the man in my dreams as he again resurfaced on the walls of my mind, looking more like Jordan than ever before, though that was still absurd. It was a dream, that was not possible, a dream where a human could change the past and future, or at least try to. I shook it off, figuring that I was manifesting the thought because of my love for Jordan and the fairy tale it created in my mind. Life wasn't like that.

Jordan was watching me now with a close eye. "What

are you thinking about?"

I quickly came up with something viable. "Just the house."

He leaned back and clutched the book to his chest.

I cursed myself and bit my tongue, my mind screaming to ask but my sanity telling me to hold back, that the day would come when I could explain my thoughts to him. Perhaps he didn't know, perhaps there really were these parallel lives, and his and mine were truly intertwined, and the man in my dreams was the puppeteer for us both. A smile grew across my face, like a mad man dreaming. Perhaps what he wouldn't say was the fact he had dreamt too. But why wouldn't he tell me when he knew so much about my dreaming? Of all the people out there, I understood.

"Are you sure you're alright, Kenzie?" He lifted one brow.

"Oh, yes fine. Just thinking about the house as a kid, that's all." I stood then and left the room like a stunned bird, leaving him in his solitude.

"Kenzie, wait." I heard him stand.

I turned on my heel very slowly, finding he was right behind me. He placed one hand on my cheek.

"I'm sorry for being such a downer." He traced his fingers behind my ear and down my neck. I felt goose bumps cover my body. The man in my dreams was screaming at me now, angry that I didn't recognize him, angry that I couldn't figure this puzzle out.

"That's alright," I replied. His grey-blue eyes searched

mine as he leaned in and kissed my neck, then my collar bone.

Time stopped as his nose grazed back toward my face and across my cheek. I was still shaken, but I felt the fear slowly fade as the heat returned to my body. I looked up at his face and put my arms around his chest. His smirk was irresistible and I leaned in for a kiss, but he leaned back with a grin instead.

"Will you forgive me?" His eyes glimmered.

I laughed. "I think that's what I was doing."

His hand traced up my spine and he pulled me toward him, our lips intertwining for a moment as I closed my eyes, thinking of my dream man and making it him; a sense of guilt washing over me as I did so.

When he leaned back, a smile lit across my face as he plucked me off the ground and I began to laugh. "Jordan! What are you doing?"

His smile stretched from ear to ear. "Having a little fun, my love."

Statement from Dr. Ashcroft,
Vincent Memorial Hospital, Boston
August 4, 2009
05:12 a.m.

Agent Donnery:
    This is painful. It seems you both wanted to come clean about it, but couldn't.

Dr. Ashcroft:
    Well, of course. I guess we both feared we'd think the other was crazy. If anything, though, we both would have understood and things would have been easier. I laugh now because it really was the same man, and my guilt was not needed.

Agent Donnery:
    Not at all. Perhaps you should trust your judgment. Just think, if you both had simply confessed, then Jordan would have had the companionship he had found with Molly, and that understanding of who he was.

Dr. Ashcroft:
    Yes, exactly. And I would have had my explanations so that I no longer felt I was burying this part of me that had

really lived. (pause) But not just that.
We would have been able to avoid all this,
too.

Agent Donnery:
    How did it feel living in that
house?

Dr. Ashcroft:
    I remember the day we first went back
there. I was so terrified because as a
child, my friends and I always teased that
the house was haunted, and here I was
waltzing in the front door.

Agent Donnery:
    Tell me about it.

Dr. Ashcroft:
    Alright I will, but this is my own
story, not Jordan's.

"Jordan, are you sure about this? It seems weird." I was waving to my mother over my shoulder, just out of ear shot as we walked down the lane.

"It's not weird to me." He tugged my hand and I walked forward.

"Well, you never thought of it as a haunted house like I did as child." I rolled my eyes, feeling the hair on my arms rise the closer we got to those dark, abandoned windows.

"I think you'll find it's quite normal inside," he reassured.

It sounded as though he'd been here more times than he led on, as though it were his beach home he went to on the weekends, while all I could think of were dead bodies in the closet and the old man haunting the living room.

We walked up the path that cut through the front yard, which was in need of some aggressive weeding. "Jordan, if it's so great, how come you didn't get a yard crew in here to take care of it?"

He shrugged. "Makes it look scary, keeps the neighborhood kids away."

I rolled my eyes again. "Just what I was trying to tell you," I murmured.

He got to the door and jammed a key into the lock. It gave with little effort.

"How often did you say you come here?" I asked under my breath, lifting one brow.

"Here we are." He flipped a switch and the lights flickered to life. "Well, I don't often turn the lights on, so that may be an issue."

The overhead light in the middle of the living room popped and went out as I jumped, nearly fainting. "Okay, and that's not weird or anything? Are you sure there are no ghosts?"

He laughed. "Could be, you never know." He turned around and gave me a wink before spreading his arms before him. "Well, here it is," he announced with pride. I found it hard to swallow.

I looked around, my mind finally able to complete the puzzle that had plagued me for so long as a child. "And this seriously doesn't bother you to come back here, to a place with horrible memories?"

He tilted his head and gave me a sour face. "They weren't all horrible, Kenzie. You don't have to make it seem like the house Hannibal was raised in. Besides, I was hoping that perhaps we could make new memories here."

My face shot to his. "*What?*" My voice sounded shocked, but not in a good way. "I mean," I paused, feeling bad as I watched his smile fade. "What?" I thought about the question, knowing what it meant to him as I forced a grin to come to my face, hoping it was at least believable.

The same grin returned to Jordan's face. "Yes." He took a step toward me and grabbed my hands with excitement. "Our town home is too small for a family."

I swallowed. "A family?" My smile was beginning to hurt my face as the urge to freak out and run away tugged at every bone and muscle in my body.

"Kenzie, I love you more than anything. Don't you want to have kids?" His eyes glittered, and I couldn't resist the endearing way he said it.

I hadn't really thought about it. At twenty-five, it hardly seemed a glimmer in my eye at this point. I looked around the room then, envisioning kids as they ran about with noisy toys, envisioning their grandparents nearby to visit. Though I wasn't ready right this moment, in all reality it was perfect.

I squeezed his hands. "Yes, Jordan, I can see it."

His boyish excitement seemed to ooze from his face. "I just feel so alive today." He let a contented breath pass his lips as he looked around.

I looked around as well; knowing what he saw was much different than what I had. Chuckling, I walked into the room and inspected everything in it, pretending to be interested though nothing here held any emotion for me but fear. "Well, if we do come here, we can get new stuff, right? Because some of this is a little dated." I was looking at the old TV, wondering if it even worked.

He nodded with enthusiasm. "Oh, of course, whatever

you want."

I looked up from the living room to the banister that led upstairs. I swallowed, knowing that in time I would learn to get the horrific images of this place out of my mind. Continuing around the corner I found the kitchen, tucked away toward the back, much larger than the kitchen in the town house.

"I knew you'd like this." He looked toward the ceiling where the room was lined with cookbooks, all sitting untouched on the top of the cabinets, as though a part of the architecture.

My jaw dropped. "Your mother must have been quite the cook."

Jordan tucked his hands in his pockets as he entered the room, as though reminding himself not to touch. Every other room in the house looked like it had been visited except this one. A layer of dust coated every surface. I understood why as soon as I saw the look on his face. It had been her sanctuary, her haven.

"It's yours now, all of it. There's nothing I'd love to see more than for you to make yourself at home and bring back the life."

I took his words to heart as I pulled a chair from the breakfast table that was tucked in the corner, bringing it to the counter and crawling on top. I ran my hand along a row of cookbooks to look at the names. She had everything from French to Greek, and in languages that looked both ancient and new.

"Could your mother read and understand all this?"

He shrugged. "I suppose, I never really knew much about her cookbooks, just assumed she knew because the food always made it to the table. I just liked to watch her."

There was a large book toward the middle with no name, so I hooked my finger in the spine and pulled it back from the stack. It was then that a fat spider fell from the top and landed on my shoulder. I screamed, toppling backwards off the chair as the book fell from my hands and onto the floor.

There was a commotion as Jordan lunged toward me, his hands grasping my waist. I let out a relieved breath and looked at him, his face solemn and scared.

"Are you alright?" he asked.

A short laugh passed my lips. "I'm fine, Jordan. Don't look at me as though I've died. It's okay." Jordan was always like this, so protective. In fact, I had been surprised he'd even let me stand on the stool to begin with.

"Well, we will have to move those, that's for sure." Jordan walked over to the book that had fallen to the ground, the crash causing it to sprawl papers all across the kitchen floor.

I picked one up that was at my feet, reading it with a curious eye,

April 3, 1963

Something happened today that is hard to explain. I always thought my life was sealed in a horrible fate of sadness, but it seems I found a way to change my luck...

Jordan ripped the page from my hand then.

"Jordan, I was reading that…" I stopped talking as I saw the look on his face.

"I just…" He looked away from me as he hastily picked up a few more papers from the ground.

As I tried to look at more, I saw that they all began the same, with a date. I gasped, seeing now that the book I had pulled was not a cookbook at all, but a journal she had kept hidden among them. My initial anger fell to sympathy as I watched him ruefully stack each page.

"Is that her journal?"

He was kneeling on the floor, stuffing the pages back inside the dusty cover. "I suppose." His voice sounded grumpy.

"Did you ever know?" I pressed.

He shut the book and stood with it tucked under his arm. "No." His voice now sounded jealous, as though he was angry that I had found it first.

I looked down at my feet, stung by his suddenly cold demeanor. "Perhaps we should leave."

He took a deep breath as he brought the book to the table and set it down, causing dust to fly out from under it. He stared at it for a moment as his hands rested on the cover. I was frozen, afraid of what he would do or say. He then slowly lifted his hands and shuffled toward me. I looked up at him, seeing his arms were welcoming me into a hug; relief washed over me.

"Kenzie, I'm sorry. I just didn't expect that. It was as

though the whole world fell away around me and I couldn't control my actions. First, you fell from the chair, then that. It was too much." He engulfed me in a hug as I fell into his arms.

"I understand, Jordan." I closed my eyes. "I didn't mean to pry. I just had no clue what it was until I read it."

He put his chin on the top of my head. "I don't want this to ruin the day though; got it?"

I nodded against his chest.

"Come on; let's go back to your parents." He stepped away and released his hold on my arms, his warmth dissipating into the air around us.

"Okay." I wiped a tear from my eye.

He grabbed the book as we left, tucking it under his arm as though it were a suitcase filled with gold. I felt my heart sink, and it was then that I knew it was going to be another bad week.

Statement from Dr. Ashcroft,
Vincent Memorial Hospital, Boston
August 4, 2009
05:21 a.m.

Agent Donnery:
    Ah, a journal much like his.

Dr. Ashcroft:
    Yes, exactly. See here, all her entries
are in Jordan's journal now, right here in
the back.

Agent Donnery:
    Are you telling me…

Dr. Ashcroft:
    Yes, I am. I'm sorry to keep that from
you, but I wanted you to find out the way
I did. See here, Jordan talks about it.
Let me read.

I cracked the journal and looked at the first page. It was dated 1959, when my mother was just a child, though the handwriting did not reflect that. I flipped the page and inspected her drawings which were scattered throughout the margins, not yet convinced that reading the entries was a good idea.

By now we had gone back to the town home, and Kenzie was at the market with her mother getting dinner. They had wanted me to go, but I declined, the itch to read about my mother's life too intense not to scratch.

A part of me was afraid of what was written here, especially after the bit I had seen as the pages lay across the floor of the kitchen like dead memories. It had caught my eye almost immediately, something so familiar to me: a time bracket, just like mine. My first instinct was to snatch the page from Kenzie, afraid of what it said though I knew I had terrified her by doing so.

I took a deep breath and rubbed my brow with my hand, delving in.

June 15, 1982

Jordan was born today. I was afraid to see him, afraid he would be deformed because of me, but he was perfect. I'm stuck here now, with him, but I want nothing else. I am tired of running away and trying to find happiness when perhaps it is right in front of me, staring at me as Jordan is now.

I need to be responsible. I need to live so that he can as well. For as much as I'd love to leave and get away, I will never go without him. I just hope he hasn't inherited my nightmare or my addictions. I will not tell him about me because I do not want to encourage him to dream the way I did. I just want him to know how much I care, and how important it is to have a normal life from beginning to end.

I drew in one shaky breath, realizing all to well what it was she had meant by addiction. I shook my head and squeezed my eyes shut. She had been like me, and though she tried, she could not prevent giving me the same fate.

I flipped past a few pages, finding one of the last she kept.

August 18, 1986

I know I'm growing ill. I can feel it. Though my life is anything but glamorous and happy, as I had always dreamed, I found today that it still has its surprises. The only reason I was staying here in this nightmare life was for Jordan, so that he could grow up in a world that functions from beginning to end as God intended, though now it seems it no longer matters.

Today was the day the neighbor dog was meant to die, but he didn't. When I found Jordan I knew right away what he had done, and that he was different. His eyes no longer held the childish wonder they should, and above all things, he himself was able to recognize that I deserved better than the life I've led for the past four years since he was born.

He has my gift, or curse, whichever lends him the better explanation. I believe he is stronger though, evolved to handle it in a way I simply couldn't. When I saw him today, I knew he was from somewhere in the future but he seemed healthy, happy; perhaps a little lost but that was all. I feel better now knowing that if he is out there somewhere, I know he's still alive and can perhaps make better of his inherited bad luck.

Though I longed to ask him what it was like in the future, about my death, about our *lives, I didn't. I do not want him to know that the illness inside me was my own fault and that the fact I am abandoning him in death is because of my own selfish needs. I see now that all I needed in life was Jordan. That it didn't matter what happened, or where I was, or what I had.*

I will take him away from this house in the hopes that he will feel more at home with me, so that he will come visit as often as his body will allow. Jordan, I'm sorry.

The words stung, as though written for me because she knew one day I'd find this. When we left the green house at the end of the lane, we had left everything behind in the hopes of starting over. After that, the kitchen rarely saw a visitor other than the path to and from the refrigerator that had been made by my father, for his beer.

I exhaled, realizing now that the cancer was much more than just that. Her death was the result of her Shifts through time and her indulgence in the same life I had. She had ended up in the same fate as I, only a fate that she could not simply rest away. Guilt washed over me as I thought about how my birth had changed everything for her. Though I had gotten stuck in a world that was sweet, my mother did not receive the same fate with the hell in which she was left.

I sighed and flipped through the rest of the pages, finding pictures I had all but forgotten, and drawings I had done for her as a child. I was afraid now of what the future was like for me and if I were also doomed for the same fate as my mother, or if I could somehow overcome it and live.

I thought about Molly then, wondering what her family had been like and if her mother had also been like mine. I wished she were here so that she could explain it to me, but she was smart to choose the life she was living, and I did not wish for her to waste the Shift just to calm my worries.

It was then that I began to wonder how many Shifters there were and if anyone other than our kind had found out that we exist. Even so, there is no way anyone would ever believe us anyway, and if they did, it would only end in war. Someone like me would never be accepted by the human race. As a nation we fear the unknown, content in dwelling in the lies that nothing bad will ever happen. Perhaps there is some secret world out there where our kind lives free, as you see on TV, a cult town of sorts. In the end I suppose I wouldn't want people to know about me and expose all my trickery, but at the same time, what better way is there to abolish my sins but to confess?

I let a laugh escape my lips as I felt the guilt inside me grow thick. Even after all the life I've seen, I still believed there would be a day of reckoning in the end. I was not a particularly religious person, not at all really, but what if there really was this world of Heaven, and what if I had ruined that dream for myself?

I heard the front door click and I quickly shut the book on my lap, looking toward the entry as I saw Kenzie and her mother peek around the corner and through the door, both huffing as they held heavy bags of groceries in their hands.

"Hey, honey." Kenzie dropped a heavy bag with a distressed face. "You want to lend a hand?"

I smiled and pulled myself out of my chair, placing the book on the side table.

"Thank you so much, Jordan dear." Kenzie's mom also dropped her bags and made her way into the kitchen where she turned on some lights.

"Beef honey. Yum," Kenzie smiled with a glimmer in her eye.

My lips curled into a smile as I watched her, hoping my mother could see us and the life I now lived. I wanted nothing more than to tell her about Kenzie, to Shift back and tell her that she could rest easy knowing I had found something wonderful, but why risk it?

I had to have enough faith to believe that somehow she knew I had made it through alright. I felt a comfort knowing that my mother had not lived the life I thought she had, that somewhere along the way there was happiness, perhaps even love. Kenzie gave me a kiss on the cheek as I lowered the bags onto the counter. I grabbed her waist as her mother filled the fridge and whispered in her ear, "I love you."

Statement from Dr. Ashcroft,
Vincent Memorial Hospital, Boston
August 4, 2009
05:35 a.m.

Agent Donnery:

Perhaps that's where some of the confusion came from. We did not understand that the mother was also writing some of the entries in this journal, we figured these were his Shifts as well.

Dr. Ashcroft:

You should have known that from the date of the entries alone. You have to understand that a Shifter cannot Shift outside the boundaries of their own lifeline, Agent. They don't exist there because they are either dead or haven't been born yet.

Agent Donnery:

I see. Yes I believe you told me that.

Dr. Ashcroft:

Have you found any more of his kind? Other than Molly, of course. I know she exists. Perhaps you need to look into her family.

Agent Donnery:
No, just him, and I suppose her, when we find her. It's hard to tell if we ever will catch her, though. If she is as calm of a Shifter as these stories suggest, we likely won't. It seems she had been raised in a manner that was open and that her parents had taught her how to control the talent.

Dr. Ashcroft:
Will you tell me if you ever do find her? I'd like to meet her. Perhaps ask a few questions?

Agent Donnery:
Probably not.

Dr. Ashcroft:
(pause) I understand. Rules, right?

Agent Donnery:
Sucks, doesn't it?

Dr. Ashcroft:
Yeah. (pause) So, are you ready to hear the end of the story?

Agent Donnery:
Yes, I'm ready to go home. I believe the sun is just about to rise, and I know my wife will be worried.

Dr. Ashcroft:
      Well, I'll try to make it snappy,
  then.

I sat on the chair opposite Jordan in the kitchen, looking up to where the cookbooks had been, then to the lower shelf were they were now. I sighed. "What happened to that book you found?"

Jordan looked up from his bowl of cereal to where the books had been as well, following my gaze. "I put it in a box, I believe. One we haven't unpacked yet."

I nodded. "Ah, I see." I didn't believe him, but I wasn't going to push. I didn't have the energy to, not today.

So far the new house hadn't revealed any ghosts, or anything else that I had manifested in my mind for the years and years I had deemed it to be haunted. Most things had already been unpacked and the old furniture moved into storage. Despite my attempts to try and get Jordan to sell all the old stuff, he refused, claiming we had plenty of money to simply store it, though God knows if we'd ever see it again.

I wriggled in my chair as it squeaked. Jordan eyed me over the top of his newspaper, his cereal growing soggy as it floated in the milk. I coughed, finding the once pleasant smell of it nauseating as it wafted into my nostrils.

"Kenzie, can you just sit still?" He pressed his brows

together as deep lines cut across his forehead. He was glaring at me.

I retorted with a sour face, "No."

He rolled his eyes. "Kenzie, what's wrong with you?" He put his paper down and took a sip of coffee.

"I'm pregnant," I blurted. "I think." I looked down at my hands as they sprawled across the counter, now sweating.

His sipping stopped as he slowly placed the mug onto the counter with a weighted clank. "You're what?"

His voice sounded surprised, and I winced. "Pregnant. Maybe."

He wasn't breathing. "How can you *maybe* be pregnant?"

I shrugged. "I don't feel well, and I missed my period." I was fidgeting with my hands. "Oh, and I took a test."

A sharp exhale passed his lips. "Well then, that doesn't sound like a *maybe*. That sounds like a *definitely*."

I brought my hand to my mouth and nibbled on my nails, not knowing what Jordan's reaction would be.

He reached across the counter and swatted the hand from my mouth. "Don't do that."

I looked up at him, his jaw tight and his eyes glimmering with unshed tears. When our gazes met he forced back a smile, but it ignited my excitement and I let my fears fade. "Is that alright?"

He laughed. "Yeah, it's alright!" He stood and lunged around the table, plucking me from my chair, making it topple over.

"We're pregnant!" I yelped.

He nuzzled his head into the crook of my neck and kissed my skin. "Does this mean we can't, you know..." His lips grazed along my neck as I shuddered.

"God, I hope not." I melted into his grasp.

"Well, should we make double sure you're pregnant?"

A loud laugh erupted from my chest. "Jordan! I'm barely a few weeks pregnant and you already want to corrupt this child?"

He spun me and set me on my feet, his smile so large that it made wrinkles across his young face. "No?"

I laughed, unbuttoning his shirt. "Well, I suppose it won't hurt, just to be sure."

Formulated from the Journals
of Patient #32185
June 17, 2009
1:45 p.m.

I took a deep breath as I walked down the stairs. I was terrified, there was no way to deny that, but I couldn't let Kenzie know. What if the child was like me? What would I tell it? Would I hide it like my mother had, or would I embrace the fact that it was unique like me and teach it how to be careful as I clearly hadn't been?

I felt my palms sweat. What if I didn't make it? What would happen if I died, just like my mother had? I lifted my shirt and placed my hand on my side, feeling the spot where I had once seen the effects of my actions, and still could. In the end, the child would always have a mother though, a mother groomed to a life suited for just such a talented child. I felt nauseated at the thought, at all the manipulation I had made to make this life what it was.

It was a lie. I was living nothing more than a lie. I needed to tell her. It had gone on long enough. At this point it didn't matter what she did or said. I could not allow her to continue to live a life that was not her own. I walked back into the office where I opened the bottom drawer and lifted out the files, revealing what was left of my mother's book, now housed among my own papers and writings.

I would show her the book, she would see then that I didn't make it up. All this age and history was the truth, and she deserved to know, especially with the possibility of that kind of child inside her.

Despite my worries, I also felt excited. I would finally have someone to share my knowledge with, a child to teach as my mother had longed to do, but hadn't. If I had known I was not alone, things would have been different these past few years. I would not do that to my child; they would know.

Statement from Dr. Ashcroft,
Vincent Memorial Hospital, Boston
August 4, 2009
05:49 a.m.

Dr Ashcroft:

   The look on your face still suggests that you're disappointed I didn't tell you about a lot of this beforehand. In all fairness, I only recently understood myself, hence the position I'm in. It shocked me, naturally.

Agent Donnery:

   That's alright, Doctor. At least you're telling me now. (pause) He must have been terrified when you told him you were pregnant.

Dr. Ashcroft:

   He was. I knew right away that he was scared, I just didn't know why. He was the one that had wanted kids in the first place, so I didn't understand the hesitation at first, but I suppose it makes sense considering he had just found out that it could be hereditary.

Agent Donnery:

   But now it doesn't matter because the child is gone.

Dr. Ashcroft:
    No.

Agent Donnery:
    I'm sorry, I didn't mean it like that.
I see that you've lost everything. I guess
they just don't teach us compassion during
basic training.

Dr. Ashcroft:
    No, they don't. (pause) But I guess it
is what it is, and I have the chance now
to try and understand everything, and the
purpose of why it happened to me. Most of
all, I can move on, alone.

Agent Donnery:
    Are you a religious person?

Dr. Ashcroft:
    Knowing what you know, are you?

Agent Donnery:
    Good point. I guess at the end of the
day all that matters is that we believe in
something, whatever that is.

Dr. Ashcroft:
    I guess I believe in love. I can see
Jordan's angle on all of this. I see why he
hid it away from me because he was ashamed.
Reading this is more of an apology than he
could have ever given me. The funny thing

is that I still believe we would have
ended up together, no matter what life and
no matter what he did.

Agent Donnery:
    I see. But now all you know is just an
unraveling layer of lies.

Dr. Ashcroft:
    It's not that my life is falling apart.
It's more like my life is finally becoming
clear. It was bound to happen eventually,
I just didn't expect it would happen this
way.

My hands were splayed across the desk as I looked at the picture that hung above my head. Why was this so hard to do? Taking a deep breath, I lifted my hands and opened the file drawer, knowing this was the last place I hadn't yet looked. I pushed back the files, revealing the journal as I gazed upon it with both guilt and wonder. With a nervous hand I reached down and grabbed it, slowly pulling it from the drawers depths. I knew he had it hidden somewhere, but why? What about her files couldn't I read?

That day in the kitchen when I read what I could of the one entry, something had sparked my interest. This wasn't just any journal, but something more; and I needed to know what that was. I looked over my shoulder toward the door, anxiety running like sand through every vein.

I only had a few stolen moments to look at it before Jordan would be done with his shower and come looking for me. At times I wished he'd had a job so that I could sneak around more often, but in his world, with his luck, he didn't need any.

I had known for a while now that there was something going on beyond our simple life. It was hard to know what it was, but I knew him well enough to know that his interest in my dreams was not completely out of concern for me. I flipped open the cover and took a deep breath, searching for the page I had begun reading that day in the kitchen. As I shuffled through, I found that nothing was in order and I figured it was from when they'd been sprawled on the floor. Finally, I saw that each page had also been numbered and was in fact, in order. *Out of order but in order?* I asked myself, trying to make sense of it.

Furrowing my brow, I flipped to the back where I found two birth certificates and a death certificate. The death certificate was his mother's, along with one of the birth certificates, the other belonging to Jordan. There were a few pictures tucked into the back flap as well and I pulled them out, suddenly shocked by the face staring back at me, a face I had almost forgotten.

His mother had a sweet innocent smile and fair skin, her hair long and black as it lay in a braid down her chest, accentuating her dark brown eyes. She was in a hospital bed, her body already frail. Her looks were breathtaking, but it hadn't been her that had shocked me, it was Jordan. Though he had told me about that day in the park when we were young, I had forgotten his face. The face that I saw in the image now, however, brought me back.

I gasped, bringing my hand to my mouth. Not only did his face bring me back to that day, but it was also the one that had haunted me for so long. It was the face from my dreams, the face of the man, the boy. Only now had I been able to see it, only now was I able to finally put the pieces together. I felt my heart racing harder with each blink, seeing the boy that had manifested himself in my dreams, growing up alongside me like a shadow.

It was him, it had to be. I was right to assume it, all along. But why was it that I could see this boy, Jordan, as though he were my best friend? Especially when I had no way of knowing what he had looked like growing up? Outside of my dreams in my everyday life, I did not know him like this. There was only that one meeting in the park when I was four, and no one remembers when they were four.

I was shaking now, my cheeks becoming flushed. Wanting to know more, I flipped to the next photo in the stack, reading the inscription, "Boston Orphanage 1994." I felt my heart stop as I looked into the face of the boy on the bus from grade school.

"No, *no*..." I whispered. I put my hand to my head, shaking it in disbelief. "Him too... *That was him too?*"

I thought back to my life in grade school and the excitement I had felt that day when that cute, mysterious boy, had sat next to me on the bus. I had long wondered what had happened to him, finding that though he had moved into the neighborhood as he had claimed...

A wave of nausea washed over me as it often did since I'd gotten pregnant, though this time it wasn't from the pregnancy, but from the rush of memories and what they meant. My mind was trying to refuse seeing the obvious; dreams I had repressed and denied for so long were now flooding my thoughts, gaining power over my entire body. The boy on the bus had claimed to be living in the green house down the lane, this house, just as Jordan had claimed when he was also the boy in the park.

I pushed the book to the side as I grabbed for the garbage can just in time to throw up. There was no denying it any longer. What I always knew was true. Coughing, I didn't hear as the door to the room creaked open and Jordan stepped in.

"Kenzie are you alright?" His voice sounded frantic.

I reached for a tissue off the desk and wiped my mouth, looking up at him, my stomach cramping. He was looking at me with concern, but I saw the way his face changed as he noticed the book in my lap.

"Kenzie, I…"

I cut him off, my emotions unable to handle formality. "Jordan, what is this?"

I held the photo up toward him and he stared at it, then me. "It's me."

Sitting up I swallowed hard. "I can see that but, but you were…"

This time he cut me off, seeing I was struggling as my stomach began to heave again. "Kenzie, I need to explain that."

What I couldn't understand is why my memory of him at this age seemed to cross over, from my dreams to my reality, as though he had traveled into both like a phantom. I grabbed for the garbage can, taking deep breaths.

"Kenzie, you need to calm down, you'll make yourself sick." Jordan knelt to the ground, lifting his hand to place it on my back, but I swatted it away.

"I think it's a little late for that, Jordan." I shook the photo in my hand. "This, Jordan. What is this? Why do I know you more than just from in the park? Why do I know your face so well, as though I'd watched you grow up? Why are you the boy from my dreams?" The questions poured from my mouth without control. I looked to the floor, concentrating on the weave of the carpet, trying to calm down. My eyes were watering and everything was blurred. I swallowed hard, pressing back the feeling of nausea.

Jordan lifted my chin with his hand, looking me in the eyes. "Kenzie, don't you ever wonder why you know me, then and now?"

I grumbled and sat back. "Don't you think that's exactly what I'm doing now?" I crossed my arms against my chest as the stomach acid burned through my esophagus.

"But did you wonder before today?"

I let a sharp breath pass my lips as I grabbed my cup of juice from the desk and took a sip. "Yes, of course I did." I set the glass back with a clank. "I was too afraid of the answer to ever ask, so I never pried."

He slid the book from my lap and brought it into his. "This is complicated but…"

"You are the man from my dreams, aren't you? Except, you know them, too. You know exactly what I've dreamt." My eyes stung with betrayal, but also a sense that I was finally getting some clarity. "You've been playing me the fool."

He swallowed hard. "Kenzie, I…" I could tell he felt guilty. "I know about the day we met on the bus. I remember it all like it was yesterday." He flipped through the pages, handing it to me and pointing. "See here."

The page was dated *May 21, 2009* at *9:34 p.m.* I skimmed over the entry, my mind remembering every moment we had shared when I had found him lost on the bus that first time, as though it was happening all over again. I felt the scars return to my face and I could feel the way the nylon nurse uniform cut into my skin. "You, this was you. But how? It says this happened last month, but..."

"But it didn't, I know." He would not look at me, as though he were ashamed of that fact.

"Why?" My voice was curt and a bit crazed at this point.

"I changed it."

"*Changed it?*" I looked back at the page, reading the end where he explained his plan to save me from the horrible life I seemed to lead. "I don't understand. You can't change it."

"But I can, Kenzie. And I did." He paused. "I'm not proud of it, I can see now that I was selfish to do so, even if I thought it was selfless at the time. Your life was yours to lead, I should have never..."

"But, Jordan, *that's not possible.*" My blood felt hot now, my stomach still churning.

"There's something wrong with me, Kenzie." His eyes met mine and I could feel every ounce of truth as he said it. "I can travel through time, or rather, I could and..."

"But that's *absurd.* Crazy," I refused to listen as I began to feel as though the word absurd had become a friend of mine. "How do I know you're not lying?" I began to crumple the page in my hands as I clenched my fist, but Jordan took it back from me.

"It's something I've inherited…"

"*Inherited?*" I interrupted.

He continued. "Yes. I assure you, I wish I was lying," he flipped back through the book and handed me another page, the one I had been looking for before.

The entry was dated *April 3, 1963*. I took it with a gentle hand, watching the page shake as I brought it to my face. I began to read, swallowing though my throat was dry.

April 3, 1963

Something happened today that is hard to explain. I always thought my life was sealed in a horrible fate of sadness, but it seems I found a way to change my luck. I was in the closet of my mother's house, hiding from my drunk and abusive father, rocking back and forth and trying to think of a happier time. I thought about that day in class a few weeks ago, when the gerbil and I got to sit in the corner and play games while the rest of the class cleaned their desks. I had done exceptionally well on the spelling bee so I won the opportunity. As I sat in the closet, I felt something funny begin to happen as the thought began to feel real, and before I knew *it, that gerbil was in my hand and I was back in class.*

At first I was frightened by what had happened, and the teacher sent me to the nurse. For the past few weeks, I relived the exact same life I already had and that dream I'd manifested in the closet never ended. It may seem strange, but I think that day I traveled through time.

Today, I will try to change why my father was coming after me in the first place. If this works, I think I may have discovered something amazing.

The entry ended, and with wide eyes, I looked back up at Jordan. "How old was she?"

He took the page from my hand. "I believe she was twelve."

"How old were…" I paused. "How old were you the first time?"

Jordan looked me in the eye. "Six. I was six that day I came and you found me on the bus."

"*Six?* You were that young?" I racked my brain, finding it made sense now, knowing that he was barely out of pre-school at the time. "But you traveled forward, she traveled back."

Jordan nodded. "Yes, it doesn't matter, as long as we can imagine ourselves at that age, it just sort of happens."

I cleared my throat, finding the nausea was returning. "And you would also assume the age you were, in either the future or past? In other words, you can't leap and stay twenty-seven so to speak?"

He shook his head. "There's no exact science. I've never really met someone like me," he paused. "Or rather, I've never gotten the opportunity to exchange stories."

I figured he was referring to his mother. "What does it feel like?"

He laughed with a hint of sarcasm. "Like sticking your body in the microwave on high."

An image of popcorn came to my head, but I shook it away. "That doesn't sound healthy."

His eyes became wide. "No, apparently it's not. That's why I've been here with you all this time. I'm stuck here."

I lifted one brow. "Stuck here?" There was a hint of anger to my voice, heightened by the fact that I was carrying this man's child.

"I didn't mean it like that." He reached out and touched my hand, and I let him, too exhausted to care. "What I meant was that I can't Shift anymore, or rather it's been a while. The last time I nearly killed myself."

I tilted my head, thinking back. "When was the last time you did? Was it when Max came and tried to kill Amy?"

He shook his head. "No, it was the night at the rugby house."

I thought back to that night, a memory I had long suppressed. "You changed that? What would have happened?"

He looked at me from under his brows. "I believe you already know what would have happened. I'm sure you dream about it. I figure you'd repressed it, though. I wouldn't blame you." His eyes became glossy as he said it, as though the anger was still there. "I tried to change it many times, but it always turned out bad. The only solution was to let you know who I was so that you would remain with me and not run off to see Max."

I took a deep breath. "I can't believe I'm hearing this."

He brought his other hand up and placed in on mine, cupping my hand in both of his. "You have to try and believe me." He let go to stand and grab the hem of his shirt. "See, you remember this don't you?"

He pulled the hem up and I saw the remnants of the large bruise he had endured that night at the rugby house. "Sure, I remember."

He ran his hand across it. "This was not from a fight. This was because my kidney was beginning to fail. See, my mother died from a cancer that she gave to herself by Shifting carelessly through time. I don't really blame her. She did live through the sixties, seventies and eighties."

I felt my nerves give up and I could no longer handle trying to understand any of this today. "I need to go lie down," I said plainly.

He had a concerned look on his face as he offered me his hand. "Are you alright?"

I glared at him. "Yeah, sure. I just found out my whole

life is a lie, and I'm carrying your baby that may or may not have the same traits you do. Things are great."

He tilted his head as he grabbed my arm. "No, I mean are you okay. You look pale."

I snorted. "Well I just threw up and my heart is racing, so of course I'd look pale."

He picked me up against my will. "If you say so."

I sighed. "I'd fight back but, I don't feel like it." It was almost painful to talk now, and I began to worry.

He laughed. "Maybe later, then." We walked toward the stairs. "I really am sorry I never told you Kenzie."

"Jordan." I changed the subject fast. "Maybe I'm not okay."

He looked at me with a sudden fear lacing his face. "What do you mean?"

"I…" I felt my head whirl as though he was twisting me in the air. "I don't know, my stomach just…"

He stopped dead in his tracks and turned back down the stairs, out the door, and took me to the car. "I'm taking you to the hospital."

I coughed then, but this time it was laced with blood and my body erupted into a cold sweat. "Jordan, what's happening?"

He got in the car, mumbling something under his breath, and it was then that I noticed the blood on his shirt.

"Jordan, look!" I pointed as he looked at himself, and then at my jeans.

There was blood all over the passenger seat of the car

now, and it was then that everything seemed to fade and I felt my body give. Though I tried to hold on I could no longer handle the rush of pain that was suddenly crippling me. In my heart, I knew the baby was already gone.

I woke suddenly as a hand squeezed mine.

"Kenzie?" Jordan's voice sounded weak.

"Jordan, is that you?" I looked toward the voice, finding his face. A sense of relief fell over me as it always did when I saw him, and it was then I realized I did not care what he said or did. I still needed him.

His face was tired and drawn. "Kenzie, I'm so sorry. This is my fault."

"Is it gone?" It was the only thing I could think about, the only thing that mattered. My baby was gone. I knew it, though I desperately hoped he would tell me otherwise.

He nodded. "They believe so..." he trailed off.

"You saw, didn't you?" I motioned for him to look at me, and as he did, I saw the truth.

"It was horrible, Kenzie. I never wanted to put you through all this."

I didn't like the tone of his voice. "Jordan, you can't change this. This is how it was supposed to happen. Don't you understand that?"

He nodded, but I didn't trust it. He squeezed my hand again. "I want the best for you, for us."

I took a deep breath as my stomach ached from the

residual pain, "This is what is best for us, Jordan. A clean slate. Now we can start over with the truth, and re-build."

He smiled, but I could see he felt lost, the look on his face like that of the man I saved from the bus. As hard as it was to believe all that he had told me, a part of me sensed the truth. I had been there all along the way, just as he had. I had pined for and loved the man of my dreams as much as he loved me here and now. I had no idea what had been happening to me, and I suppose if I had known all along, I would have tried to stop it, but here I am, with all I have.

"Do you want something to drink?" He rose from his stool. "I could use some coffee."

I nodded. "Perhaps some water would be good."

He leaned down and kissed me on my forehead.

I held onto his back as he pulled away, whispering in his ear. "Jordan, it's alright. This is not your fault. You don't need to change it." I let go and he stood tall.

"I know, Kenzie." He turned then and walked toward the door, pausing for a moment to smile before leaving.

I leaned my head back onto the pillow, thinking about what I'd lost. The baby was only two months old, no more than a tiny being. Perhaps the child saw what was destined for it when I found that book yesterday. Perhaps it knew by the way I had reacted that this life was not the one it wanted. I thought about the Kenzie in my dreams and the Kenzie I would have been. I had envied her freedom and her bravery, but perhaps that version of myself also envied me in a similar way.

Does it really matter if you change a moment in the end? For all the struggles I saw on her side of things, there were also the struggles here. In that other life I would have never been beautiful, while here that beauty haunted me. All I know is that it is what it is, and now it's over. The best I can do is deal with the cards I have been dealt, and try to make the best of it.

I heard a crash in the hall as a woman screamed and I sat up in horror. I felt my blood curdle then as my mind began altering itself. Where the memories of our discussion about the journal in the office had once lived now lived the memories of the discussion never occurring at all. I put my hand over my mouth as my head began to ache, finding that Jordan was out there trying to change my memories and the past, though it seemed it still ended with the same horrible fate.

I pushed myself off the bed and sat up, wincing as I grabbed the I.V. drip and ripped it out of my palm, the needle leaving a deep bruise. I stood on weak legs as I heard doctors running down the halls, rushing past my room. I began to walk toward the door, afraid of what I would find, but determined to see. As I rounded the corner, no one noticed me but what I saw left me clinging to the wall for support.

Jordan was on the ground in a puddle of blood, his shirt soaked through the side. He was still conscious but I saw there was little life left; he was dying. All attention was on him now as a crowd of people bustled around him, and I lost a visual. Filled with fear, I pressed forward, moving people out of the way until the crowd parted and his eyes met mine. I saw then the despair and sorrow, and I understood why he did what he had. If there was any doubt left in me, it was now gone, replaced by the truth and the driving force behind his life.

He blinked as his eyelids became heavy, a doctor finally noticing my presence as he walked away from Jordan to me, taking my arm and leading me back into the room. I never saw Jordan again.

Dr. Ashcroft:
They tell me he's stable, but non-responsive.

Agent Donnery:
This is true. They are trying all they can, but they need a kidney. He has type O blood, so it's hard to find a donor.

Dr. Ashcroft:
You're speaking to the gallery, Agent. I know this. There's a 16% chance.

Agent Donnery:
Unfortunately you're not a match either.

Dr. Ashcroft:
I also know that, Agent.

Agent Donnery:
And his family members are all deceased, which I know you also know, so…

Dr. Ashcroft:

No, I understand what you're telling me. You're trying to say that there is little chance to save him.

Agent Donnery:

We are trying hard. We want him to live for obvious reasons. Just wanted to make sure you are aware of the facts.

Dr. Ashcroft:

I appreciate it.

Agent Donnery:

Well, I better let you be. You probably need some sleep.

Dr. Ashcroft:

Yes, that would be good. Thank you.

Agent. Donnery:

No, thank you. This will be a tremendous help.

Dr. Ashcroft:

One last thing, Agent. If he lives, what will happen to him?

Agent Donnery:

Nothing other than questioning. It's not as though he can go anywhere anymore. You've made that clear. This other one though, we'll need to find her. It's not

safe to allow them to run around changing
things. One day it could change something
huge, and we may not have a nation or
world to answer to because of it.

Dr. Ashcroft:
    (laughter) I understand. Tell your
wife hello for me, and that I'm sorry I
kept you.

Agent Donnery: I will.

I watched Agent Donnery leave as I lay back against the pillow. I was exhausted but still awake. Reading the stories seemed to put everything into perspective, and I finally felt free for the first time in my life. I ran my hands across the book in front of me, wondering if Agent Donnery had meant to leave it or not. I pulled it to my chest and hugged it, thinking of Jordan and falling in love with him all over again.

I felt at peace, a feeling I hadn't felt since I was very young, before all the dreaming. The light outside was just beginning to rise above the nearby hill as it hit the blinds, splaying a striped shadow across the hospital floor. I had worked in this hospital for a while now, and I knew they had given me the nicest room on purpose, something reserved for those with great healthcare.

I wondered then what they knew about Jordan, if anything at all, or if they simply thought it was a failed kidney. I thought back to the events of yesterday, my mind now harboring two memories in Jordan's attempt to save his child. His efforts were proof in my belief that you can't always change the future by changing the past. In the end I was still here, and no matter what, it was still another miscarriage.

I exhaled as I released my grip on the book and closed

my eyes, allowing sleep to set in, too tired to push it away. There was a knock on the door then, and my eyes flickered open. I watched as light from the hall flooded the room and a shadow entered. It wasn't until the door was shut that I saw it was a girl that stood there, dressed from head to toe in black. I felt my heart stop as a sharp breath caught in my throat, recognizing her from Jordan's descriptions.

She stood like a shadow near the corner, her turquoise eyes just as I had imagined, but her skin was not the pale white that Jordan had suggested. I tilted my head, noticing it was now kissed with a bit of rose.

"I tried to tell him, but he wouldn't listen." Her voice was angelic as it filled the room, echoing the same way it had that day in Biology.

"You're Molly." I was still trying to process the fact that she was really here, like a fictional character come to life.

She nodded. "I am."

I nodded back to her as she approached my bed. "I'm sorry I couldn't stop him in time. Though I tried, he didn't listen. He never listens."

I laughed.

Molly smiled. "I'll admit that I knew what he was going to do, so I met him out there in the hall..." she pointed over her shoulder.

"It's dangerous for you here." I watched her, her lashes long as they fluttered.

She tilted her head with a smirk. "No, not really. I know how to stay out of the way, if you know what I mean."

I smiled, noticing that she still had not changed based on the stories. "You still seem young. Why? I thought you couldn't Shift and remain the same age?"

She trailed her hand across the blankets on the bed, looking around as though taking in the feeling of this moment. "I'm the same age because I can be, because I Shift differently than Jordan."

I nodded. "Jordan described you to have much fairer skin. Did you go on vacation?"

Her eyes darted to mine, the noticeable rose to her cheeks hard to deny. "Not really, I just became more alive." She blinked and looked away.

"Ah." There was little I could make of her replies, so I changed the subject. "Have you seen him?"

She smiled. "Yes. I'm actually here to take you to see him."

I pressed my brows together. "Why help us? Why be there all along and yet let this happen?"

She watched me as I sat up, her lips parted as she breathed steadily. "Because it was meant to happen. It needed to happen." She stopped and lowered her eyes. "Well…" I could tell she was struggling now. "Not all of it. My goal was to keep him from Shifting, but he's so stubborn." She shook her head and eyed the book in my grasp with strange recognition and belonging.

I placed it beside me and rolled off the bed, making sure to keep my gown shut at the back. Molly walked over to a nearby cabinet and found a change of clothes hanging inside.

"Here, wear this." She shoved them toward me.

"What about you?" I looked her up and down. "They know what you look like."

She shrugged. "No, they won't see me, remember? I know where they are."

I nodded. "Oh right, you've been there."

She laughed. "You could say that."

I found her laughter as enchanting as Jordan had explained, the air around her relaxed and solemn. I got dressed and followed her to the door. She peeked out and around the corner, ushering me forward with one hand.

I followed her down the hall to the elevator. When we got in, she pressed the button for intensive care and looked up at the reader above the door as we descended.

"Is he in bad shape?" I looked at her as she continued to look up, her head covered by her hood, leaving only her chin and nose peeking out.

"Yes and no. Nothing worse than you've seen before, as far as the bruising goes, though now it's on both sides since both of his organs are failing." She said it as though it were no big deal, as though she had a solution.

The elevator door opened and she stepped out like she owned the place.

"Where are you from, Molly? I mean, where is your base?" I followed after her as fast as I could though my stomach still ached, the familiar feeling of the nausea I had while pregnant remaining.

"Around here." She did not look back as she turned a

corner and I followed.

"When were you born?" I kept pressing, fighting for the answers Jordan could never ask.

She stopped as she came to the last door in the hall, looking back toward the reception desk as she opened it and walked in. I also looked back at reception, being quick as I darted through the open door, shutting it behind me with a gentle click.

"I haven't been born yet." She was whispering now.

"What?" My voice was sharp but quiet. "Then how..." My voice trailed off as I saw Jordan, the beeping of the monitors filling the air with an ominous beat. I walked slowly toward the bed, putting one foot in front of the other. His eyes were shut, his chest rising ever so gently. I glanced at his vitals, seeing they were dangerously low.

"I'm going to save him." Molly's voice cut through the silence.

I looked at her, her eyes staring at Jordan. "But..."

"Mother, this is my destiny. This is what I want more than anything."

I felt my heart stop. "*Mother?*"

She looked at me, removing the hood from her head as a cascade of curly auburn hair tumbled down her back. "Yes. Mother."

"But..." I put my hand on my stomach. What did she mean? She had been lost, miscarried.

"It is true that I can Shift just like he can, only I've learned to travel outside of my life." There was a proud smile on her face. "When I was seven I found the book grandmother and father had left for me."

"Seven?" I felt my brow begin to sweat.

"Dad always told me I was so pale, so cold. It's because I was technically dead." She watched me. "But now." She looked down at my stomach. "Now I'm alive." She was filled with pride. "Grandmother helped me. I went and saw her, told her the things Jordan couldn't, and together we made a plan."

I felt a lump rise in my throat. "But you…"

She cut me off, her smile fading as she looked back at my stomach. "No, he did die, my brother. But I did not."

I took a deep breath, feeling my legs going numb as I moved to the chair in the corner. "Twins?"

She nodded, "It happens more than you think. You miscarried because he did not want to live this life, but it made room for me." She paused. "Dad needs me, Mother, and I need him."

I looked down at my stomach, my hands still cradling it, her.

"I do not want to live without him as I have. I love him, too." She looked back at Jordan, touching his hand. "I have his blood. He can have one of my organs." She touched her side.

"But how, Molly? They would never allow it." I shook my head, my brow furrowed. "You cannot do that, you would die." I was referring to the child inside me, and the surgery that would be inflicted.

"They will. Tell them I am his cousin. That's all they need," She handed me some forged papers that she'd had in her pockets as her eyes began to well with tears. "Mother, you don't want to raise me alone. Trust me, I know. As much as you hate what he's taken from you, one day you will see what he gave you in return. You love him, perhaps not right now, but you will remember."

I tried to understand. "But what about you?"

She shrugged. "I do not need to Shift anymore. If I do this then I solidify my life as a regular being, and I am happy with what God decides to bring to me. I just want my father back."

"Okay." I rose from my chair, unsure of what to do next. Molly walked toward me then and wrapped her arms around my sides. "Please, Mother, for both our sakes."

I let out a sharp, derisive breath, seeing the comedy in all this. I put one hand on the back of her head, running my other down the length of her hair, amazed by how similar it felt to my own. "We need to get you out of that hood, then. They know you too well like that."

She looked up at me, stepping back and pulling it over her head. I grabbed it from her hand and stashed it under the bed. Looking at Jordan, I told myself this was the right thing. For all the decisions he had made for me, this was mine to make in return.

Looking at Molly, I saw that she was thin like me, her body tall as she knelt down beside Jordan. "Someday, Daddy, you will understand why I did this." She kissed his hand.

"Alright, come with me. We're going to talk to the head of hospital. They'll trust me. We need to get this done before

Agent Donnery comes back."

Molly smiled. "Thank you, Mother. I know they will trust you. I know this will work."

I shook my head. "Please Molly, no more telling me the future. It takes the fun out of this."

She laughed. "Alright, I promise."

I put my hand to my stomach, wondering if this would hurt me as much as it would hurt her.

August 4, 2009
7:33 p.m.

By sundown I had managed to convince them she was a legitimate relative. God knows why they believed me, but they did. As far as they were concerned, they had a willing individual that was legally and adult, so no one cared. It seemed they had a grasp on the importance of the situation, even if they didn't know the facts.

"How will you get back?" I looked down at her as she lay in the cold operating room beside Jordan, her hair tied back into a net and her face as cold as I had imagined before.

"Don't worry about me, I'll make it one last time, I know it." She squeezed my hand.

"Of course you do." I squeezed back, admiring the brave woman I had somehow managed to raise alone.

"I'll see you soon enough, Mother. I promise." She gave me a faint smile as someone entered the room.

"Dr. Ashcroft?" A nurse touched my arm. "I'm sorry, but we have to ask you to leave."

I looked back one last time as the nurse led me out, giving Molly a smile of thanks, of love.

"Doctor?" A voice roused me and I rubbed my eyes.

There was a pinch in my side as I sat up, and I felt what had happened to Molly.

"Doctor, have you seen your cousin?"

I looked at her with alarm. "What?"

The nurse looked frantic. "Your cousin. We can't find her anywhere."

I looked around. "No but, did it work? Is he okay?" I knew Molly was fine, I could feel it. All I cared about now was Jordan.

The nurse gave me a quick nod. "Yes, but, Molly... She's gone. We brought her back to her room after we removed the kidney, but when we came to check on her she was gone. We fear she may die if she's not found soon."

I grabbed my stomach, feeling it lurch. "Well, um..." The nurse stood, distracted.

"Don't worry, we will find her." She took off then toward the front desks as a doctor summoned her.

I looked around the dark waiting room, then at the clock. Rubbing my eyes I stood, knowing by now she was already gone, and they would never find her.

I walked toward the water cooler and grabbed a cup, pressing down the latch as the liquid splashed inside and the cooler bubbled.

"Good to see you up and about." The voice was eerily familiar and the one I had been dreading since the moment Molly had come for me.

I froze, squeezing my eyes shut. After a few minutes I was able to gather myself and I turned. "Agent, good to see you so soon."

He gave me a look that told me he knew what was going on. "Where is Molly?"

I shrugged.

He sighed and motioned me toward the chair. I sat, sipping on my water, my eyes darting about the room.

"Listen, Kenzie." He brought his hands into his lap. "I felt as thought there was some connection here I wasn't picking up on. I see it now." He looked at my stomach.

"I, uh…" I took another sip of water.

"I honestly don't care, Doctor." He looked toward the ceiling, his body slumping with exhaustion.

I wrinkled my brow, surprised by his reaction.

"When I got home, my wife hugged me and my little girl gave me a drawing she had made in pre-school. It was then that I realized I'd do anything to protect them and anything to keep our family whole." His breath dragged in his throat. "I may not completely understand what is going on here, but I can tell you it's harmless. One child or one father with just one kidney will not risk Shifting again. This I know."

I swallowed. "Agent, I honestly didn't know about her."

He laughed. "I don't figure you did. You look like hell."

I smiled. "Thanks." I thought about the boy I had lost then, wondered why he didn't want to be a part of this life or this family.

Agent Donnery stood. "As far as I saw, this whole thing never happened. Just a false alarm." He winked as he pulled the tapes of our recorded conversation from his pocket and handed them to me.

My mouth fell open. "Really?"

He laughed. "Just go home, Doctor. Have some peace for once."

I felt relief and excitement pass over me.

He grabbed my hand. "Perhaps I'll see you again someday, Doctor. Perhaps when you have that second child." His grasp loosened as he turned away from me before I could utter a word, leaving me alone once more.

I walked toward the nurse's station, the whole hospital in an uproar to find a girl that had escaped surgery. The girl that was right here, with me. I touched my belly and looked down the hall toward Jordan's room, sneaking past the doctors and slinking through the door.

As the door clicked shut, I heard a soft murmur. "Kenzie?"

I turned, seeing Jordan laying there, his eyes barely open. "Kenzie, what happened?"

I ran to the side of his bed. "Oh Jordan, you're okay." I grabbed his face, kissing it over and over.

He tried to laugh but stopped, his stomach too sore to handle it. "I take it you're no longer angry with me?" His voice cracked.

I smiled. "No, I'm not angry."

He looked at me. "And the baby?"

One chuckle passed my lips. "She's alright." He didn't need to know that his attempt to change things hadn't worked, and he didn't need to know about the twin just yet. The moment would come, but now was not the time.

His eyes got wide, "She?"

I swallowed. "It's just a hunch." I wouldn't tell him about Molly either, figuring that one day he'd see and that hopefully then he'd understand the love of a family, and the fact that he was never alone.

After twelve hours of labor and eventually an hour of pushing, our little girl came into the world. She was a healthy six pounds and three ounces, and as they handed her to me, I already knew what I'd see. Her turquoise eyes were brighter than I remembered as she blinked and gazed at me, her face rosy and her hair barely sprouting from her head.

Jordan came to my side, his brow beaded in sweat, afraid of the unknown. There was a small scar on her belly as I ran my hand across it, a very light pink that showed despite her new skin but enough that I could recognize just what it was. Jordan looked over my shoulder with a smile that was quick to fade as his body froze.

"Let's name her Molly." I grinned with pride and looked up at him.

His eyes were wide as he looked around the room and at the remaining nurses, now just leaving. "What is this?"

I laughed as Molly stuck her hand out toward Jordan.

He let out one surprised laugh. "Why didn't you tell me?"

"I wanted it to be a surprise, that's all."

Jordan reached down and grabbed her tiny hand. "But how?" I could tell he was struggling to understand. "She saved me, didn't she? And now..."

I cut him off. "And now she's just like you, Jordan. So you can be stuck here together."

He stared at her for a moment before formulating another question, his eyes still wide in amazement. "Do you think she'll remember it, like you did?"

I tilted my head, watching her curious eyes. "I'm not sure. I guess we'll find out."

The doctor came in then and inspected her, his face filled with concern. "May I take her?"

I nodded, knowing what his concern was about. He would surely find that Molly had been born with one kidney, the other removed in a fashion that wouldn't make sense. As a doctor, I knew how confusing it would be to them, but I also knew that at some point they would give up and Molly would come back to me.

Molly's curious case was surely a gift from God. And though I doubted God held any hope for our family, it seemed this was His way of saying that He was still here for us, despite all that had happened.

When I look back, I think that I still lived a lucky life. One filled with magic and mystery, adventure and love. Though it's nice to live in a perfect world, it is better to believe that it is, in fact, very flawed but beautiful because of it. I watched as Jordan came back into the room, walking toward me and grabbing my hand.

"But how?" he asked again, still lost.

I shrugged. "I'm not sure how or why she came to us

so soon, but I do know that she wanted a father, and I could not deny her that affection. She is just like you, Jordan. Just as strong willed and determined. She knew what she needed to do to prevent your death, but to also put an end to our bloodline. With one kidney, childbirth for her is a major risk and so is Shifting. It was her way of forcing herself into a normal life, and though she may know what the future holds, it will be different because you're in it."

Tears formed in Jordan's eyes. "I never knew. I never thought it was possible for a Shifter to move like that."

I squeezed his hand as hard as I could muster, my body exhausted. "All she needed was the journals from you and your mother, the pictures and the memories that you laid out so well." I saw his eyes flash, and I knew what he was thinking. "You cannot think like that any longer, Jordan. Your mother wanted you to live a normal life, and you know that. She hoped that you would be born normal, but when she realized you weren't, her hope was lost. You cannot save her anymore. We need you here with us, as a family."

Tears rolled down his cheek and he nodded with a shaking lip. "I'm sorry my mother never got the chance to meet her, to see how we had changed it all."

I laughed. "But she did, Jordan. This was entirely your mother's idea. Molly told me that."

He began to cry, and for a while he was silent, but as the morning turned to the afternoon, I think he managed to find a sense of peace.

"I'm so sorry, Kenzie. I never meant for all this to

happen. I didn't know."

I let out a heavy breath as he woke me from a light nap, hearing his words. "It's not worth worrying about anymore, darling. We're alive and together now. All the rest is history and it won't be repeated."

Jordan's face curled into a smile. "I love you, Kenzie."

I yawned before letting out a gentle laugh. "I know."

"Here, Molly, pass me the ball!" I yelled from across the court, putting my hands up.

She laughed. "Nice try, Dad. This is a one-on-one game, so I can't pass you the ball."

We were both breathing heavily as sweat coated our brow, feeling hot, though the air was crisp and turning into fall. We stopped for a moment and I put a hand on my hip, squeezing my side.

"Does it hurt?" Molly walked up to me with the ball in her hands, a solemn look on her face that reminded me of back then, when I first saw her.

"Just a little tight, is all." I held back a wince, feeling the residual pain that still lingered as a reminder of what I had done to myself.

"Jordan, I don't regret what I did."

I froze and looked at her, her voice changing as she addressed me by name. I had never told her about what she had done, as a sort of experiment, to see if she could remember, and also to hopefully hide the truth from her.

"I know about it all; I could never forget that. I knew my decision to Shift for the last time was not without good cause, and I would do it again if I had to." Her turquoise eyes blinked as she walked over to the bench and grabbed her black sweatshirt.

"You know?" I was still gasping for air.

Molly laughed. "Of course I do, Daddy."

I laughed and walked up to her, giving her a hug. "Then let me thank you for what you did for all of us. You had a bravery that your grandmother and I could not possess."

I felt her squeeze me like she never had before, and for the first time since she came to me, years and years ago, I felt we had finally connected. "Do you want to hear about Grandma?" she asked, looking up at me.

The words sparked a flood of tears as she said them, my mother's face smiling at me across my memory. I swallowed hard, my voice cracking. "I would very much like that."

October 14, 2028

What is fate but a way to order life? When I chose to Shift my entire world, I hadn't expected it would only delay the inevitable. I only wish that I knew more about my real life, the one I left behind many lives ago. I have learned now that I cannot hope to change the future or past. I can only hope that as I try my best, fate will shine on me. Time spent wishing that things were different is time wasted, life thrown away and forgotten. I will never be young again, but I have growing old to look forward to and that is all the adventure I need. Indulging in the power to Shift was like taking the long road to learning to live in the present moment of everyday life, but now that I know, it is something I will never take for granted, ever again.

Jordan McKay

Still Want More?

Log onto:

www.ParallelTheBook.com

and click on *Resist the Shift* to register and read the

Alternate Ending

See what would have happened if Jordan had *resisted* the
Shift, and learn more about this incredible story...

In *love* with *Parallel*?
Preview *Abra Ebner's* Debut Series

THE FEATHER
BOOK SERIES

Feather
Guardian
Raven

Here...
Beginning on Page 318.

The Feather Book Series was Abra Ebner's First look into writing, and as such, she challenged and experimented with the parameters of what makes a writer, creating a powerful series that defies structure, and is bound to leave you enchanted...

ABOUT ABRA EBNER

In Chelan, Washington with her friend Jana, a budding writer...

Abra (like Abracadabra) Ebner loves to write and believes that by helping others discover the magic of writing the world will be a happier place. She lives in Washington with her husband and two cats where she writes a little bit of everything: *Science Fiction, Fantasy, Cookbooks, Self-help, Chick Lit,* and *graphic novels.* She loves to travel and has extensively, visiting Germany, England, Switzerland, Scotland and studying at the Queensland College of Art in Australia. She graduated with honors and has not forgotten her graphic design roots as she still designs everyday. Abra is one of the founders of *Crimson Oak Publishing,* a company that was originally started for her books but now also consults with, and helps other ambitious self-published authors find their way to success.

Visit Abra's sites:

www.ParallelTheBook.com
www.ParallelTheBook.Wordpress.com (blog)
www.FeatherBookSeries.com
www.FeatherBookSeries.Wordpress.com (blog)
www.CrimsonOakPublishing.com
www.TheAuthorsOutline.com

Email and Comments:

info@CrimsonOakPublishing.com

FEATHER

BOOK ONE

ABRA EBNER

PREFACE

Once upon a time, the Gods created a being far greater than anything in existence. These beings, the highest form of human life, were closer to God than even the angels, and their beauty far more appealing than any earthly creation.

The Gods, upon seeing such a beautiful creation grew jealous. The being needed no love, longed for no power, and hungered for no nourishment of either mind or soul. Their flawless creation was angelically perfect, and therefore appallingly wrong, for nothing could be more perfect than the Gods themselves.

As the being flourished, troubled by nothing, the Gods grew dark and vindictive. In their hatred they mused and the plan they constructed was horrid, inhumane, and dark. They chose to split the perfect soul for eternity, the Gods finding themselves ultimately endangered by their creations power and strength. In one swift movement they ripped the being apart, creating two hearts, both sharing one soul.

One half was the creator, the life and energy of the earth, and the mother of man. The other half was the power and protection, a warrior of worlds. In this, they created Male and Female.

As the Gods schemed in their eternal greed, they chose to make their creation a game, no more than mere pawns for their enjoyment. As punishment, they scattered the beings among the humans of earth, both halves separated and eternally locked in hunger and longing for the love of their shared soul.

The female half was the holder of their life, the emotion and beauty of the soul. In her, she protected this delicate power, never abusing its energy and forever giving to the earth and nature. Despite her possessions, she was lonely and lost in love, weak, sad, and alone.

The male half, the powerful half, was left lifeless and drained of the energy only the soul could give him. In the male's life on earth, he searched for his strength, the female, and the power he could ultimately gain from it. Their lethal lust for that soul was so great, that it drove them into madness, anger, and despair.

Upon meeting their soul mate, the male half was found hungry, and vicious, murdering their other half in their greed, and ultimately leading to their demise. But despite their vicious love, many survived long enough to understand their power, and in finding each other, they unlocked the secret to their lives.

Together, the two halves created a whole, a life force greater and more powerful than anything on earth. Though eternally tormented by jealously and hunger, they were better together than apart, the ultimate test of eternal love.

A NEW DAY

"*E*stella, take this." Heidi thrust a thick envelope toward me as a sad tear grew in her eye, her hand trembling and weak as it floated in the air between us.

I looked at the envelope with caution "Oh no," I shook my head, my face contorted into a sad frown, "Heidi no, I couldn't." I squeezed my eyes shut, unable to accept the gift.

"Please Estella," she paused, her voice now choking in her throat, "I just want to see you happy. I am old and tired, my life is ending and yours is just beginning." She walked toward me with a stern look on her face, the envelope still held out in front of her in her stubborn stand. Her eyes scanned mine in frantic waves and I could see she loved me like her own.

I grabbed the small manila package between my trembling fingers, treating it with delicate care. The contents were beyond what I could ever deserve, but the needs in Heidi's eyes were deep, and I found myself unable to say no.

"Thank you," I looked at the ground as the familiar sadness stung at my heart.

Heidi leaned in and hugged me, her small arms

squeezing the breath from my lungs. "I'm sorry I couldn't have been more of a mother to you," she whispered, her breath hot as it fell across my ear.

She was crying now, and I felt the tears seeping into the shoulder of my blouse.

"Heidi, you are the closest thing to a mother I've ever known, don't think any less." I put my arm around her frail shoulders as she trembled into my chest, the guilt in me rising as I forced back my desire to stay, to save her from her lonely life.

She pulled away, a strong look now flooding her tear stained face, "You go, make me proud," her eyes seeped bravery, "and find your happiness." She patted both of my shoulders with surprising strength as her long nails dug into my skin with a sting of pain.

"I promise, I will come back soon," I tried to smile as I dropped to pick up my last bag, but nothing came.

Heidi followed me to the car in her housecoat and slippers as I threw the last bag in the back seat of the old rusty green Datsun. I was finally able to afford the car after my summer working at the Market downtown. I did everything I could to scrape enough money together, to make my escape from the city.

Heidi's eyes had dried and I looked at her with nostalgic love and admiration as I climbed in. The old vinyl seats yawned against my sweaty skin and I winced at their searing heat. I squeaked the door shut, slamming it with as much force as I could muster before putting my hands on the plastic wood grain steering wheel. She waved to me with hopeless vigor as I coaxed the vehicle to life and forced it into reverse.

"I will visit soon!" I yelled from the window as I drove off, "The college is not too far."

Heidi took a sad and tired step forward as she made a final attempt to wave goodbye. I would miss her as my foster mother, but this was my time to make something of my sad life. The upbringing she had given me was all I could have hoped for, but something inside me was driving me away, pushing me to another place.

As I drove down the crowded streets, the shadows cast by the towering buildings of downtown Seattle always left me somewhat disappointed. The tiny house where I had been placed when I was ten glared at me as it disappeared between the apartment complexes of the west side in my rearview.

I took a deep breath, exhaling with a labored heart. I had decided the city was not for me. After years of adoption and rejection I couldn't stand its cold cement and moist dirty air any longer. Why the city had let me down I was unsure, but as the depression in me grew deeper as the years passed, it had become a sort of cancer. There was death here, and everyone took their happiness for granted. I would have given anything to feel a smile, to muster out a happy laugh.

I rolled my windows up, closing out this world as I headed north toward the Cascades. As the hills of Seattle whizzed by, each growing less crowded with houses, I felt a sort of liberation. The stern grip I'd had on the steering wheel slowly released and soon I was casually driving with one hand. My lonely life had never granted me the experience that was ahead of me, the chance to be with nature as my heart had so longed.

The college brochure had promised a tranquil and secluded experience and that was just the thing I was hoping my dark heart needed. College had always been a goal for me, and despite my graduation from high school, with a bachelor's degree that I had earned taking night courses, it still didn't satisfy my insatiable need to learn.

As the sun finally released onto the calm valleys of northern Puget Sound, the density of forest began to creep ever closer to the road and I felt a strange pull from the plants that sat there, each bowing toward the concrete as though a wall between it and the other side of life, much like my mind. I envied their freedom, their simple happiness and ability to adapt. I on the other hand, had never belonged, and despite how hard I tried, I always stood out. The world hopelessly saddened me, as though somewhere in my past life, it had let me down, my soul now darkened by my evil existence.

I reached into my bag, retrieving my bottle of medication and popping one pill in my mouth as I habitually did every day for the last twelve years. Each clouded thought further stifled by the power of Prozac. I allowed myself a second to close my eyes as I once again opened my windows, releasing the seal as the wind whipped through my angelically white hair. As the sun touched my pale skin, it felt warm and soothing like a bath of heavenly light.

Opening my eyes, I felt discouraged that even a moment like this could not muster a smile.

Even as a baby I had never laughed, never let out even so much as a delighted coo. Smiling was something I did because I had to in order to fit in. I learned what was funny from my peers, and practiced for hours in front of the mirror, my facial muscles stretching with pain in a way that came so naturally to everyone else. Tears never came either, though I knew what I had was sadness, I never felt that was the true definition of the feeling either. It was as though someone had ripped my soul out, leaving me helpless and empty.

I thought about all my adoptive parents, and how many times each tried to create a happy life for me, how relentlessly they urged me into activities designed to muster a laugh, though one never came. It was an inevitable truth that each failed as they rejected me back to the social workers, apologizing for their failure as parents. After a while, I gave up and moved in with Heidi and her other foster kids, for what I planned to be forever. I was like a poisonous berry, beautiful on the outside, damaged and sick on the inside.

I exhaled from deep within my charred soul as I finally reached the town of Sedro-Woolly, where I turned onto highway twenty, heading east into the North Cascades. The small town of Sedro-Woolly was far north, close to Canada and the San Juan islands, and just far enough from Seattle to leave it all behind. The town was the gateway to my future, and a new life.

As I headed into the wilderness, the trees that edged the roadside seemed to welcome my presence as the branches swayed in the light wind. The air seemed magical, and I saw the glimmer of bugs flying between thick rays of light like fairies in the trees. With my windows opened, the gentle clamoring of water casually whispered in my ear as I passed spring after spring, cascading down the granite rocks and into the roadside reservoirs.

The mountains closed in around me like a blanket, casting deep shadows on the road, but not the same depressing shadows I had grown up around in the city. These shadows revealed a whole other world beyond the dirty streets and sadness, a world of soulful life. For the first time, I felt a soft warmth flicker in my charred soul and I gasped, the feeling ripping the breath from my lungs.

Rounding the corner with caution, the trees parted in a dramatic wave and the sun poured into the car. The river that had followed the road burst open into a large lake that was choked back by a small dam. The water sparkled cleaner than I'd ever seen in Puget Sound and the glimmer made my eyes water. The air that poured into the car was crisp and moist from the glacial waters and I breathed deep, allowing it to heal my polluted lungs.

I stared in disbelief, wondering how I'd let this whole world hide from me for so long. As I followed the lake, I kept glancing toward it, feeling that it would disappear as fast as it had come. I blinked hard a few times, my mind wondering if this was just a twisted dream, a taunting memory set up to cause even more pain.

Like a meandering stream, the road wound to the right and I crossed over the lake on a delicate bridge. I felt a rush of something cold enter my body as though the water were pulsing through me, becoming a part of my blood and filling every vein. I allowed the feeling to control my thoughts, and I imagined a tidal wave washing through my scarred mind, cooling each itching gash.

With a sudden pulse, just when I thought I couldn't have seen anything any more gorgeous, the lake further expanded and an even larger dam loomed before me, grand in its amazing power. I took in the complex construction and it amazed me to believe that as a human race, we could create something so powerful. I could see the college now, nestled into the hillside on the other side of the dam, I was almost there, almost free.

As I turned from the main road toward the complex, I slowed as my car rolled onto the cobblestone blocks. The gentle vibration was calming as the cobbles shuddered under my weight. The college had utilized this dam as the crossing to the school and a part of me felt like it was a bridge to my fairy-tale castle.

To my left was the drop to the lake that I had drove along on my way up and as I peered over the ledge, my head felt the gripping vertigo as my eyes focused on the rocks below. To my right, the water brimmed against the wall, swirling in its attempt to escape, the churning water anxious and foamy. The lake itself was a milky crystal blue and sharp rocky peaks surrounded it as they reached into the even bluer sky. The unique coloration was unbelievable and I recognized it to be Diablo Lake, where the College sat along the waters ledge.

As I neared the other side of the bridge, I noticed a gorged waterfall drop like a graceful veil from a far peak and into the lake on its final decent. Its raw power humbled me as I watched in silence as it misted the air around it, rainbows flashing in its wake. As the wild wind whipped toward me across the water, I noticed a sort of untamed beauty that felt so normal to me.

I closed my eyes and held my breath as I saw the gust of wind tickle the small waves of the lake on its approach toward me. As it finally fell through the window of my car, I found it to be wet and cool as it wrapped through my long hair, beckoning it to dance. My body shivered from the cooling touch and my arms erupted with sudden goose bumps.

When I reached the other side of the bridge I released my breath, my body heavy and grounded as my car rolled onto the gravel drive, the water no longer flowing below me like a force of energy greater then I could control. I circled Diablo Lake and just a few hundred feet farther east, the road became even rougher as my tires struggled to find their grip. I drove with caution up the hill toward the front of the small cluster of buildings, my curious mind now beginning to rumble.

An anonymous donor had created the Cascades College a few years back. Its purpose was to provide a Masters in Environmental Studies through hands on experience and practice. There were also primary classes but mainly it was a place to get your hands dirty and experience the real world, in its truest sense.

When I had learned about the College I had remembered that it was the first time I'd felt my heart truly beat. Something about its design, location, and description felt more like home than anywhere I had ever been. I needed to be close to the earth, close to the place where life began.

I was never the nature lover type, but my choice to come here had been purely selfish. Ever since I could remember, I possessed a strange talent for growing plants, a green thumb if you may. But my talent did not simply involve using the right fertilizers, and making sure to water. My talents seemed to involve something much more magical and indescribable, something I was here to figure out.

I turned my car off with a heavy sigh as I sat in front of the main learning center, the large 'Welcome' sign looming over me. I felt the flicker beat again in my heart and it again ripped the breath from my lungs. Taking in the small modern buildings, I began to wonder if this was still just a dream, just a figment left by my heavily sedated mind.

A tall thin red headed man seemed startled by my abrupt arrival as he jumped from a bench by the office doors and ran toward my parked car with a smile plastered across his face. He couldn't have been much older than I, but instantly seemed to act years younger. He was bounding down the hill, his legs becoming perilously tangled as he tripped with inherent clumsiness, regaining his composure in an embarrassed but well rehearsed manner before continuing toward me. He was wearing a green plaid short-sleeved shirt and your run-of-the-mill pair of hiking shorts and Columbia boots.

He breathed hard as he placed both of his hands on the window and knelt down to my eye level, locking his gaze on mine. "New arrival?" he asked, his voice full of carefree delight.

I looked at him with nervous eyes as fear gripped my stomach. "Yes," I managed to squeak.

His eyes were a light blue like mine but full of life and happiness. "Great," he paused, sticking his hand out toward me through my window, "I'm Scott."

I stared at his hand for a moment, allowing my shock to subside to comprehension. Finally, I deduced that Scott was harmless and I grabbed his hand between two fingers and gave it a soft shake.

Scott yanked it back just as quickly as he had thrust it forward, unfazed by my reluctant personality, "Well, it sure is great to meet you. Would you like some help with your things?"

He opened my car door and I cringed as it shuddered and scraped, rust falling to the ground. "Um..." I was processing the information as quick as I could, "Sure. That would be great." I pulled myself out of the seat. "Thanks," I added, smiling as well as I could.

He stood there with his hands on his hips, looking like a dog ready to be thrown a bone. "So what's your name?" As soon as I was out of the way he jumped forward, lunging into my backseat and loading his pale scrawny arms with my three somewhat small bags, the makings of my whole life.

"I uh…" I stuttered as I grabbed my throat, begging it to stop. "My name is Estella." I finally managed to gather my thoughts as the time caught up around me. My medications always caused me to think slow, like fighting a fog of information that was always clouding my reflexes.

"Alright Estella," he grabbed a sheet from his pocket, maneuvering his full arms and struggling to bring it to his face, "Looks like you got your own cabin." His eyes got wide with excitement as though the cabin was his own.

I nodded in agreement. I had worked a few extra shifts at the fish counter of the Market to make that possible. I wasn't about to bunk up in a group dormitory again, not like I had for a good bulk of my life at the orphanage.

"Well then," he smiled with a sweet glow as he urged me forward, "Follow me."

"Thanks," I grabbed my shoulder bag from the passenger seat and rushed to keep up.

"So, Estella…"

"Oh you can call me Elle," I quickly corrected him.

He looked back at me as I followed behind him, "Ok then Elle, what brings you here?"

I looked at him sideways, what else would I be here for? "For the Master's course," I said ruefully.

"Oh really!" he looked back at me again, this time analyzing my face more closely. "Aren't you a bit young for a Masters?"

I shrugged, watching my feet as they struggled to

stay on pace, nerves again gathering in my stomach. "I got my degree while I was young."

"Really?" he sounded shocked.

"Well," I felt embarrassed and my cheeks began to flush, "It's just that, it came so naturally." I paused, breathing hard as we passed under a large pine that left a thick bed of needles on the ground, "It wasn't very difficult for me. I had a lot of time on my hands."

The fact that I never had friends made me result to anything that could pass my time and mostly that was homework and studying. I was a first class nerd and social reject. Even when I did try to make friends, my awkward existence eventually scared them off. I knew that at some point, Scott would come to learn this as well.

His eyes smiled at me, "Then I am impressed. I'm in that program too, but I'm not quite as young as you, I'm twenty-one. I kept pretty much on pace with things through High School." He watched me with curiosity, "I suppose we'll have the same classes. There aren't many people here."

I nodded, thinking about the fact that that was how I'd wanted it, quiet and secluded. As we rounded the path, I finally spotted a small cabin perched on the hill.

"So, that will be yours," he announced. We approached fast, climbing onto the porch as our boots echoed beneath us. He threw down a bag to open the door and I noticed there was no lock. "I will just set your bags here in the corner. Does that work?"

I nodded again, "Yeah, thanks Scott."

He thrust his hand toward me again, still the same energetic spark to his face, "Well, good to meet you Elle." He still didn't seem fazed by my standoffish behavior. "I guess I will see you tomorrow in class?"

I shook his hand and tried to give him another smile, though I was never able to succeed in getting the happy notion across. "Yeah, I guess I will. Thanks again."

I shut the door behind him as he bounded down the hill with the same awkward lumber as before. As I looked around the small square cabin I was pleased to see there was a lot more then I'd first imagined. I had my own bathroom, small shower, and a tiny kitchenette with a small fridge. My bed was a full size, bigger than I'd ever had and I began to feel somewhat spoiled.

I reached in my bag and grabbed out the thick envelope Heidi had given me and I slid it in the crack where the fridge met the cabinet, thinking I'd save it for an emergency. I circled the inside perimeter of the cabin, placing one foot before the other, inspecting every square inch of my investment and opening the blinds as I went so to let the light in.

After deciding everything was in order, I sat on my bed and pulled one of my bags toward me. From inside I grabbed out a small stack of moleskin journals and placed them on the shelf above my bed. I had began documenting my life the day I was able to write, it soothed me to be able to get it out, keep my soul open for happiness to come in, though it never did.

Deep in the bag, I found the framed note from

my real mother. It was the only thing I had from her. The beautiful script and rough edges played at my emotions and every day I read it in anticipation,

Estella,
You are beautiful, and it pains me to leave but some day you will find the beauty you seek living inside your darkest soul. You are safe now.

The poetic words puzzled and saddened me. I had searched for her when I was younger but found nothing about her or where she'd gone or even if she was dead or alive, and my soul remained black.

Placing it on the wood side table, I glanced back to my bag where I reached in and pulled a small tattered brown box from its depths, treating it with extreme care and delicacy. Opening it as though something may fall out, I retrieved a small pot containing a petite purple plant that was sleeping inside. Grasping it with two hands, I set the Purple Clover on the sill and touched its butterfly leaves as it reacted to the light and stretched its petals toward the sun like an opening umbrella. I had decided to take just one tubular with me from my vast garden in Seattle, just one child to start a new life with.

After unpacking the few clothes I'd had, and leaving some in the bag out of laziness, I finally laid on my bed, letting my platinum hair fan out around me. After a moment of silence, I pulled myself back up where I reached in my bag, grabbed my book, and leaned back into my pillow where I began to read as the darkness of the night crept in around the cabin. Soon, only the small light of the single lamp shown across the lonesome room, the sharp contrasts eerie against the walls of the unfamiliar place.

The hours had passed faster than I'd expected as I glanced away from the page to the windows. The blackness there was infinite and my heart began to race as I allowed the world of my book to fall away from me. I pulled my head off the pillow and sat up, throwing my legs to the floor where I stood. As I approached the cool pane I was shocked to see only a few faint lights glimmer from the compound that surrounded me. I had never seen or felt something like it in my life, darkness and quiet, all at once. I leaned toward my lamp and switched it off, allowing the lights outside to magnify.

I crept to my door where I placed my hand on the cool brass handle and opened the door, walking in slow quiet steps onto the small deck, not wanting to disturb nature's slumber. I clenched my eyes shut as tight as I could as I tilted my head to the sky, allowing myself the suspense of what I would surely find there. As I opened them, I gasped as the tiny diamonds that littered the sky sparkled greater then I'd ever seen and in far vaster numbers than I could imagine.

I had read about the stars, seen images and studied their matter but never would I have expected the expanse that welcomed me now. The city lights of Seattle and the almost constant thick shroud of clouds made star watching nonexistent.

My body was full of sudden weight and I began to feel dizzy as the strength from the star's mass caused my heart to race. A light breeze whipped around my cabin, twisting my hair around my shoulders and it felt like the breath of God. I could smell the pines and the sage tickle my nose and a feeling I had never felt crept through my limbs.

For a moment I couldn't help but feel I may at last smile, but the wind subsided and my dark soul remained empty. As the stars twinkled ever stronger, I realized I was getting close. There was something out here I needed to see, something I was meant to do, but what that was, for now, would continue to elude me.

FEAR

$\mathcal{T}$he sun streamed through the blinds as I woke to the quiet. My restless sleep left me groggy and clouded as I reached in the bedside table for my medication. Putting one hand to my head as it began to ache, I felt suddenly nauseated. I hadn't expected the dead silence of the night when I was so used to the rumble of the city. Eventually, I knew I would grow to love it, but the transition period was a little rocky.

I urged my lethargic body to sit up as I scanned the cabin, realizing nothing had changed from the night before. I threw one pill in my mouth in one mechanical movement and forced it down my dry throat. Rubbing my eyes, the cloudiness began to fade and I was finally able to throw myself out from under the covers and place my feet on the cold wood floor where I worked to gain my balance.

Staggering to the bathroom as I grabbed a ruffled pile of clothes, I closed myself within and splashed a handful of cool water on my face. Outside the small window, the chirping of birds was deafening but sweet and I stood on my toes to peer through the dusty glass. Down the hill I spotted the cafeteria building and my stomach rumbled at the thought of food. I hadn't eaten dinner due to my dumbfounded amazement with the night sky and I knew that it would be best to at least attempt a piece of toast.

As I slid on my jeans, struggling to force my tired legs through each pant leg, a sudden sharp knocking rapped against the front door of the cabin. I jumped in fear, my body going rigid with shock. I looked around as I scanned the mess I had made unpacking; half hoping I had just imagined the sound. To my regret, there was another sharp knock, this time even louder and more obnoxious. I dove to the floor where I threw my shirt over my head, catching the hem on my ears as I ripped it on and stumbled through the bathroom door, nearly crawling my way to the front door.

I grabbed the handle for balance as I flew it open, the sudden burst of light blinding me. I struggled to focus my eyes, shielding them with my hand as my gaze finally landed on my visitor. I wasn't surprised to see Scott standing like an awkward idiot before me, smiling in the same eccentric fashion he had yesterday.

"Well hey there Elle." He paused as he looked at my rumpled clothing, "I didn't wake you did I?"

I was still stunned from the sudden burst of light so I just shook my head in defiance. My lips pursed and annoyed.

Scott's smile ceased to falter. "I was just going to go get some food before class," he pointed down the hill toward the other building. "Just thought since you were new, you'd like to have a guide." He shrugged.

I swallowed hard, still too tired to attempt an empty

smile. "Sure," I said in a flat voice, cursing myself for my lack of confidence, "I'm starving." My face was in shock, people usually tended to avoid me, but not Scott.

I pulled my long hair the rest of the way out of my shirt as I grabbed my bag. Giving the cabin one last scan, I gingerly shut the door behind me. Grasping my boots from the deck, I sat on the ledge to pull them on as Scott stood on the path, whistling to himself and looking up into the branches of a large evergreen that shaded the path. I couldn't quite understand him. He was so unfazed, so unobservant of my awkward existence.

I finally stood, smoothing my navy thermal shirt over my jeans and collecting my thoughts. Taking a deep breath, I mustered what courage I had and walked off the deck and toward Scott.

"Ok," I paused a few feet from him and his attention fell to me, "I'm ready."

Scott smiled again, "Perfect." He summoned me forward, "You're going to love the food here, I promise." He attempted a wink but instead it ended up looking like a twitch.

We hiked down the hill and I took in my new surroundings. There were five buildings in my view and I noted each carefully, eager to find my place here. The structures looked modern and clean, built into their surroundings in such a way that hardly any dirt had been disturbed. The massive beam frames looked far stronger than necessary, and the windows were at least an inch thick. I knew the winters here were long and harsh and the snow pack so great that most of the trees, even now in late summer, were still bowing from the painful weight forced onto their limbs.

Scott noticed the curious look on my face and took it upon himself to elaborate, "That over there is the bird and wildlife lab," he pointed to the far left toward the bottom of the hill, "That will be our second class today."

"Birds?" I asked, puzzled.

"Yeah," he choked, "they really are an integral part of the ecosystem here." He looked at me with wide convincing eyes. "And down over there," he pointed to the right, "That is the greenhouse."

My eyes became wide with interest, "That's more like what I'm into."

Scott watched me with an amplified look of content to his face, "And over in that cluster is the astrological lab, the water lab, and the hatchery."

I nodded in comprehension. Despite the fact that I was nervous around people, I was thankful to have Scott, even if I was uncomfortable being this conversational. I had never managed to keep friends, or even really make them to begin with. My soul was too depressing to be around and most people mistook my silence for cockiness. I had always thought I was at least reasonably attractive, with my crystal blue eyes and smooth porcelain skin, but looks aren't everything and people still looked at me like I was a monster.

The gravel below our feet crunched as we arrived at the cafeteria. The front entrance was gated on both sides by two large timbers and the walls were mostly glass, allowing the light to bleed into the space. My skin glowed milky white in contrast to the other students and visitors filling the hall. They had obviously spent most of their lives outdoors where I was always shielded in the city shade, a prisoner of my own mind.

We walked to the counter and I grabbed a plate. There were droves of fresh berries and grainy breads and what I deduced to be tubs and tubs of granola. I cringed at the sight. I hated granola more than anything, the needless chewing and tasteless texture frightened me. Settling for a soft bran muffin, I grabbed it from the basket and placed it on my plate and then watched wide-eyed as Scott piled his plate high with berries and tofu scrambled eggs.

"I can't get enough of this stuff." Scott mounded another scoop of eggs on an already dangerously teetering stack and then grabbed for his silverware.

I followed him to a table in the far corner where the sun warmed my back as I sat. "So what made you come here?" I asked, watching him with acute curiosity as I tried my best to be social.

Scott looked at me over his glasses with a mouth full of blueberries, his teeth grossly stained. "My mother is an environmental researcher," he paused, wiping juice from his chin as it dribbled from his gaping mouth, "She's out in the woods of Alaska right now but she will be back in about six months. She was always my source of inspiration."

I nodded as I picked at my muffin, my appetite somewhat depleted, "That's nice." I felt my insides sink at the thought of having a mother.

Scott swallowed a load of eggs, "So what's your story? You seem like you've got a heavy mind." He was analyzing my sadness like a Petri dish.

I thought for a moment, finding the right words to say that wouldn't cause him to turn and run. "Well," I flicked a sugar crystal off the table, "I was an orphan." I watched his face for some sort of reaction but one never came. "And I've always had this thing with plants, with nature," I blurted.

He looked at me surprised, only a slight twinge of confusion on his face, "What thing is that? Like an Affair?" He gave me a smug confident smile, something I didn't think he could posses.

I faked a grin and rolled my eyes, finding his version of sarcasm a little sadistic. "No not like that," I tore at my napkin, "like a mother thing. The plants…" I paused, trying to see how I could explain without sounding like a complete nut bag, "they love me. They react to me even when I don't take care of them at all. No matter what, they still flourish under my care." I held my breath after I said it. It had always been a strange talent of mine and certainly not something a normal girl could do.

He looked at me and I could see he hadn't gotten it, "Mother nature then right?" He let out a small chuckle.

I rolled my eyes and released the breath from my lungs in relief.

"So then you're a tree hugger," he said as a matter of fact, looking at me as though it were a typical occurrence. "We've got two types here, animal activists and tree huggers."

He chewed as he pointed at me with his fork, "And you're a tree hugger."

I lowered my gaze, feeling somewhat hurt and very annoyed. I was no hippy, which was for sure. I had never been an obsessed recycler or taken to eating granola, yogurt, and tofu. I knew that what I had was a different passion, a real passion, not a means to fit in.

Scott noticed my pained expression, "Oh, sorry." He looked concerned, "I didn't really mean to offend you," he let out a nervous laugh in his attempt to erase his prior remark.

I looked up at him, "Oh no Scott, don't worry you didn't." I felt bad for him, he was really trying, "I don't really have feelings, well at least no feelings other than pain, so don't feel bad."

Again, he gave me the same dense confused stare and I could see that he and I were going to make great friends. He didn't seem to understand me, and that was good.

"Well good." A bubbly smile was again plastered to his freckled face, his glasses smeared with blueberry juice where he had grabbed the rim to readjust them onto his thin nose.

He finished his whole plate as I stuffed the muffin in my bag for later, feeling an acute loss of appetite after the depressing conversation and also the fact that I had to watch him eat. Scott grabbed my plate as he stood, throwing them with expert aim into a nearby tub as we left the building.

"So, looks like we're off to the hatchery," he looked

at me as excitement filled his eyes. "That's my favorite class," he whispered, as though there were anyone around to even care.

It was a sunny day, the weather of summer just turning into fall, yet still somewhat warm. I followed him down the hill to the crystal blue lake as he half skipped in front of me. The building was old and water stained like an antique boathouse and it was the full length of the dock, about eighty feet long. Once inside, I noticed how its shape reflected its function. To the front was a long segmented tank that spread down the side of half the room, each filled with a dozen fish, divided based on their age and relative size.

Scott ran like a child to the ledge of the tank and looked deep within, "Hey Elle, come see."

I approached the tank in short wary footsteps, I'd never really cared for fish, especially live ones. Anytime I got in any lakes or oceans they would nibble at my feet as though I where I giant chunk of floating wonder bread.

I peered deep into the multifaceted turquoise water, the pearl green scales of the fish glittering like dark clouds as they twisted their way around their bleak confines.

"Hey look!" Scott pointed to the fish now circling in anxious rings in front of me. "He likes you."

I sighed, looking down at the struggling fish as it tried all it could to get closer to me, in any way possible. I felt sorry for the poor thing, a runt, stuck in a glass box for the rest of its life. With reluctant will, I raised my trembling hand where I let it hover above the water in my rippled reflection. I watched as the trout swam at the shadow, following the shelter I was creating for it as my hand swirled above the water.

Scott watched in amazement and I noticed his shocked expression out of the corner of my eye. Ashamed that he had seen what I'd done, I slammed my hand back into my pockets, feeling my pale skin blush to a dramatic red.

"How did you do that?" Scott came to my side, watching the once anxious fish now swim with tranquility, still as close to me as possible. "He was like, following you."

I shrugged, "That's what I was saying. They love me." I felt like a freak and I was waiting for him to blow me off, call me a weirdo and never talk to me again.

"Well," he gave me a stupid grin. "Then I guess they do," he shrugged.

I stared at him in disbelief. How Scott had made it this far in life amazed me. His dense demeanor and oblivious personality would never survive in the city; he'd be eaten alive. As I tried to calm my nerves, the room filled with students, each eyeing me with curiosity and disapproval and I shrank to the back. A few minutes later, a frumpy, frizzle haired professor entered the room and began to preach before everyone was even settled, her voice lisping like a drowning snake.

"The fish are our friends," she droned with passionate respect, and I could tell this was going to be a long hour.

I watched Scott as he stared in obedience toward the front, alert in his love for marine life. Soon, my eyes wandered to the other students. People of all ages filled the room, each plainer than the next. I felt like I had a giant arrow pointing directly at me, the one thing that didn't belong, but then again, when had I ever belonged? My blonde hair stood stark against the muddy colors of the people around me, and at one point, I noticed the teacher could barely stop staring at me, an almost entranced look on her face.

At the end of class, Scott turned to me with elated and glossed over eyes, "That was amazing," he gasped, throwing his bag over his shoulder. His happiness bled from him like a deep open wound and I longed to know how that felt.

I watched him as a pathetic lump grew in my throat, not wanting to ruin the moment for him, "Yeah, sure was." My voice was sarcastic but there was nothing I could do to help it and I hoped he hadn't noticed my unconvincing attitude. Luckily he hadn't.

"Well Elle, time for the birds," he gave a playful nudge, "We'll get to plants soon though, don't worry." He winked at me and grabbed my arm as he led me out the door and back to the gravel path.

We walked in silence to the bird and wildlife lab as I began to doubt my presence here, surely no one would take me seriously. Scott wasn't absorbing the fact that my strange abilities weren't just with plants, it was with everything in nature. I just tended toward plants because the extraordinary pull I had for them was safe. With animals, you never knew what was going to come at you, bulldogs were the worst, not that they wanted to hurt me, but the drool was gross.

Scott pulled the heavy door of the lab open and we walked into the stark white classroom. Students were socializing as they roamed from table to table in casual circles. I followed Scott to a station toward the back and we settled onto the tall stools. I analyzed his face as he sat poised on the stool like a kid fresh from etiquette school and I wondered why he hadn't had more friends.

Looking around the room, I noticed that all the windows had grids and I assumed it was to prevent the birds from flying into them. To the far left was a large aquarium-like enclosure that stretched from the floor to the ceiling and inside I saw a slow squirrel moving amongst the branches of its confined habitat like an old man. There were six rows of desk stations, all big enough to hold two to four students. The room felt sterile, like a doctor's office, but I liked it.

Even though the overall space was bright and refreshing, it still did nothing to boost my sullen mood. After a few moments of idle chatter, the students began to settle, taking their seats in a routine manner as a door toward the front of the room creaked open, the handle slamming against the wall before bouncing back.

I looked around with wondering eyes at all the students, all as still as statues and as quiet as death as though frozen in time. I looked to Scott for an explanation as fear and confusion began to fill my mind.

He gave me a nervous glare as he folded his hands

politely before him, "Professor Edgar is very strict," he hissed between clenched teeth, "You've got to remain as still as possible, as alert as you can be, or…" he paused as the clumping sound of heavy footsteps entered the room.

My eyes widened in terror as the door to the front of the classroom slammed close and a tall figure took the stage with a large hawk poised on his strong arm. What shocked me most was the professor's youth and I deduced that he must not be any older than twenty, possibly even younger. His face and eyes were like ice behind his tinted glasses and large lab coat. I shook my head as a sudden fog filled my mind, and I felt a flurry of anxiety grip at my chest. My heart rate quickened as though my life was being threatened and I struggled to remain calm, focusing on his face instead.

The professor's youthful skin was radiant and unflawed. He had a prominent chin and thick eyebrows that framed his strong face well. The glasses he wore shielded his eyes, making it hard to tell the exact spot to which he was looking. The pitch black of his hair contrasted beautifully with his pale skin and for the first time, I felt I wasn't the only one that stood out.

My heart rate remained elevated and the flutter in my chest began to sting with a sharp unbearable twang. I started to wince as I struggled to control the pain, my head now ripping open in agony. Something was attacking me and it felt as though they were drawing the very life from my bones and I found myself now struggling to remain calm.

Scott noticed my trembling as he eyed me with a

tense look, hoping I wouldn't attract any attention. I shot him a worried glare as I struggled to take deep breaths but my lungs began to seize, causing my cheeks to flush as a sudden rush of blood streamed straight to my head.

"Class," the professor boomed. I wasn't sure if the professor had even noticed me, but I prayed he wouldn't. "The red hawk is a fierce predator."

I noticed the squirrel in the tank leap from its branch and scurry into a small house in the far corner as beads of sweat gathered on my forehead.

The professor froze as though his shoes were suddenly full of lead, scanning the class with his dark eyes which seemed to take on a new, almost ominous glimmer. His mouth was pursed into an angry line and his nostrils were flared. The hawk sat steady on his arm, unfazed by his carrier's sudden mental disruption. As his eyes landed on each student, I saw them squirm on their stools, each praying the following words were not directed toward them.

I was stifling my heavy breaths as his eyes met mine and halted, remaining on me as he took one singular step forward and then stopped. My whole body went weak as though I were no more than a puppet, my limbs tingling as though someone was forcing sand into my veins. Placing my hands on the table to prevent myself from fainting, the world around me seemed to slowly dissipate as I felt something inside him pulling me closer.

His eyes were burning even darker now, mesmerizing me with terror and I prayed that it would stop, begged for anything to interrupt this painful and silent attack. No matter how hard I tried, I couldn't look away from his perfect face, his gaze becoming harder to handle as I began to sweat more profusely. It felt like an eternity had already passed as we stared at each other, my mind turning to a stormy dark. His brows furled even deeper, the lines on his face now cutting into his angelic white skin, making him seem years older. A student bravely adjusted his stool as it scratched across the floor and the professor broke his stare, his face somehow lost. I softly gasped for air and the world around me returned in a rush of warmth and I rubbed my neck as though I had been choked, finding it sore as though it had really happened.

"Elle," Scott whispered, his voice frantic and scared. "Are you ok?" His throat sounded dry and his voice was cracking.

"Yeah," I took a few heavy breaths, regaining what composure I could and summoning a courage I had never known.

The professor staggered to his desk, looking away from the curious class to hide his faltering expression. His body language looked as though, like me, he was having trouble regaining his composure. I watched with observance as he leaned one strong arm against the mahogany desk, the hawk continuing to sit steady, unchanged in his composure to the class. After a brief moment of reprieve, the professor turned back and the stinging in my chest subsided. As his gaze fell on mine I noticed that his eyes were now serene, and calm, void of the murderous black of before as though now a whole new person.

"Class," he started again, wiping a bead of sweat from his brow, "This hawk has been injured." He motioned one shaking hand toward the hawk.

I struggled to understand what had just happened as everyone looked toward the professor, confused. Why had we both reacted so strongly toward each other?

"Our lesson today," he continued, "will be in the preservation and health of this creature."

He began to make his way down the aisle and my heart rate quickened. As he grew closer, I noticed his gate was far too smooth and sophisticated for his age, but there was something there that suggested otherwise. His nose was in the air as though from another time completely and the way he carried himself exuded ages of perfection.

"He has a broken wing," he continued, now glaring at me with shameless authority, his dark eyes still hiding the exact point of his gaze.

As he approached our table, I felt my breathing become very shallow and the aggression in his eyes blazed as my already fair skin turned even whiter.

"And your name is?" He finally halted in front of me.

My palms spread across the table as I tried to remain calm, holding my breath in utter shock. His eyes beckoned for me to look into them, and even behind the tinted lenses, they seemed to glow.

I stuttered nervously, "El..." my voice was hoarse and low, "Estella."

I saw his eyes react to my name as I said it, flashing

what had appeared to be a bright blue. He stood there quite still for a moment and I noticed the students around me staring with looks of grave pity and vindictive interest, all relieved to not be where I sat.

"Estella," he repeated. A smile curled across his face and his voice was like honey as he breathed my name.

A strange part of me still felt a pull toward him, his almost floral scent wafting toward me and tickling my nose. Despite the fact that he was the creepiest person I had ever encountered, there was a dull sense of intrigue and admiration.

"Can you help heal this Hawk?" His eyes blazed a calmer grey as he looked at me, head tilted in contemplation.

I looked at him horrified, if I even so much as touched the bird people would notice there was something strange about me. I knew that my abilities to heal were not normal and far too obvious in a situation like this. The hawk stirred on his arm, its piercing gaze looking at me in a way that seemed like prey.

"I – uh," I tried to reach out and gather my thoughts through the thick clouds of my mind, "Wh – what should I do?" Fear filled my eyes but no tears would ever come. I felt the hairs on my back raise as the tension in the room shrouded me in terror.

The hawk tilted his sorrowful head at me as though comprehending the words I was saying, mimicking his handler as his talons twitched on the sleeve of the professor's dark shirt. Without warning, the bird turned its blazing gaze from me to the professor as he too looked toward the bird, as though having a brief conversation over the matter.

I blinked once and they both shot their stare back toward me, my chest once again beginning to sting. I felt myself leaning back on my stool in an attempt to resist his pull, to get as far away from him as possible. The hawk jumped from his arm to the table and the whole class gasped in suspense. I took a few calm breaths, knowing the bird wouldn't hurt me but my heart was still pounding hard in my chest and I couldn't help but take a moment to absorb the feeling, a feeling rare to me.

The hawk hopped toward me, its poise never faltering despite its broken wing and assured pain. I felt the bird's discomfort sting my chest and I winced. As he approached, I could almost hear his thoughts, filling my dark soul with a thin haze.

"Grab its wing," the professor boomed as he looked down on me, his startling strength and towering height astonishing me inside my fogged comprehension. "Feel the bone so you can share with the class," he hissed, a crooked smile crossing his smooth young face.

I looked away from him as a wince grew in my throat, my gaze now locked on the warm amber eyes of the hawk. Little by little, I released my grip on the table and raised my trembling hand toward the injured wing. The hawk watched me with confidence, never shying away from my advancing touch. His amber eyes glittered like coins as he looked into my thoughts, finding calm there.

With extreme caution, I lowered my hand onto its

powerful wing, stroking my touch over the ridge of his elbow and down the length of his feathers. The bird opened his beak, breathing deep as it relaxed its wing into a full span. The students toward the front of the room stood from their chairs, anxious to get a better view. In slow movements, I again grabbed the bird's wing, bringing my other hand up to cradle its chest as I felt the bone, finally finding the protrusion halfway down its bicep. Closing my eyes in regret, I felt the bone molding beneath my touch as it healed with shocking speed. My stomach churned as I felt it, my nerves crushing my confidence like a rock. I had never been confronted like this before and I was certain that this absurd incident would grant me my one way ticket back home.

I looked to the professor with sheepish eyes, begging him not to notice. He nodded in approval, his hungry stare locked on my hand as I continued to massage the hawk's wing, now nearly healed. I jumped as the satisfied hawk clicked its tongue, ruffling the feathers on his back as he jumped away from me and repositioned his wing against his smooth brown body as though no harm had ever been inflicted.

I looked at the professor as he continued to stare at me with a solemn mask. He stood there for a brief moment as the hawk returned to its perch on his arm, and its feathers puffed in happiness; both eyes glinting with playful light.

Just as fierce and fast as he had come, the professor spun on his heel and marched back up the aisle. "That will be all today," he boomed with a threatening pitch to his voice as he exited with haste through the same door he had entered, not another word or explanation said.

My breathing returned as I felt my lungs re-inflate and the fog in my mind cleared. It was all a blur, the way he'd looked at me, the way the hawk had known something about me.

Scott put one hand on my back to support me, "Are you alright?"

His words disappeared like a dissipating cloud as my head felt faint, and my eyes rolled back into my head; the room fading to dark.

Hooked? Got to
www.FeatherBookSeries.com
to find out more.

The Feather Book Series
by Abra Ebner

Available on:
Amazon
Mobipocket
Sony E-reader.

3310654

Made in the USA